PEKING DUCK
AND COVER

PEKING DUCK

AND COVER

VIVIEN CHIEN

St. Martin's Paperbacks

First published in the United States by St. Martin's Paperbacks, an imprint of St. Martin's Publishing Group.

PEKING DUCK AND COVER

For information, address St. Martin's Publishing Group, 120 Broadway, New York, NY 10271.

www.stmartins.com

ISBN: 978-1-250-33877-8

Our books may be purchased in bulk for promotional, educational, or business use. Please contact your local bookseller or the Macmillan Corporate and Premium Sales Department at 1-800-221-7945, ext. 5442, or by email at MacmillanSpecialMarkets@macmillan.com.

St. Martin's Paperbacks edition / August 2024

Printed in the United States of America

10 9 8 7 6 5 4 3 2 1

for Holly:
From eat-in "chickens" to JP drains, thanks for
always being there.

ACKNOWLEDGMENTS

I am deeply grateful to my agent, Gail Fortune, who continues to support me through all my ups and downs—writing and otherwise. It is through her guidance and powerful pep talks that I continue through the process of finishing a book with any amount of grace.

Thank you to my fabulous editor, Lily Cronig, who has guided me through this installment of the Noodle Shop mysteries with a gentle hand, a sharp eye, and much encouragement. I think this is the beginning of a beautiful friendship.

To the ever-impressive ladies of St. Martin's Press: my publicist, Kayla Janas, and my marketing gal, Allison Ziegler, who make this series sparkle and shine more than any high pigment eyeshadow I've ever found. Thank you for your skill.

To Mary Ann Lasher, the artist extraordinaire behind all these lovely covers. I brag about you at parties.

To my copy editor, John Simko, I so enjoy our time working together, so much that I enjoy it. (That is not a typo, he gets it. P.S. John, don't fix that.)

A massive thank you to Jennifer Enderlin for believing in this series and allowing "this voice" to be heard. I'll never be able to express how much it truly means to me.

To the wonderful people at St. Martin's Press, thank you for the job you do every day. You put books into the hands of people all over the world and that, my friends, is just plain fantastic.

I am also grateful to my friends and family, my "ride-or-dies," and my partners in crime. It is with your unconditional love that I continue to propel myself forward through this journey called life. Special shout-out to the friends who let me know when I have spinach stuck in my teeth. I'd be lookin' a fool without you.

Lastly, but NEVER least, thank you from the bottom of my heart to all my readers. You're amazing humans, and I've said it before, and I'll say it again, I'm the luckiest author to have the lot of you. Your kindness, support, and generosity have held me together through the hardest of times. It makes writing this series even more special than it already is. Hugs to each and every one of you. And don't forget: If no one told you today, you look absolutely amazing.

CHAPTER 1

New year, new me. Isn't that the phrase? When you're Asian, you have the opportunity to experience that twice a year. And you better believe that I, Lana Lee, take full advantage of that fact every calendar cycle. Because sometimes, let's face it, you don't follow through with your January 1 resolutions like you thought you would.

Though Chinese New Year doesn't revolve around the act of resolutions, I still allow myself a fresh start, just in case I fall off the goal wagon by, let's say, January 15.

Normally I would hold out a little longer, struggling to make that next trip to the gym or remembering that I'm supposed to be eating less carbs versus more. But when you have Ian Sung, property manager of Asia Village, breathing down your neck in preparation for the upcoming Lunar New Year festivities, it's a bit difficult to put down that doughnut. If Mama Wu at Shanghai Donuts—which is conveniently located right next to Ho-Lee Noodle House, my family's restaurant—didn't make such a fantastic sugar raised doughnut, I probably wouldn't have had to consider an empire waist for my New Year's Day outfit.

It was a mere ten minutes before nine a.m. when Ian waltzed through the doors of Ho-Lee Noodle House with a white wax paper bag and a to-go coffee cup. He'd known me long enough to learn my weaknesses and how to get me to comply with his requests.

"We're not even open yet," I bellowed while accepting his peace offerings. We were two days away from the celebration that would encompass Asia Village and he had entered full-on bossy mode.

He held out an arm and ushered me over to the nearest table. "Exactly. I'll have your full attention."

Stifling a laugh, I seated myself facing the door so I could keep an eye on any activity going on in the plaza. If Ian thought getting my full attention right before the restaurant opened was an actual thing, I kinda felt sorry for him.

Aside from his delusional thinking, I would best describe Ian as a charmer. No doubt that he was incredibly good looking, but . . . in a sinister way. You know that bad guy who always shows up in movies, the dashingly handsome one pretending to be the good guy? On the surface you want to believe him, but deep down you know better, you know he's up to no good. You're just waiting for him to show his hand and prove you right. Well, that's Ian. As of yet, though, he hasn't shown any signs of actually being the evil antagonist I imagine him to be.

I opened the bag he'd handed me and removed the sugar raised doughnut, which was shaped like an eight . . . or an infinity symbol . . . Choose your perspective. I inhaled the sweet dough as I took my first bite, the sugar granules sticking to my lip gloss.

"Now, I know I don't have long before the Matrons get

here, so let me run through my thoughts before you say anything." Ian began to fidget with the knot of his silk tie.

Dressed to impress in fine French suits, Italian leather shoes, and a Rolex watch that cost more than I make in a year, he is one photo shoot away from ending up on the cover of *GQ*. Of course, I don't admit these types of thoughts to other people. I have my own dashingly handsome man, thank you very much. And frankly, if you ask me, one is enough.

"You have the floor," I replied.

Ian pulled a folded piece of notepaper out of the inside pocket of his suit jacket. Unfolding it, he glanced at me. "I need to confirm that all of the food is handled. You and Ho-Lee Noodle House are in charge of the main menu, the Bamboo Lounge will be handling alcohol and appetizers, and Shanghai Donuts will provide the desserts. I checked with Mama Wu when I picked up your doughnut this morning, and she confirmed her end. What's going on with Penny and the Bamboo Lounge? Are they all set to go?"

Since I was in mid-bite of my doughnut, I gave him a thumbs-up. We'd been over this several times already. Penny had ordered mass amounts of alcohol at the beginning of the year in preparation for the party, so that was one hundred percent covered. And she'd been tacking onto her regular weekly food orders to avoid any supply chain problems that might occur with bulk ordering.

My mother had chimed in on the topic and voiced her annoyance that our restaurant wasn't serving the appetizers as well. But I knew it would make life easier for us, and the budget.

Removing a ballpoint pen from his pocket, he checked off the first line and then read the next. "What about the tables, chairs, and tablecloths? They are being delivered Saturday morning, correct?"

I set my doughnut on the tea saucer in front of me, lest I shovel it down like a scavenger. "Yes, Ian, all that stuff is being delivered Saturday morning like we have discussed on multiple occasions since I first confirmed the order. *Also*, along with that is the acrylic cover for the koi pond."

"Oh good, that was next on my list," he said, checking off another line.

"Why are we going over this yet again? We just met about fine-tuning the details on Monday."

He huffed, pinching the bridge of his nose. "Because, Lana, we have no room for error on this. It is by far the largest party we've ever had at Asia Village, and we don't want to have egg on our face, now do we?"

"A lot of this is riding on me too, you know." I wiped my hand on the napkin Mama Wu had supplied in the bag. "I'm pulling Megan in . . . not to mention two of her bartenders for this whole shindig. I've made all the appropriate calls and double-checked my work. I'd appreciate a little bit of confidence in my abilities, Ian."

He tapped his paper with the tip of his pen. "What about the lion dance performers?"

I pursed my lips. "Really?"

"Yes, really."

A gentle tapping on the window of the front doors caused me to look up. The clock above the door told me it was nine a.m. on the dot, and four familiar faces stared back at me. The Mahjong Matrons had arrived.

Aside from their status as reigning champs of the infamous Chinese tile game, the elderly widows were my most reliable customers. They showed up at the same time every day, ordered the same exact things, and even sat in the same booth. On top of all that, they were also the absolute authority on everything going on in our tight-knit Asian community. If there was something to know about someone, they knew it.

"Excuse me," I sang to Ian, taking a small amount of pleasure in making him wait.

I unlocked the doors, pulling one open, and with a grandiose sweep of my arm, welcomed the Matrons in. "Ladies! It is so good to see you; it feels like it's been forever."

Helen, the true matriarch of the group, tilted her head. "Good morning, Lana. What has gotten into you?"

The other ladies followed behind her, marching into the restaurant with piqued curiosity at my exuberant behavior.

"Yes," Wendy said, studying my face, "are you feeling well?"

"It's just good to see the four of you; it feels like it's been ages," I said, closing the door once they'd all filed in. "Matter of fact, it feels like two years."

Helen and Wendy headed over to their usual booth by the window, which provided a great vantage point to look out into the plaza. But the other two ladies, Opal and Pearl, stayed behind to observe me further.

Pearl, older sister to Opal, looked me up and down. Her hand extended, and I felt like she was going to check my forehead for a fever, but she paused, and instead took a step back. "You're not sick, are you? We were just here yesterday."

I laughed, shaking my head. "I know you were; just feels like it's been forever."

I started to move in the direction of their table, and they followed, though with some hesitancy.

Opal noticed Ian, who had risen from his seat, tapping his fingernail on the back of the chair. In a quiet voice, she nodded, and reached for her sister's arm. "Ah, I see why Lana is happy to see us. The boss is here. We are a happy distraction."

Ian blushed. "Good morning, ladies. I promise I won't take much more of Lana's time."

Helen called from the table. "I should hope not, Mr. Sung. We have much to do today."

Ian cleared his throat and sat back down.

"Just a minute," I said to him, passing our table. "Let me grab their tea and place their order real quick."

Had they not been a few feet away, I'm almost positive he would have complained. But he knew better than to say anything in front of our elders.

A few minutes later, I returned with their tea and let them know that Peter, my best friend and the restaurant's head chef, was working on their order.

I sat back down, grabbing for my doughnut. "Okay, you may proceed."

Getting back to his list of to-dos, he began rattling off something to do with something, but I had my eyes on the Matrons. I knew they were eavesdropping, as it was second nature to them, and I wondered what they thought of him being here.

It was pretty well known around the plaza that Ian had a thing for me, and that it was not mutual. The Matrons adored Adam, my current boyfriend, and kind of fawned over him any time he'd stopped by the restaurant while they were around.

"Lana, have you heard a word I've said?" Ian tapped his pen on the table.

Turning my attention back to him, he widened his eyes and scrunched his well-manicured brows. "Well, have you?"

I set my napkin down, picked up my coffee cup, and

took a sip. "Uh-huh." My eyes slid back over to the Mah-jong Matrons, who were, of course, pretending as if they weren't listening in.

Ian smirked. "You haven't heard a thing I've said, have you? I'm not going to keep bringing you doughnuts if you refuse to cooperate."

"I heard you," I replied with a groan. "You want to have a rehearsal in the parking lot with the lion dance crew before the actual show on Saturday. I already know. They're scheduled to meet with me tomorrow morning."

He folded his arms over his chest, leaning back in his seat. "And what did I say after that?"

"Right. After that. Well, you said . . ." I paused. I could feel five sets of eyes on me.

Helen, who was not only the matriarch but the loudest of the four, twisted in her seat. "He said he wants you to announce the winners of the raffle after the show is over, dear."

"Exactly," I said, nodding along with Helen. "That's what I was just about to say."

Ian pursed his thin lips. "It is critical we save the raffle until the *very* end of the night so everyone stays for the whole event. We can't have people leaving early or immediately after they've eaten. How will that come off to other guests if people just eat and leave?"

The event itself was free to the public, but if you wanted a ticketed table there was an entry fee that would help cover the cost of the show. As an incentive, if you purchased a seat, your name would be entered into five different raffles featuring goods or services from any of the fine shops in our beloved plaza.

Ho-Lee Noodle House was contributing a two-hundred-dollar gift certificate—which my mother argued with me about, by the way. She wanted to cap the prize at one hundred, but I convinced her that if we really wanted to stand out from the others, we were going to have up our ante.

I'd also let it not so accidentally slip to Yuna, the receptionist at Asian Accents hair salon, what we were up to, and within the day it spread like wildfire around the entire plaza, causing the other shops to chip in more-competitive prizes. Yuna is basically the future generation of the Mahjong Matrons. I thought it would be a good test to see how efficient her rumor-spreading skills were, and it didn't hurt to give her some practice.

My plan worked even better than anticipated, and when the fliers went out advertising all the great prizes, we had a sold-out event. So despite all the hard times Ian gave me, he knew I was good at this and wouldn't let him down. Even factoring in my short attention span in the morning hours.

Ian tapped his fingernail on the black Formica tabletop. "Donna will be there. It is absolutely crucial that everything go off without a hitch. No excuses, no exceptions."

He was referring to Donna Feng, property owner and widow of the original proprietor, Thomas. She'd taken on the role but was not at all hands-on like her late husband had been. She allowed Ian to do all the heavy lifting while she kept an eye on the finances and the bigger-picture items.

And though she didn't grace us with her presence every day like Thomas had, she was an intense woman who demanded excellence at any cost. Which probably explained why the look in Ian's eye was so severe as he delivered his warning.

If I hadn't felt sorry for him in that very moment, I might have brought up the concept of what it means to jinx something. But I didn't have it in my heart to tell him that by demanding its perfection, he'd just given the whole evening the kiss of death.

CHAPTER 2

- - - - - - - - - - - - - - - -

Ian left shortly after making me promise four more times that I had heard everything he so kindly repeated for my express benefit. And now with him out of the way and off harassing some other participant, I could focus on getting the Matrons settled up with their bill and move on with my morning.

I returned to their table with a check and a platter of almond cookies.

Helen grabbed for the bill as she always did while the others made their customary fuss about allowing her to pay. Word on the street was that when her husband had passed away, he'd left her a healthy sum of money that allowed more than enough wiggle room in her budget.

She shushed them and angled her head upward, giving me the once-over. "Ian Sung is so worried about business all the time. He is not thinking about what you need to do to prepare yourself for the new year."

I had a feeling I knew where this was going, but I allowed them to enlighten me.

"Yes." Opal nodded in agreement. "I am sure your

parents are preparing the appropriate reunion dinner. Your mother takes great care in this tradition."

I nodded. Asia Village would be closing early Friday evening so everyone could be home with their families.

Pearl raised an index finger, pointing it in my direction. "And I'm hoping that you have been cleaning up your house. Things should not be messy on New Year's Day."

I thought about the pile of dirty laundry on the floor in front of my closet that my dog, Kikko, had transformed into her play pile. "Yup, I've just been cleaning every chance I get."

Wendy said, "I suspect you are not telling the truth. But there is still time; you must correct this as soon as possible."

The other three nodded.

My cheeks reddened a little at being caught in my innocent fib. It had been a busy few weeks, and I'd let some of my daily chores at home go by the wayside. Especially the laundry. Our unit didn't have a private washer and dryer, so we had to drag our things to the designated laundry facility a few doors down from our apartment. Not exactly my favorite thing to do, especially in the winter months.

Helen placed her money with the check and handed it to me. "I know we don't have to worry about you buying new clothes. This is something we all know you're good at doing."

I took the bill tray with a reluctant smile. "Yes, my outfit is all taken care of." The idea was to wear completely new clothing on Chinese New Year as a symbolic fresh start. It was the one tradition I made sure to always partake in.

"But not your shoes, right?" Pearl reminded me. "The shoes must have been worn at least once. No exceptions."

"Nope, shoes have been worn before." I felt proud of myself for at least accomplishing that.

"Wonderful," Wendy said with a clap. She reached for an almond cookie, shaking it at me. "We will leave the rest to you and hope everything turns out in your favor."

I smiled and thanked them, excusing myself to cash out their bill.

When they left, I set an alarm on my cell phone to remind me when I got home to take care of that laundry. My life was too topsy-turvy these days to take any chances.

An average day in my world is truly nothing to write home about. I wake up far earlier than I want to, head to Asia Village—a mecca of all things Hello Kitty, noodles, and Asian-knickknack related—where I manage the family restaurant and deal with a variety of eccentric people. And in some instances of said people, "eccentric" is putting it nicely.

The Mahjong Matrons are my first customers of the day, every day, except Sundays when our restaurant has shortened hours. The adjusted hours are because as a family, we go to dim sum at Li Wah's on the east side of Cleveland every Sunday morning. There are no excuses as to why you can't show up. Not even the threat of nuclear devastation.

So, other than that, the Matrons are always there to greet me, and to be honest, it's become quite comforting. My life could be spiraling out of control, but at least I knew the Matrons would show up.

There was only one time in history that *all* four ladies failed to arrive as they should, but those were extreme circumstances, and yes, I had thought about calling the National Guard.

Once they left for the day, I'd go about my business of tallying the books, making sure food and supply orders got done, then waste time listening to gossip from at least three people about what in the world Elise from the Asian grocery was thinking when she got that pixie cut, *or* whatever the latest "tea" was being spilled around the plaza.

Peter's mom, Nancy, who was one of my mother's best friends, worked the split shift from eleven a.m. to eight p.m. She'd cover my lunch, and then before I left for the day, I'd cover hers. After that it was off to the bank to make our daily deposit, and then . . . finally, I'd head home.

Now, it should be noted that heading home is always my very favorite part of any given day. Home is where my dog lives, and where I co-habitate with my best friend from college, Megan Riley. She manages a local bar, so our hours conflict on more days than they don't, but it gives us the space we need to avoid crowding each other.

Evenings usually consist of snorty kisses from Kikkoman, my black pug—Kikko, for short. After we've said our hellos, the two of us peruse the apartment complex greens for the perfect tinkle locations. I count that as my exercise most days.

I spend a lot of my free time with Adam Trudeau, Fairview Park Police Detective and boyfriend. During the week we're usually too tired from our positions as functioning adults to do anything wildly exciting. But on the weekends we do make an effort to accomplish more than just stuffing ourselves into pajamas and sitting around bingeing various Netflix series.

Then comes blissful sleep, which I don't do as much of as I should. Wake up . . . rinse and repeat.

But I'd be lying if I said that was all that ever happened. There is another part of my life—a much more adventurous part—that creates a lot of controversy amongst half of my friends and *all* of my family.

It seems that I have a knack for solving crimes, and to be frank, I have no idea where this particular skill or propensity for justice comes from. I feel it in my gut. That's my best answer. For that I've been called an empath. I can't seem to let these things go or wait while other people—of the law enforcement variety—sort things out. My older sister, Anna May, said it's because I'm bossy and need to take charge of things. I'd prefer to say that I'm a self-starter. I mean, it's all in the way you sell it, am I right?

My most recent brush with the law had been just a few weeks ago while I was visiting my aunt Grace in Irvine, California. I was there for a food industry convention, but fate had other plans for my trip. A friend of my aunt's had been the victim of some wrongdoing, and much to my surprise, she enlisted my help. You wouldn't see that kind of behavior coming from my mother, but they are without a shadow of a doubt, completely different people.

What struck me most were two things—more riveting than crime-solving—that happened while I was away. The first being that Anna May and I actually got along. Which never happens at home. I'm afraid that it didn't last as I'd hoped it would though. It seemed that as soon as we hit Cleveland air space, our old ways of butting heads resurfaced. However, with that being said, I do think we have a better understanding of each other, and maybe, just maybe, we're not *quite* as hard on each other as we used to be. But, it's only been a few weeks, and I reserve the right to change my mind at any time.

The other thing that happened was some kind of internal shift of character that I often have a difficult time putting into words. I don't know if it was the salty air or the extreme amount of sunshine that did it, but I felt like a different person. I no longer found myself wishing away the parts of me that didn't live up to everybody's expectations. It was the first time I didn't hear myself say that I was giving up my treacherous pastime of amateur detecting to make someone *else* feel better. For once, I was more concerned with my own feelings, prioritizing myself, and it felt good. It felt liberating.

I can't say that my parents were happy about this newfound version of Lana, and I'd had a lively discussion or two reminding them that I was an adult. My thirtieth birthday was barreling toward me at an accelerated rate, and the helicopter parenting was becoming a bit much. But parents will be parents, and as my mother so forcefully reminded me, "You will always be *my* baby."

Of course, it wasn't as if I was hoping for any new travesties to come my way. Preferably not, if I'm being honest. It wasn't like I was a glutton for punishment or anything. But the point was, I would be ready to take on anything that dare come my way.

So, regardless of what anyone said or thought—including the former version of me—the new Lana wouldn't be giving up her sleuthing ways. And you could take *that* to the bank.

CHAPTER
3

Friday morning was the definition of commotion at Asia Village. Most of the prep had to be done prior to Saturday because of the customs involved with the first day of the new year. Peter's mom, Nancy, would be opening the restaurant with me because I had to meet with various contractors and there was no way I'd be able to wait tables and run around the plaza.

When Ian first approached me about being his right-hand woman on this project, I'd hesitated. I couldn't understand why he always wanted me to do everything with him. Hadn't he, by now, thought that maybe he should get an assistant, or at the very least, a trusted event planner? Adam suggested that the answer was simple: Ian wanted to be around me through any excuse he could think of. Though I was inclined to agree with Adam's sentiment, I didn't want to add fuel to the fire by admitting I suspected the same thing. Ian had for the most part been very respectful of my relationship. But did I think if he saw a window of opportunity, he'd take it? Absolutely.

What floored me was hearing the words coming out of

my mouth agreeing to take on the responsibility. I think it was largely because I had a vision for it. I wanted to see the day play out as I thought it should. And the best way to do that was to do it myself. Ian still got to make the last call on everything, but I got what I asked for more often than not.

I'd arrived at the plaza around eight a.m. Mr. Zhang from Wild Sage was already there and had let in the team of people who were hanging red paper lanterns and decorative couplets around the plaza. Our sky-lit ceiling was already adorned with strings of twinkle lights that held lanterns all year long, but they were white, yellow, and pink. For the holiday, they all needed to be red.

Mr. Zhang stood outside his shop, hands behind his back as he observed the workers carrying their ladders to the next location. When I approached him, he broke his attention and smiled at me, his temples crinkling as the gesture reached his eyes. "Good morning, Lana."

"Morning, Mr. Zhang," I replied with a smile of my own. "You're looking well today."

None of us knew exactly how old Mr. Zhang was. It was possible that he was older than time itself. But he was spry and quite the character. He'd been a friend and a father figure to the late Thomas Feng.

Wild Sage was a cool shop filled with herbs, tonics, and Chinese remedies for any ailment you could think of. I hadn't asked him his opinion of the new shop, Eastern Enchantments.

He bowed his head. "It is kind of you to say so."

"We'll see you at dinner tonight?" I asked.

Mr. Zhang had become my grandmother's boyfriend of sorts. My mom didn't like to use that word, so she often said he was her "man friend." I was happy for A-ma though. She deserved a little romance after being a widow for so many years.

To my surprise, my mother had invited Mr. Zhang to the reunion dinner at my parents' house, and A-ma was absolutely elated. It was a symbol of acceptance.

He nodded. "Yes, I will be there. How nice of your mother to invite me . . . Lana, I must ask, are you prepared for the new year?" His voice was laced with concern and innocence.

I suspected the Mahjong Matrons might have shared that I had not been keeping up with my laundry duties.

"I did about three loads of laundry last night when I got home from work," I assured him. "And I made sure to sweep and vacuum as well."

He nodded his approval. "Good, I would not wish to see you ill-prepared. There has been much upheaval in your life since you have begun your journey here."

My cheeks felt hot. "It hasn't been all bad." Though I'd become more comfortable with myself and the things I'd been through, I didn't want to discuss any of that. It felt a whole lot like over-explaining. I felt my right foot take a step toward the restaurant, inching away before a lecture could begin.

He seemed to notice, and his eyes traveled down to my feet. Mr. Zhang smiled. "You have much to get done today, I will not keep you."

My stomach fluttered as I felt immediate guilt. He always meant well, and deep down I knew that.

As if reading my mind, he removed a hand from behind his back and patted my forearm. "Do not worry so much, Lana. I understand better than you know."

With an apologetic smile, I said, "See you tonight then?"

"Yes, I will see you later."

With a final wave, I went on my way, trying to pace my strides to Ho-Lee Noodle House. As I unlocked the doors and let myself in, I wondered what warnings I would receive from the Mahjong Matrons today.

I straightened up the dining area until Nancy and Peter showed up at eight thirty. By the time they arrived, I had wiped down any menus that needed it, made sure place settings were at every table, and straightened the chairs. My mother was a stickler about crooked chairs. Don't ask me why that was one of her things, it's just something I've known about her since I came out of the womb.

I locked the restaurant doors behind them, trying to stifle a laugh at the juxtaposition of their appearances. Peter's tall, skinny frame appeared more pronounced standing next to his mother, who was about six inches shorter than he was. Though she was also slender, Nancy was an appropriate weight for her size, whereas Peter was more often than not referred to as a "toothpick." It didn't help that his all-black wardrobe was intentionally one size bigger than actually required for his body type. He did it for comfort and probably for style as well, but it always had people asking him if he'd been losing weight.

So while Peter looked like he was gearing up to attend a rock concert, Nancy was dressed in a chic black-and-tan houndstooth wool coat over a cream-colored angora sweater and pleated charcoal dress pants. Her black hair—which she swore wasn't dyed—was well past her shoulders, and she often wore it styled with large curls that framed her round face.

They shared the same mouth and nose, but that's where their resemblances stopped.

Aside from these observations in contrast, I also noted

that Peter looked somewhat frazzled. Which was highly unusual for him since he was normally so zenned out that it unnerved me.

"What's your deal?" I asked, poking him in the middle of his back as he walked away.

Peter lifted his black baseball cap momentarily to smooth back his shaggy hair and mumbled, "Nothing." He readjusted the hat low over his eyes and kept walking toward the kitchen without another word.

Nancy laughed. She paused, stopping me in my tracks while Peter disappeared into the kitchen. "He is a little bit stressed about the rules for the holiday. Since he can't use some utensils tomorrow, he will have to prepare many of the menu items today."

"Oh," I replied. "I completely forgot about the whole knife thing and not cutting off good luck."

"He will survive," Nancy said with a smile. "As he always does."

We continued our walk back to the kitchen. "Lou will be in a little earlier to help with that, so hopefully it's not as bad as Peter's imagining." Lou was our night cook and always willing to help out if we needed an extra set of hands.

"I will help as well." Nancy pushed open the swinging door and we stepped into the kitchen. Peter was adjusting his wireless headphone and grumbling to himself when we walked in. He always left one earbud out so he could hear what was going on, but there wasn't a moment of his shift that he wasn't listening to heavy metal. He claimed it calmed him down, and who was I to judge the relaxing properties of Metallica.

Nancy disappeared through the next set of swinging doors to the employee lounge area—which was really a trumped-up term for the nook we used to eat our lunches in peace. I'd grown up in that particular nook, Anna May and I coloring and watching cartoons while my parents ran the restaurant. I'd also studied for tests back there, learned how to tie my shoes, and even found my first chicken pox mark at six years old while watching *Scooby-Doo*.

I leaned against the counter next to Peter, feeling sympathetic. "We're gonna get through it. It'll be a smooth day and—"

Peter held up a hand before I could finish. "I'm not even superstitious, man."

"I know."

"But your mom . . . and my mom . . . like whoa. I got the third degree on the way to work that I better not try and sneak in any cutlery tomorrow. Like, for real?"

I could see Peter was not the person to admit my laundry activities to, so I just nodded along.

"And you know, I hate being talked at first thing in the morning."

I did know, firsthand. "It's just one day," I said, unsure of how to proceed.

Peter lowered his voice. "Just keep my mom outta the kitchen for like two hours. I need some peace and some jams."

"No problem." My eyes traveled to the adjoining room. "I'll go talk to her now."

He gave me a thumbs-up, pressed something on his phone, and turned to prepare the grill.

Taking that as my signal of dismissal, I went into the employee lounge and found Nancy sitting at the two-seater table.

"He wants me to leave him alone, I bet." Amusement danced in her eyes.

I nodded. "Out of everyone, you know how he gets first

thing in the morning. The times he's driven me to work, we usually don't speak a word."

She chuckled. "I'll leave him to his cooking then. Do you have anything that needs to be done?"

"There's a box of decorations by the cash register. Would you mind hanging those up around the dining room? I have a few things I need to tend to back here."

"No problem. I enjoy hanging decorations." She rose from her chair and straightened her black dress shirt. "I'll let you know when the vendors start showing up."

When she left, I shut myself in the shoebox I call an office. A little paperwork needed to get done before the day got away from me. While I massaged my temples, I went through the receipts from the previous night and tallied the totals. We hadn't done too bad for a Thursday night, but I wanted more business. I always wanted more business though, so that was nothing new.

Mainly so I could do things like give Peter a bonus for his extra hard work, and for dealing with customs that he didn't particularly want to participate in.

When I say that I have schemed to make the extra business happen, I am not exaggerating. Since my time as restaurant manager, I have done promos, held a speed dating event (didn't go well), participated in the Cleveland Night Market (also didn't go well), and catered an upscale party for none other than Donna Feng (which, yes you guessed it, didn't go well). But did I give up? Not a chance. We aren't quitters in the Lee family, that much I can say.

I wasn't going to let any of those failed endeavors stop me going forward either. Perseverance can be a challenge, but it is a worthwhile pursuit.

My hope was that the celebrations tomorrow would

bring a lot more business to the plaza in general. I'd noticed the mayor of Cleveland's name on the list and was
only partially surprised because he was a friend of the
Feng family, after all. He'd been at every one of Donna's
parties in recent times, so I was glad to see that tomorrow's
festivities weren't an exception.

I'd also noticed a few familiar news anchor names from
WKYC, a handful of journalists from *Cleveland* magazine, the *Plain Dealer*, and of course, our very own mayor
of Fairview Park.

I was beyond excited, especially since I'd put a lot of
work into this project. It was truly going to be a night to
remember.

CHAPTER
4

I made it through a half hour undisturbed before I heard light tapping on my office door. "Come in!" I yelled.

Nancy opened the door a few inches and poked her head through. "The lion dance performers are here."

Setting my pen down, I pushed my chair out and shimmied around the corner of the desk. It was a tight squeeze between that and the filing cabinets.

Nancy pushed the door open farther so I could follow her out, and I grabbed my coat from the peg next to the threshold before exiting. She turned to look at me as she led the way. "The Matrons are also here. They were concerned that you weren't there to greet them today."

"I forgot to mention that you were filling in for me when I saw them yesterday morning."

Out in the dining area, a group of casually dressed Asians had gathered around the Mahjong Matrons. A tall man with a shaved head stood near the edge of the group, holding a large drum and flanked by two women, one of them holding onto the head of the lion costume.

He noticed my arrival and came over to greet me,

extending a hand. "You must be Lana. I'm David Hong. It's good to meet you in person finally. Put a face to the name."

As we shook hands, I said, "Same. Thank you for doing this on such short notice." His skin was cool and his palms calloused. On first appearance, though he was covered in winter garb, you could tell he was built and physically fit. It could have been the veins popping out of his neck, or the fact that his sweatshirt clung to his chest in a flattering way. The kind of way that tells you he goes to the gym without him having to tell you.

The others turned to face us, all smiling and extremely chipper. Four women and three other men made up the dance troupe.

David stepped to the side, and with a sweeping motion introduced the woman standing next to him who was empty-handed. "This is my sister, Rhonda. We run the family business."

I sensed a bit of tension as Rhonda took a step forward. She stood right in front of her brother as if she were trying to cut him out of the conversation. And instead of offering me her hand, she gave me a childlike wave, spreading her fingers out as her hand flapped back and forth. "Hi Lana, nice to meet you! I've heard a lot about you from Kimmy. I'm the one who recommended the party rental company, RE: Event Rentals."

I waved back in the same manner, which felt unnatural. I've always believed in a firm handshake. It sets the tone. "Nice to meet you as well. And thanks for the suggestion. I was scrambling to find someone who'd be available on such short notice."

"A family friend started working there," she said. "And they can use all the clients they can get their hands on."

David cleared his throat but said nothing. I had the

express feeling that he wanted to take the conversation back over.

But Rhonda continued on with a bat of her eyelashes. "He's like a second brother to me, and I want to support him with his new job any way that I can."

I studied her face as she yammered on, seemingly oblivious to her brother's impatience. She was a pretty woman with youthful, petite features and it was hard to guess at her age. Especially factoring in her mannerisms. I knew that Kimmy had mentioned she was a few years younger than us. But I had no idea what a "few" meant to Kimmy.

The two of them knew each other from the Black Garter, a gentleman's club in a neighboring city. Kimmy had been the one who helped me book their dance troupe for the party, and I was thankful for the help because I'd been lost on finding someone in such a tight window of time.

Kimmy had been serving drinks there afterhours to help make extra cash for the past year, and in the meantime had made friends with a lot of the dancers, Rhonda being one of them.

I wasn't anyone to judge, and from what Kimmy had said, Rhonda was quite talented. Her specialty being acrobatic in nature. Kimmy had shown me a video of their troupe in action, and I was sold by the end of it. When informing my parents of the decision to hire them for the party, I'd left out the specifics of the association. What they didn't know, they couldn't judge. Plus, I didn't want to out Kimmy's affiliation.

Kimmy moonlighting as a cocktail waitress at the adult venue was the best-kept secret in all of Asia Village. Not even the Mahjong Matrons knew. I knew, and of course, Megan and Adam. Oh, and Peter, naturally. But that's where the train stopped.

Kimmy's family would undoubtedly send her to the

mountains of Tibet if they thought she entertained such a career path. But times were tough, and Kimmy needed extra income. I'd always thought it was odd that her parents never questioned how she was able to sustain her lifestyle on the meager salary they paid her. But maybe they assumed her position was the same as mine—relying on credit cards to get by. It's not a habit I'd recommend for anyone.

David repositioned himself so he wasn't standing behind his sister. On his other side stood a woman similar in size to Rhonda who was holding onto the head of the lion costume. "This is Angela," David said. "She's going to be—"

Rhonda clapped her hands together. "Are we ready to head out?"

The slight was obvious to me, but everyone involved acted as if it hadn't happened. Angela—the slighted—gave me a polite nod before turning away and heading to the doors.

Immediately I was curious about the relationship between the two women, but I'd have to save any questions I had for later.

The Matrons—all looking entertained—had risen from the table and began slipping their coats on. Helen stood in front of the others and said, "They have welcomed us to come watch the preview. How could we say no?"

I turned to Nancy. "We shouldn't be long."

"Don't worry," she replied. "I'll watch over everything."

The thirteen of us marched out of the restaurant in single file like a gaggle of ducks. I slipped on the double-breasted peacoat I'd just bought myself for Christmas. It was light gray and hugged my frame so I'd at least have a little bit of a figure. Winter did nothing for my body structure.

Passing Shanghai Donuts, I inhaled the sweet bakery smells that Mama Wu was busy preparing for the day. She waved through the window, and I returned the gesture with a smile. Ian had apparently decided that a doughnut was not necessary for me this morning. I made a mental note to pick one up later. I tended to "eat my feelings," and it was a stressful time for me right now.

As we neared China Cinema and Song, Kimmy came jogging out of the store. "Hey, what are you guys doing?" Her family's shop sold the largest collection of Asian entertainment in all of Northeast Ohio. If you wanted a Chinese movie, an imported CD, or movie posters, that's where you went.

"Bare-bones dress rehearsal," I said. "Wanna come?"

Kimmy shrugged. "Sure." She disappeared back into the store, most likely to grab a coat.

In this new age of digital takeover, business had been difficult for them, but they still had their loyal customers who kept them going. I was currently in the process of helping Kimmy find ways to increase business. I liked doing that sort of thing, and we were candid enough with each other that I could give her my honest opinion on whether I thought something would work.

Yuna and Mr. Zhang were standing together outside of Asian Accents, both with their coats on. Their heads turned as we approached.

Mr. Zhang stepped forward. "We shall join in watching the preview," he said with a good-natured grin.

Yuna waved at me with excitement. "This is so exciting! The lion dance is my favorite part!"

If I were a different person, say like Kimmy, I probably would have told Yuna to take her excitement down a notch. It was a little much this early in the morning. Instead, I nodded in agreement.

Once we'd reached the entrance of the plaza, Kimmy had caught up with us, still trying to stuff one of her arms into her puffy coat. She sped up next to me. "What's Peter's problem?"

"He's upset about tomorrow and all the restrictions."

"I tried texting him and he was like 'okay.' And I'm like 'okay?' . . . and then he was like . . . 'yeah' . . . and then I was like—"

"Kimmy . . . I'm a little preoccupied right now." I exited through the doors that Rhonda held open. "Maybe we can talk about that later."

Kimmy had a snappy comeback ready. I could tell by the look in her eye. But Rhonda pinched her arm, intercepting any chance she had of razzing me. "Hey you! I didn't know you'd be here today."

Kimmy held out her arm and gave Rhonda what I could only describe as a half hug. "I'm here every day. It's like the Hotel California. 'You can check out' and all that . . ."

She raised an eyebrow. "I don't know what that means . . ."

"It's a song," Kimmy said. "Probably too old for you to know. Which is not making me feel better about myself, by the way."

"Who doesn't know the Eagles?" I asked.

Rhonda turned to me. "Who are the Eagles?"

Kimmy smacked her forehead. "Never mind, young blood." She elbowed Rhonda playfully in her side. "This conversation is giving me gray hair."

Rhonda laughed. "I'll google it later. You have me intrigued."

The two women hung back as we made our way out into the parking lot, where I was quickly distracted by the team of workers erecting a large metal stage in the north section of the open area. Caution tape had been used to partition the space we needed for the show, and I was extremely interested to see how this was going to work.

We'd been fortunate enough not to have any more snowstorms in recent days, and no further snow planned in the forecast until after the weekend. Which would be perfect. However, the reason for that was it'd been too cold to snow.

The temperature was beginning to rise. We were now riding at a steady twenty-three degrees, an improvement from last week's brisk seventeen.

Since the stage wasn't completely finished, the dance team would have to mimic how it would work tomorrow. The plan was to have a tented area behind the curtain where they'd come out of.

David sidled up next to me. "We'll begin with some firecrackers. Two dancers will be out on stage at opposite ends. After the first firecracker display, I'll come out with a drum. Unlike this one, it'll be much larger and on wheels. One of the dancers will pull it across the stage while I drum. Then once I've crossed to the opposite end, the ladies will come out in the lion costume. We'll act out a few of the traditional dances before winding ourselves through the audience."

We continued to walk closer to the metal structure as he pointed this way and that.

"Right here"—he pointed to the center of the stage— "will be a ramp, and this is where we'll descend into the crowd." He turned around and pointed at the entrance of the plaza. "And finally parading back through the doors.

"After we're safely off stage, more firecrackers will be set off. We'll set off a few smaller ones and then conclude with a finale."

"Okay, wonderful," I said, nodding as I envisioned the event coming to life. "I was wondering how we'd get everybody back inside at the end of the night. This will work perfectly so I can announce the winners of our raffles once you've wrapped up."

"We'll just do a quick run-through." He patted his drum. "I want to make sure that everyone knows the direct path we will be taking inside and the appropriate places to pause to engage with the audience."

He left me standing with Kimmy and the Mahjong Matrons, who had been off to the side listening to our discussion. He rallied around his team, and we watched as he pointed to the stage and back to the door, most likely repeating everything he'd just said to me.

Two performers—a man and a woman—stood at opposite ends of the stage. They sped through their dance, and then two more performers came out, one with a tambourine and the other with a small drum.

The four danced around one another—talking through the motions as they went along. You could see the skill with which they worked as a team. They circled a final time, and then in twos they went off to the side. Now David came forward.

He beat on the drum with authority, setting the rhythm to which they all moved.

Then, the lion's head poked playfully through the curtain, jerking to the beat of the drum.

I watched as it began interacting with the others on stage, and slowly they all began to move toward the entrance, pausing intermittently to include a dance move in front of their imaginary onlookers.

David commented as they went along: "Pause here, interact with the crowd."

Just as they neared the doors again, the head of the lion continued moving forward as the rear of the costume held its position. This caused the tail of the lion to be pulled from over Rhonda's head and knocked her off-balance.

Thankfully she caught herself before face-planting into the concrete, but it didn't completely stop her from falling. She landed on all fours, cursing as her hands slapped the pavement.

"Ow! Stop rushing through your steps!" Rhonda yelled, hoisting herself up on the palms of her hands. She stomped forward to acknowledge the person manipulating the head of the costume. "How many times do I have to tell you to focus on your counts?! Are you a total idiot?"

"Rhonda! Don't be so harsh!" David snapped back. "Angela is still trying to learn."

The woman controlling the front end of the costume removed herself from beneath the lion's head and ran a shaky hand over her tousled hair. Her face was flush from exertion and probably also embarrassment.

Rhonda's face reddened. "You take her side with everything. This is unbelievable." She dropped the back end of the costume. "It's bad enough that you gave her my position as the head of the costume. Maybe you two should do the dance yourselves." She stomped her foot like a child and stormed back into the plaza, leaving all of us staring in shock at her outburst.

I leaned toward Kimmy. "Is it just me or did that seem like an overreaction?"

Kimmy snorted. "That's Rhonda for you. I wouldn't call her the world's most rational person to begin with, but from what I've heard, she's not taking too kindly to the new replacement within their team."

"What's the deal with that? I noticed something off between those two back at the restaurant. Are they just oil and water, or what?"

"No, it's more than that." Kimmy leaned in close, her voice hovering at a whisper. "That's her brother's new fiancée."

CHAPTER
5

Kimmy was ready to dive headfirst into gossip mode, but I shushed her because the Matrons were doing that thing again where they pretended like they're not listening, but they totally were. On top of that, we had Mr. Zhang with his eagle eyes and Yuna with her impeccable memory retention. No doubt before the morning was over, the young receptionist would have recited the events word for word to anyone at the salon who would listen. With that in mind, I didn't want Kimmy to inadvertently out herself and the association she had with Rhonda. Plus David was coming this way and I didn't want him to think we were standing around bad-mouthing his sister.

I tugged on the sleeve of her puffy coat and forced a smile as David approached. Attempting to keep my tone light, I asked, "Is everything okay with Rhonda?"

He shook his head. "I'm really sorry about that. It's very unprofessional. She's been having a hard time lately with the changes in the crew. But I didn't expect her to have an outburst like that in front of everyone."

Angela shuffled over, standing slightly behind David

as if she didn't want to intrude on our conversation. I hadn't paid her much attention when we'd met inside the restaurant. She was small in stature, quiet—and in a way, unassuming. Though she was naturally beautiful, with minimal, if any, makeup, she didn't have much of a presence. She seemed the sort of person who would blend into any room and be easily forgettable. I didn't see her being a threat to anyone.

I attempted to give her an encouraging smile, but the longer we stood there, the more I began to worry. "Is this going to be a situation tomorrow?" I asked David.

"No, I'll have a chat with her." David's head turned in the direction of the door. "Rhonda knows how important this is, and Ian paid a lot of money for a grade-A performance. It has to be perfect. Our company would not settle for anything less."

Kimmy tsked. "You know what? Let me go talk some sense into her. Maybe she needs encouraging words from a . . . friend. Instead of family or whatever."

David held up a hand. "This is between me and my sister, I can handle it. I appreciate—"

Kimmy batted at his palm. "Nonsense, it's no trouble. I have a certain way about me that tends to get through to people." Without giving him a chance to argue the point, she walked away.

David huffed. "I'd rather she didn't get involved."

"If there's one thing to know about Kimmy, it's that she's got a determined mindset," I explained.

Helen caught my attention. "If the show is over, we will go inside now."

I noticed that the other performers had moved inside without us realizing it. I nodded, a shiver running through my body as a gust of wind blew through the parking lot. "Yeah, it's cold out here. We'll be in right behind you."

Yuna turned to Mr. Zhang. "Come on, Mr. Zhang, you can hold onto my arm."

He bowed his head and latched onto her elbow.

After the others were out of earshot, Angela spoke up for the first time since joining our little huddle. "I feel awful because I know this is my fault. I got distracted and lost count." She tucked her chin inward and pouted.

Her emotional display seemed insincere somehow. As if she'd practiced this exact reaction a few times before to garner sympathy when she was in trouble. I don't know what made me think that, call it a hunch, but in the time or two that I'd dabbled in investigating, I'd learned quite a bit about tell signs. However, I didn't know Angela well enough to say either way.

David wrapped a consoling arm around her shoulders. "It'll be okay, things will straighten themselves out, and we'll all be one happy family soon enough."

Angela collapsed her head against his chest. "I hope you're right about that. I don't want to be the cause of a family feud."

"What exactly is the problem anyhow?" I asked, unable to hide my curiosity.

David shrugged. "Rhonda has it in her head that Angela is trying to replace her in our family business. Which is absolutely ridiculous. All because I wanted Angela to have a chance at leading the lion dance this season. Rhonda has been in that role for several years; it's okay to give someone else a turn every once in a while."

I didn't want to throw in my two cents. I probably wouldn't have acted out in the way that Rhonda had, but I'd probably have some similar feelings about being replaced.

If David was waiting for me to agree with him, he didn't show it and continued right on talking, much like Rhonda had done earlier. "My sister and I are partners until the end. No matter who I marry, I'd never allow it to be any other way. Angela knows that too." He squeezed her shoulder. "She just wants to be a part of it."

Angela nodded, keeping her head firmly planted against his chest. "It's true. I always wanted a sister, and I was so excited to be a part of this family. I didn't think this would happen . . . We're already enemies before I've even married into the family."

"Well, maybe she'll come around." I said it half-heartedly because frankly, I didn't know anything about Rhonda either. Family dynamics could be rough, and having a sister wasn't always the cakewalk you wished it to be.

"She's going to have to," David stated. "There's no other option. This marriage is happening, and I refuse to choose sides. But, if my sister pushes my hand, I won't have a choice."

I happened to catch a glance at Angela's face. I swore her lips curved up in satisfaction. But maybe it was just the frigid temperature getting to me and I was imagining things.

Once the performance team had left and David had gone over a few final details before he and Angela left as well, Kimmy stopped by the restaurant to inform me that she'd smoothed things over with Rhonda. "I appealed to her rational side," she said with confidence.

"What does that mean?" I asked.

"Money," Kimmy replied. "Do it for the money and forget about that harlot."

"Do you really think that slip of a woman is that menacing? I'd hardly consider her to be of harlot status."

"That's what they always say, isn't it?" Kimmy asked. "It's always the quiet ones."

I decided to let the whole thing go. It couldn't be my problem. Not today and certainly not tomorrow.

After Kimmy left, I went about my daily duties and tried as best I could to focus my thoughts back to the subject at hand. When I saw my parents for dinner later that night, the last thing I wanted to admit was that I'd gotten sidetracked by family drama that wasn't even ours.

CHAPTER
6

Adam had the pleasure of being roped into this family event, and was on driving duty tonight, toting myself and Megan to my parents' house.

My parents live in Parma, which—fun fact—is the largest suburb in all of Ohio. Growing up there proved challenging at times because it wasn't exactly the Asian capital of Cuyahoga County. But we got by and I think it equipped both Anna May and me with thicker skin.

When you're a kid, it's not the coolest thing ever to be different, and we'd been teased more than a few times because of it. At that age, you want to blend in, be a part of a group, and sometimes kids can become downright nasty when it comes to things like that. The trick is to get through it, not let any of those insecurities stick to you as you develop into adulthood. Once you become un-apologetically comfortable with who you are, life opens up and things are much easier. You have to learn quickly that other people's opinions of you are not your concern. Not exactly the easiest lesson in your teens.

Anytime I visited my childhood home, I became nostalgic. Reminiscing about playing on the swing set in our backyard or meeting up with the other kids on our block to ride our bikes down to the neighborhood park. I found myself sharing sentiments with adults from previous generations—we always think our youth was a "simpler time."

Adam pulled into the driveway behind my sister's car.

The three of us were decked out in the traditional colors of the holiday. The requirement was to wear completely new clothes, except for your shoes. Which I was grateful for because there's nothing worse than being trapped in a pair of stilettos that hadn't yet been broken in.

Megan had chosen a respectable knee-length, gold dress with matching heels.

Last week, I'd taken Adam shopping for a red dress shirt, which was a completely new experience for him. His closet didn't even approach that spectrum of the rainbow. Then when I told him he had to wear khakis instead of black pants, I could swear he mumbled something about running away to Mexico, but I pretended like I hadn't heard a thing. Black was a no-no, and my parents would sooner throw him out of the house than allow him to sit through a meal if he showed up in his usual attire.

I, myself, was outfitted in a red dress with capped sleeves and a flowing waistline to cover up some of the doughnut pudge that sat around my midsection. As I'd gotten dressed, I reminded myself that after this weekend was over, I was going to make it to the gym come hell or high water.

Adam had kept the car running because the temps had dropped back down below twenty. I removed my seat belt and stared out the window. Normally I loved Chinese New Year, and the family dinner we had the evening before. This year seemed even more special because now my family considered Adam and me serious enough to invite him along. But I couldn't shake this sense of dread that sat in the pit of my stomach. It had been with me on and off since the practice rehearsal that morning.

"What's wrong?" Megan asked from the back seat.

I rested my elbow on the window ledge. "I don't know. I just have this sense of yuck that I can't seem to shake."

Adam placed his hand on my leg. "Is it because I have khakis on?"

Even though it was dark in the car, I could sense the smile in his voice. "Oh hush," I said. "You look wonderful."

"I look like I work at Verizon," he quipped.

Megan laughed. "I bet if you went to Target, people would ask you where the toilet paper is."

Adam joined in her laughter, and I tried to feign a smile. "All right, let's go in before this becomes improv hour." I reached for the door handle. "I'm probably just frazzled with everything going on."

Adam turned off the engine and we all exited the warmth of the car, scurrying to the back door of my parents' house, my teeth chattering the entire way.

Inside, we were greeted with a cacophony of laughter. I could hear my grandmother, Mr. Zhang, Anna May, both my parents, and a voice that sounded familiar, but I couldn't quite place. It wasn't until we reached the living room that I recognized the dashing man sitting next to my sister with sandy blond hair and eyes the color of well-steeped green tea.

"Hello everyone!" I filled my voice with cheer, trying to pretend I wasn't surprised to see Henry Andrews—Anna May's on-again, off-again, unofficial boyfriend. There was a lot of controversy around their relationship because Henry wasn't legally divorced, only separated.

My parents rose from the couch. My mom clasped her hands together. "Oh good, you're here. We can eat soon!"

A-ma and Mr. Zhang stood as well. They were adorable in their semi-matching embroidered red jackets. While we all exchanged pleasantries, A-ma snuck over to me and slipped a red envelope into my palm, closed my fingers around it and gave my hand a squeeze. It was tradition to give these envelopes with wishes of good fortune and luck during the coming year. Usually the elders give to the younger members of the family, and lucky for me I still counted in that category.

Adam passed by me, outstretching a hand to Henry. "Hey man, long time no see."

As Henry outstretched his arm, the Rolex he never seemed to take off peeked out from inside his suit jacket sleeve. He grabbed Adam's hand, the dimples in his cheeks appearing as he smiled with genuine interest and gave him a hardy handshake. The two men had gotten along pretty well during our last sit-down together. "Good to see ya, buddy." His other hand patted Adam on the back. "It's been a while."

"Thanksgiving," Adam replied.

Anna May blushed, and I immediately wondered if something had changed in his marital situation. I mean, why else would he be here?

Henry nodded. "That's right. Turkey time. I had to unbuckle my pants after dinner." He patted his belly, chuckling. "I have a feeling Mrs. Lee is going to produce the same outcome."

My mom beamed with pride. She loved anyone who adored her cooking.

I went to hug my sister, giving her an extra squeeze. "You're just full of surprises these days," I said through a gritted smile.

Since coming home from our trip to Irvine, Anna May hadn't mentioned Henry's name, not one time. If I got the opportunity to pull her off to the side, I would have lots of questions that needed answering. I was so shocked, I didn't have time to be mad about the fact that she hadn't shared any new details with me. Her relationship with Henry had been such a big to-do in her life that I was more hurt than anything else that she hadn't shared whatever new developments had clearly happened.

Whispering in my ear, she replied, "We'll talk soon. Not now, okay?"

I nodded into her shoulder before we separated, and she went about the act of hugging Megan and greeting Adam.

After we'd all exchanged pleasantries, my mother suggested we head into the dining room.

I sat on the side near the window that looked out on the driveway, Megan and Adam on either side of me. Even with the extension panel on my parents' dining room table, we were snug with a party of nine. The table seated eight, so Henry and Anna May were smooshed next to my grandmother and Mr. Zhang, while my parents sat at the heads of the table.

I rested my hands in my lap, feeling uncomfortable. It felt like time had stopped and we were trapped in this awful moment of awkwardness. It was all close quarters and unspoken words. Adam must have sensed it because he draped an arm around the back of my chair.

My mother disappeared into the kitchen, and I wished I had followed after her, but I thought it might appear odd because I never did that. Normally my sister would trail after her, dutifully helping serve the food. But today she just sat there, her body leaning against Henry, closer than needed—even with the tight space.

My dad was first to break the awkward silence that

was beginning to develop. "So"—he clasped his hands together—"how did things go at the plaza today? We all set for the big day tomorrow?"

I nodded. "We are ready to go. Nancy helped set up the dining room decorations, and all the food is prepped. Peter just has to pull it out of the cooler and cook it."

"No knives, I hope," my dad said, leaning forward. "You know your mother will have a fit."

"Oh, I know," I said. "And he knows too, maybe too well."

Adam raised an eyebrow. "What's the deal with knives?"

Anna May replied. "Using anything sharp on New Year's Day represents the cutting off of good fortune."

Adam tilted his head. "I didn't realize your mother was so superstitious."

I snorted. "She's selectively superstitious."

"I can hear you!" my mother yelled from the kitchen.

We all laughed.

Idle conversation came a little easier after that, and the evening resumed. My curiosity about what had transpired between Anna May and Henry was beginning to calm itself, and now my stomach was consuming my thoughts.

A few minutes later, my mom brought out a large platter of steamed dumplings. She playfully smacked my sister's shoulder. "Come help me."

I could tell Anna May was holding in an eye roll. She had more restraint than I did. With a tight-lipped smile, she rose from her chair and followed after my mother.

My stomach growled, and I felt my mouth begin to water as I eyed the giant plate of dumplings.

Next, my mom and sister came back with a plate of freshly fried spring rolls and a giant bowl of longevity noodles, which are also known as yi mein and symbolize long life. They retreated back to the kitchen for the final dishes, and I knew what was coming next, the thing I dreaded most of all.

The two returned, my sister carrying a dish with a Peking duck and my mom carrying two platters with a giant catfish on each. The head and tail securely attached . . . for the sake of tradition, representing a good beginning and end to the year. "There's two this year?"

"Yes, we have more people now and one fish will not be enough."

My mother set one fish in front of Mr. Zhang, symbolizing that he was an honored guest and that he would eat first. Then to my surprise, she set the second fish in front of Adam.

"Why are you putting it right there?" I asked.

She clucked her tongue. "Adam is my future son-in-law. It is an honor to have him as our guest."

Adam cleared his throat, reaching for his water glass.

In that moment, I could feel the color draining from my face. Every set of eyes, including our fishy friend, stared at me.

Henry gave Adam a sly smile. "Is there something you'd like to share with the class?"

After gulping down half the glass of water, Adam shook his head. "No secrets here."

Anna May sat down, her eyes focused on me, ignoring Adam's 'no frills' response—something my sister never accepted. "I'm sure you guys must have talked about it."

Megan kicked me from under the table. We exchanged a glance, her eyes shifting behind her, and without actually speaking, I knew she was asking if I wanted to bust through the window behind us and run away. Everybody knew I didn't discuss the details of my relationship with my family. Especially with my mother, who had been trying to marry me off since I graduated college.

My dad didn't like to talk about it either, because in his head I was still five years old. I noticed he had begun fidgeting with his napkin.

Between the comment my mother made, witnessing my dad's discomfort, and the catfish staring at me, I was ready to actually jump out said window.

Mr. Zhang spoke quietly to A-ma, filling her in on the topic of conversation.

My mother took her seat. "Let's eat," she said, as if we hadn't been talking about anything at all. "Mr. Zhang and Adam, please eat first."

Anna May continued to stare at me. "Are you going to act as if I hadn't just asked you a question?"

Henry placed his hand on Anna May's shoulder. "Easy, counselor."

I reached for my chopsticks. "I'd rather not discuss it, if it's all the same to you." I proceeded to grab dumplings, noodles, and two spring rolls for good measure. My eyes slid over to the duck, who also still had its head. "I'm sure there's a lot of other things we could be discussing."

My dad had busied himself with carving a few slices off the side of the duck, and I plucked one off the plate for myself.

Anna May pursed her lips. "Well, fine, we won't talk about it . . . as long as you don't get married before I do."

Now it was Henry's turn to pale.

Adam covered a laugh with some fake coughing, and my dad groaned.

Mr. Zhang sampled the fish. "Ah, Betty, this is cooked perfectly."

Adam had pulled himself together and also took a bite

of the fish. "Mmm, yeah, Mrs. Lee, this is the best catfish I've ever had."

My mother blushed. "Oh thank you, everybody. It is my joy to cook for family."

Now with the formalities out of the way, it was time to dig in.

I glanced over at Megan's plate and noticed she had about half the food I had on mine. I started to second guess the number of dumplings I'd shoveled onto my plate. But when I turned toward Adam's plate, I noted he had double what was on mine, and that made me feel slightly better about myself.

A-ma laughed quietly to herself. She was watching me look at everyone's plate. When our eyes caught, she gave me a thumbs-up, and pointed to her own plate, which looked similar to my own. She perked up in her seat, and said, "Eat! Good!"

It made me laugh a little bit too. I smiled back and returned her thumbs-up. Even though my grandmother and I couldn't speak to each other in conventional ways, we seemed to understand each other enough. Her English was sparse, and though she practiced with my mom and dad every day, she spent more time speaking Hokkien, the Taiwanese dialect that my mom's side of the family spoke. And yet, sometimes, I felt like my grandmother understood me better than anyone else around me.

After a few minutes of comfortable silence, my mother paused and asked, "So you do not talk about marriage?"

"Mom." I closed my eyes and inhaled deeply. We had guests and I didn't want to cause a scene.

Mr. Zhang gasped. "Ah, did you hear about what happened at the plaza today with the performance team?"

My mother turned to acknowledge Mr. Zhang. "No, did something bad happen?"

I sighed a breath of relief as Mr. Zhang began relaying the story of what went on between David, Angela, and Rhonda. He'd apparently gotten the details from the Matrons about David's new engagement and the problems it was causing in their family dynamic.

It wasn't exactly a topic of discussion I wanted to speak on either, but it was better than the previous option of marriage. I had to give it up for Mr. Zhang. Out of everyone at the table, I wouldn't have expected him to be the one to rescue me.

When no one else was looking, he winked at me from across the table.

CHAPTER
7

Somehow we'd managed to keep the rest of dinner free of marriage talk. It could have been due to the fact that Megan, Henry, and Adam all kept the conversation revolving around different topics that had nothing to do with wedding bells. Mr. Zhang also helped out when he could by talking about the plaza or some herbal remedy he'd added to his shop.

Or it might have had something to do with when my mother began clearing the table and my father followed after her. They'd been missing in the kitchen for longer than it took to place dishes in the sink, that was for sure.

My mother came back with a serving tray of ti kue—which is a sweet rice cake that's eaten to symbolize prosperity. It has three ingredients: glutinous rice flour, sugar, and water. You basically mix it all up, steam it until it's cooked through and through, and boom, you have a weird little sticky cake that keeps the Kitchen God from talking too much about all the things you did wrong the previous year. I wonder if it was something that would also work on Anna May.

We stayed well past midnight—because it's the one day of the year when you're actually required to be a night owl. Something to do with ensuring a long life for your parents. Of course, it was me who'd have to wake up super early to open the restaurant tomorrow.

My dad announced that he'd gone all out and purchased some Chinese firecrackers to set off. My dad—the rebel—had cleared it with the neighbors so no one called the cops on him. That one made Adam chuckle.

We bundled up and went about moving our cars onto the street. Henry and Adam went to assist my dad toward the apron of the driveway, while the rest of us gathered on the front patio. Megan linked her arm through mine as we huddled closely together, both of us shivering within a matter of seconds. "Remind me to find a nice pantsuit next year," she said.

My teeth chattered as I laughed. Even though I was freezing, I felt a child's excitement. I'd loved firecrackers since I was a kid, and the effect was not lost on me as an adult.

The firecrackers began to pop and sizzle as the flames snaked down the length of red paper tubes that were strung together.

A sense of hopefulness washed over me as I watched the fire flicker and dance down the driveway and into the street. Perhaps it was the symbolism of scaring away evil spirits, something I never gave much thought to in the past. Or maybe it was my deep appreciation for the act of beginning anew—fire burning away the old remnants of the past. It made me think of the mythical phoenix rising from the ashes, reborn . . . stronger.

Whatever the cause, I wanted to hold onto this feeling for as long as I could.

CHAPTER
8

I'm not used to waking up early on Saturday mornings. I don't like it. It feels wrong and somehow cruel. That's not to say I never do it. But I keep it to a minimum and always make up for it on Sunday.

The wistful hopefulness from the previous evening was still with me, but I felt the sharp rap of worry chiseling away at my peaceful demeanor. Kikko poked her head out of the blanket at the foot of my bed. She appeared confused that I was awake and stared at me longer than usual. I shrugged and whispered, "Time to make the doughnuts." She tilted her head at the word "doughnut." Of course, she would have no idea that I was referencing the mid-1980s commercial for Dunkin' Donuts. If she did, well that would just be plain weird.

I slipped out of bed, hoping not to wake Adam. It was his day off and he would be accompanying me to the plaza. But I wanted to let him sleep in as long as possible. It was rare that he got to anymore.

With my socks and boots on, I outfitted Kikko in her ~nk plaid flannel winter jacket. I'd never met a dog who enjoyed clothes as much as she did. Willingly, she'd lift her front paws up while I placed them through the arm holes. Especially during the most frigid months of winter, she'd run away from me when we got inside, refusing to take off whatever outfit I'd put her in.

Throwing on my coat and grabbing her leash, we headed out into the courtyard of our apartment complex. I was the only one outside walking around at this hour. The sun was still struggling to peak out from behind the heavily clouded sky. A light wind shifted the large gray masses, but much like myself, they seemed reluctant to get moving.

Kikko was a ball of energy, snorting along as she sniffed the frost-covered lawn. As she circled her tinkle spot, the grass crunched beneath the weight of her paws.

On a normal day, she'd linger and drag me to every tree she could find. Then we'd circle around the bushes, so they got a little bit of sniff time too. But when it was below freezing, Kikko was determined to get back inside. Who was I to complain? I didn't want to be out there either.

Inside, I gave her a treat before going about the process of preparing my life blood—or as others call it, coffee.

I ran through the day in my head, knowing it would be nonstop the entire time. The larger table and chairs would be set up above the koi pond. And two-seaters would decorate the perimeter, leaving enough room for people to get to and from the various shops. It was Ho-Lee Noodle House's job to make sure everyone was served and taken care of. Megan would be assisting with the serving duties, and even Kimmy had volunteered to help us out since both her parents would be working at the entertainment shop.

It was a fixed menu, so I wasn't as worried. But that

didn't mean I wasn't still running through every possible catastrophic outcome.

I poured an extra cup of coffee and headed back to my bedroom. Adam stirred at the sound of the door creaking open. He covered his eyes with his forearm, then inhaled deeply. "Is that coffee I smell?"

"Yep, freshly brewed."

He uncovered one eye and peeked at the mug I presented before propping himself up. "Thanks, doll." He took the cup from my hand and blew me a kiss. "I need this before I even think about getting ready."

His outfit for the day—a mustard yellow, fitted, button-down shirt and blue dress pants—were hanging in a plastic garment bag on my closet door. The shirt was really more of a golden color, but he claimed it was "mustard." I'm not sure if that was better or worse, but I went along with it.

I pulled my red dress out of the closet and gave it a final inspection. It had a mandarin collar adorned with two button knots. The long sleeves were embroidered with delicate dragons that would wrap around my arms. The empire waist billowed out just below my bust, the skirt sitting at knee length. Respectable, yet fun.

The footwear had been a little tricky because I knew I had a lot of walking around to do, but I didn't want to wear flats for the party. In the back of my closet, I'd found a pair of red wedges with dragons embroidered on the heels. I'd bought them several years ago at a vintage clothing shop in Lakewood and had only worn them once because they were a little dramatic. But they were perfect for tonight and matched my dress to such precision, you'd think I'd actually planned it that way. The shoes, however, were for the party only. During the day, I'd gotten a pair of red and gold silk embroidered ballet flats from Esther Chin's shop, Chin's Gifts. I'd worn them around the past couple of weeks so they wouldn't be considered new.

I slipped into my dress and then moved over to my vanity. I'd been a makeup fanatic since my early teens. I remember the first time my mom let me pick out a Bonne Bell Lip Smacker, I'd felt so grown up. Now my makeup collection was oversized with various eye shadow palettes, contouring kits, different types of eyeliners, lipsticks, glosses, blushes, bronzers, highlighters—you name it, I had it. My addiction to cosmetics hadn't gotten any better since Rina first opened her shop at Asia Village. I saw everything just as it was coming out and always had her save me one of each new item. Between the Ivory Doll and the plaza's bookshop, Modern Scroll, it was a miracle I had any money left over for things like food and rent.

Adam was watching my reflection in the vanity mirror, his eyebrows scrunching as he sipped his coffee.

"What?" I was applying some concealer under my eyes, hoping it would hide the dark bags that had formed overnight.

"It just amazes me every time I watch your routine. You have it down to an art."

"This is about thirteen years of experimentation," I replied.

He set his coffee cup down on the nightstand next to the bed and threw his legs over the edge, standing and stretching out his arms. "I'm glad all I have to do is shave. I don't know if I'd have all the patience for that."

"Rina sells some men's skincare products. I could hook you up." I twisted around on my stool and winked at him.

He laughed. "You're all talk. I'm still waiting on those Speedos."

I faked a gag. "*We* never agreed on those."

"It's your loss, doll." He kissed me on the top of my head. "I'm going to shower and shave."

When he left the room, I smiled. Every time we were together, I felt like I hit the jackpot. How truly lucky I was to have met him. Though the circumstances of our meeting had been grim, something good had come from it. You could say he was my silver lining.

We had our moments, sure. Doesn't every couple? But overall, he was the best partner I could ever ask for.

Thinking all those lovey-dovey thoughts, I was a little caught off guard when I turned back to my mirror. Studying my features, I immediately noticed a hint of concern in my eyes.

Maybe it was just nerves. Today was a big day, after all.

However, if I had known this would be one of the last normal mornings I'd have in a long time, I might have savored the moment a little bit longer.

CHAPTER
9

Dressed and ready for the day, Adam and I got into his car, which he had been so kind to warm up before I even stepped outside. While he'd been doing that, I'd written Megan a note reminding her that she'd need to be at the plaza no later than five o'clock. I stuck it on the outside of her door and patted Kikko on the head one last time before leaving.

The party wouldn't officially begin until six, but Chinese New Year was an all-day celebration and Asia Village would be packed with people from the moment it opened until we locked the doors for the evening.

It wasn't typical to have the celebratory gathering so late in the day, but Ian had wanted a dramatic firecracker finale at the end.

I also wasn't used to having Adam with me on a workday. Sure, he'd been to the restaurant countless times, and it's where we'd first met. But he never saw me handling the minutiae of the day.

The entertaining aspect of him coming along, however, was going to be him working together with Ian. I could still see Ian's jaw clenching as I informed him that Adam would help with the table placement. With everything else I had going on, there was no way I'd be able to do it. After airing my complaints to Adam about my growing task list, he had so kindly offered to take over that function.

When we arrived at Asia Village, I instructed Adam where to park. "Look at the stage," I said, tapping my passenger-side window as we headed toward employee parking. The performance area was completely constructed and seemed larger than I remembered it being last night when I'd left the plaza. "It's fantastic. I can't wait to see what it'll look like with the backdrop curtains on it."

"It seems like a lot of to-do for a twenty-minute show. It's also going to be as cold as Antarctica once the sun goes down."

I clucked my tongue. "Don't pooh-pooh on my parade. It's going to be fine. As long as it doesn't snow, it'll all work out. Plus, everyone will be huddled around each other, so we'll generate body heat." That last sentence didn't sound convincing, especially to a freeze baby like me. But Ian wanted a firecracker show in the middle of January, so I was just running with it.

Adam shrugged and parked the car, and we exited with haste, rushing to the door to escape the wind.

I said a silent prayer that the heavy gusts would simmer down by that evening.

At exactly nine a.m., a stocky man about three inches taller than me with a grown-out buzz cut and a slight limp walked into the restaurant. He introduced himself as Nelson Ban, my contact from the party rental company, with a firm handshake and a tight-lipped smile. He had an air of assertiveness that told me he liked to be in control of a situation and fancied himself an alpha male. Not to say that he wasn't extremely polite, and his confidence did put me at ease. I like to hire people who knew what they were doing so I didn't feel like I had to babysit.

I introduced Nelson to Adam and Ian and left them to it. I had a lot to accomplish and didn't want to waste too much time on pleasantries.

The rest of the morning and afternoon moved along without incident. Adam worked in tandem with Ian, and they managed to behave themselves with minimal pea-cocking. At least that's what Adam reported back to me once the task had been completed.

Peter had shown up in somewhat of a pleasant mood. He hummed along to whatever heavy metal was playing in his headphones and didn't mention even once the fact that he couldn't use a knife.

Nancy handled the restaurant while I went about set-ting the banquet tables. And shortly before five o'clock my parents, Megan, and Kimmy arrived to help with the re-maining odds and ends.

The musical entertainment—three extremely skilled women I'd met at the Cleveland Night Market—set them-selves up at the opposite end of the plaza's entrance.

Their musical sampling would be whimsical and lighthearted and feature traditional Chinese instruments. Upbeat yet classical sounds of the erhu, pipa, and guzheng. A complement to a holiday dinner that resonated with hope for the future.

Shortly before six, large quantities of people began fil-ing into the plaza, heading in the direction of Ho-Lee Noo-dle House, where they were told to check in for seating.

Vanessa Wen, our teenage part-time helper, was handling the functions of hostess for the evening. I watched on as she efficiently began seating the guests, her bubbly personality shining through as she smiled and directed people to their tables.

Kimmy zipped by me, almost running into a family of three as Vanessa ushered them to their table. I reached out for my friend's arm, and nearly got pulled along with her.

Her head whipped in my direction, and it looked as if she was ready to attack until she realized it was me.

"What's the rush?" I asked her, releasing my grasp. "Everything okay?"

Kimmy's eyes darted around the room. "Um, yeah . . . I think so. I'm trying to track down Rhonda."

"I don't think they're here yet." I felt a lump forming in my throat. "Why? What's wrong?"

"Nothing," Kimmy said, still searching the room. "I'll let you know."

Before I could ask any more questions, she had zig-zagged her way through the banquet tables.

I wanted to follow after her because I didn't like the expression on her face, but Penny Cho stopped me before I could go any farther. It was time for the drink service to begin. A few of her staff from the Bamboo Lounge along with some servers from Megan's bar went systematically around the tables collecting drink orders. I handled dropping off the teapots along with extra glasses of water.

When I took a moment to collect myself, I noticed that I'd lost track of Adam. My eyes landed on the table reserved for our family, and I saw that he was sitting with another man and my father having a chat. It took me a moment to acknowledge that the third man was, in fact, Henry. Again, I had no idea what was going on with him and Anna May and had yet to talk with her about it.

I searched the area for her, but she was nowhere to be seen. Before long, I was distracted by our landlord, Donna

Feng, who had just arrived, and decided it would be best to head over to greet her.

Donna stood at the entrance of Ho-Lee Noodle House, dressed fabulously in a shimmery red wide-leg pant suit. The usual French twist bun that she styled her hair in was secured with a red and gold comb I caught sight of as she turned to examine the plaza. Her eyes swept over the length of our makeshift banquet hall. "Oh, Lana, you have done such a beautiful job," she cooed, embracing me in a hug. "I am so proud of what've you created here. The place is completely transformed! Maybe I should have made *you* my second-in-command."

I laughed nervously. "That's a tall order. And Ian's doing pretty good, don't you think?"

Donna pursed her lips. "He's fine, I suppose. But he seems to need a lot of help. When he told me he'd enlisted your services, I was befuddled. He should have been able to handle the bulk of this on his own."

"Well, you know, parties like this need a woman's touch."

She placed her hand on my wrist, as if confiding a big secret. "My darling, that is the absolute truth. Men would be lost without us, I can assure you."

"Where are the twins?" I wanted to change the subject before Donna got carried away with her passing idea of giving me Ian's job.

"Oh, they're around here somewhere." She glanced around behind her. "You know these teens of mine can never stand still. I practically had to drag them here tonight."

"Do you know where your table is? If not, I can show you where you're seated. We have you at the best table, right in the middle of the plaza."

Donna clapped her hands together. "Oh that's wonderful. You know I love to be in the center of it all."

After I left Donna at her table, I pulled aside Robin, one of the servers from the Zodiac I knew fairly well and whispered, "This is a VIP table and she's the head honcho. And the mayors of Cleveland and Fairview Park will also be here soon. So please make sure they are served each course without delay."

Robin replied with a curt nod and a "You got it, Lana."

As soon as she'd walked away, I spotted my party rental contact from this morning, Nelson Ban, ambling around, craning his neck to search through the tables of guests. I had a feeling he was looking for me, so I headed in his direction.

But before I got the chance to reach him, Kimmy pulled me off to the side. "Hey, Lee, have you seen Rhonda yet?"

I shook my head. "You're still looking for her? She and the rest of the team should be here soon. Why? What's the issue? You didn't say before."

"Well, there might be an issue. I don't know yet. Maybe, maybe not."

"Kimmy, I love ya, girlfriend, but I'm kind of in a hurry and I'd rather you just tell me now. You're making me nervous."

"Right, sorry. It's just there's this guy here that comes to the Black Garter all the time. I don't know if she knew he was coming, and I wanted to ask her."

"Maybe she told people at the club to help fill the event?"

Kimmy peered around me. "Yeah, maybe. Okay, I'll let you go then." She rushed off in the opposite direction.

When I turned back to head toward Nelson, he was nowhere to be found. Shrugging it off, I went back to my event duties. If it was important, he'd find me one way or another.

And so it went. The servers brought out the appetizers: spring rolls, dumplings, and turnip cakes. My stomach began to growl, but I knew I'd have to wait it out until I was confident that everything was in order.

The lion dance team arrived as the guests were enjoying their appetizers. One of the performers, dressed as the God of Smiles, danced comically around the room, entertaining the guests with their theatrical antics.

I noticed that Kimmy had found Rhonda and they were huddled off to the side near China Cinema and Song most likely gossiping. Against my better judgment, I decided to head over and see what was going on.

Rhonda smiled as I neared them, again acknowledging me with the same childlike wave.

"You guys all ready for tonight? I hope there aren't any issues with one of the guests?"

Rhonda sucked in her cheeks, then exhaled loudly. "Everything is good to go. I invited a couple of people from the Black Garter to come hang out and watch the show. Figured it would be good for business on both our ends."

Kimmy nodded. "Yeah, sorry, Lee. Didn't mean to give you the wrong idea."

"No problem," I replied. "As long as I don't have to kick anybody out."

Rhonda's eyes widened. "Actually, there is someone who you *could* kick out."

Kimmy clucked her tongue. "Oh, stop it. Don't go causing drama over stupid crap."

I looked at the two of them. "What's going on?"

Rhonda pointed toward one of the tables. "My brother's dumb ex-girlfriend, Whitney, is here. She has a lot of nerve showing up after their breakup. With how messy it all was, she shouldn't show her face anywhere he's performing. I don't know if he even knows she's here or how he'll react."

Kimmy placed a hand on Rhonda's shoulder. "You've got to stay out of it. Let David worry about Whitney."

I felt a pit forming in my stomach. "If she didn't actually do anything, I can't just kick her out. I hope this isn't going to turn into a problem."

Rhonda pursed her lips. "No problem. I'll make sure it doesn't affect the performance."

It felt like a good time to remove myself before any more stress was added to my plate. "I'll leave you ladies to it then. Good luck on stage."

"Thanks, Lana. We won't let you down."

Near the end of dinner, when I noticed many of the tables had their plates cleared, I snuck over to where my family was seated for a few minutes. Sitting on the edge of my seat so as not to get too comfortable, I rubbed Adam's back lightly to get his attention. He was facing away from me, still in discussion with my dad and Henry. He twisted in his seat. "Did you know Henry was going to be here?" he whispered.

"Not a clue," I said in a low voice. "I haven't really had time to talk to Anna May." I pulled my chopsticks out of my napkin and reached for a piece of duck. "My parents don't seem at all surprised."

Henry and my dad were talking about the Cleveland Browns, both being huge football fans.

Adam noticed me observing their conversation. "I got roped into going to a game. He's got box seats or something fancy and invited me and your dad."

"Better you than me," I teased. Neither one of us were sports fans. Adam was more into cars and motorcycles, and I had no complaints about that. I'd sooner go to a car show than a football game any day.

Playfully, he pinched my thigh. "If you don't behave, I'm going to ask if I can bring you along."

"I'm sick that day." I took a bite of duck, the first taste I'd had since the evening began. Peter had cooked it to perfection. The meat itself was tender, and the skin crispy, but not dried out or overdone.

"Try again, doll."

Reaching for a dumpling, I replied, "Oil change? Jury duty? Annual doctor's visit? Hair appointment? Oh, Kikko needs to go to the vet!"

Adam laughed. "I see you have a plethora of excuses at the ready."

I pointed my chopsticks at him. "Hey, I'm an expert, remember?"

A dainty hand squeezed my forearm. "Figures I'd find you over here. Slacking on the job."

I found it was Megan standing over me with a smarmy grin. "That David guy flagged me down because he couldn't find you. They're beginning their preparations outside. About twenty minutes from now they'll be good to go. Also, your mic is ready." She pointed toward the entrance to Ho-Lee Noodle House.

My stomach flip-flopped. "Ugh, I hate this part . . . Everyone staring at me."

"You'll do fine," Megan replied, patting my shoulder. "Now up and at 'em. Let's get this show on the road."

"Okay, okay." I placed the chopsticks on my plate and poked Adam's shoulder. "You better put together a real nice take-home plate for me. Or I'm going to be cranky."

"Me too," Megan chimed in before slipping away back

toward the Bamboo Lounge, probably to pick up another drink order.

Adam shook his head and laughed. "Good luck up there, babe. I'll see you outside."

The mic was attached to the rolling lectern we'd placed outside the restaurant. I pushed the "On" button and gave the top of the microphone a gentle tap. The sound echoed through the plaza, and I was aware of the fact that many heads were turning in my direction.

"Good evening, everyone!" I said, my customer-service voice a go. "Thank you for joining us this evening. Asia Village wishes all of you a happy Lunar New Year!"

There was light applause and a sharp whistle that I knew was my dad. I could feel my face reddening.

"We would like everyone to join us outside for a special performance and firecracker show. Please grab your coats and head out to the parking lot. The show will be starting in fifteen minutes. If you'd prefer to stay inside, feel free to watch from the doors. The lion dance will end inside the plaza, and then we'll announce the raffle winners."

Everyone stared back at me.

"Thank you again for coming, and enjoy the show!" I set the microphone back on its stand, which seemed to cue everyone to clap again. I gave an awkward Miss America–style wave, then disappeared into the restaurant to grab my coat.

I hurried outside before the bulk of guests made their way through the doors. I wanted to make sure I was able to direct people to the right areas. We had ropes up to make sure that none of the attendees would get too close and potentially get hurt by the firecrackers or the grand finale.

But even with the ropes in place, I didn't want anyone to have any funny ideas. Especially any of the children.

To my surprise and delight, most everyone came outside. The air was cool and brisk, but the wind had dissipated and there was a certain stillness to the atmosphere.

The harsh lighting of the stage was a deep contrast to the darkness of the surrounding area, and it felt obtrusive somehow. As if we were disturbing the natural order of things. The only other light came from the moon itself.

A shiver ran through me, and I hugged my coat closer to my body.

I saw Adam's tall figure walk through the plaza doors as he made his way through the crowd with ease. He stood next to me, placing a reassuring arm around my shoulders, squeezing me close to his body.

"Where's my family?" I asked.

"No clue what happened to Anna May and Henry, but your parents are near the entrance. Your grandmother and Mr. Zhang are watching from inside because it's too cold for them."

I tried to see if I could spot them by the doors, but I was too short and there were too many people standing in my way.

As I turned my attention back to the stage, I could see movement behind the curtains. Before long, two dancers came out into view, just as they had in rehearsal, and went to opposite ends of the stage.

Ceremoniously they danced around their respective corners and prepared to light their firecrackers.

People in the crowd were clapping and cheering, making the surrounding energy palpable. Thankfully everyone was enjoying themselves in spite of the cold temperature.

Soon both sides of the stage erupted in bursts of fire and light. The crowd cheered. Pops, crackles, and booms filled

the otherwise empty parking lot. A few traditional fireworks went off in the background, lighting up the night sky.

Adam pulled me closer, kissing me on top of my head.
"Happy New Year, babe. This is awesome."

I felt a sense of pride, not only for a job well done, but
for my culture and the traditions that were kept alive for
all these centuries. It made me feel part of something bigger than just myself, a long lineage of proud customs.

As the firecrackers simmered down, I noticed a head
poke out through the curtains. The two dancers jogged
over to the opening, then disappeared behind it. My heart
thumped. That wasn't part of the show.

I took a step forward wondering what could possibly be
going on.

David's head poked through the curtain, searching the
crowd. My gut told me this couldn't be a good sign.

Adam's body tensed next to mine as he matched my
step forward.

David and I finally locked eyes. It was clear that he was
upset. Once he'd gotten my attention, he disappeared back
behind the curtain.

I started to rush toward the stage.

Adam followed me step for step as we went up the ramp
to the stage at a quickening pace. I could hear the crowd
mumbling amongst themselves. The clapping and cheering had subsided.

My hand shook as I reached my arm out to pull open
the curtain. Just as soon as I'd done it, it felt as if someone
had punched me in the stomach.

Adam pulled me back by the shoulder, burying my face
in his chest, protectively cradling my head.

But it was too late. I'd already seen Rhonda's body limp
and lifeless on the ground, the lion's head lying next to her,
its mouth wide open.

CHAPTER
10

Time has no meaning when this sort of thing happens. I didn't know how much time had passed since I'd opened the curtain on the tragic scene of Rhonda's untimely demise. Adam was still clutching me tightly, and I heard a female sobbing somewhere behind him.

Adam whispered in my ear, "Stay right here, and don't turn around. I'm going to let the audience know to head back inside."

I nodded my head, though it felt more like I was twitching uncontrollably. He knew without me even saying so that I couldn't go back out there. I was an absolute mess.

He released his hold on me, then addressed David. "I'm a detective for Fairview PD. Call nine-one-one . . . now. And don't touch anything while I'm gone." He pointed to the remaining troupe members, who'd kept their distance. "That goes for you guys as well. Everyone stays put until we get some badges in here."

I stood there with my back to Rhonda's body, a morbid sense of curiosity pulling at me to turn around—like daring yourself to uncover your eyes during a gruesome scene in a horror movie. You know you don't want to see it, you shouldn't, but yet . . .

I focused on listening to Adam address the crowd. His baritone voice barreled across the parking lot. "Sorry folks, the show has been cancelled. Please make your way inside, for the time being. We're going to ask that no one leave at this time."

"What happened?" a voice yelled back at him.

"Right now we just need everyone to go inside and stay there. More information will come later. Thank you." He said the last bit with a firmness that couldn't be dismissed. Adam was good at making clear boundaries whether he was on duty or off.

I heard some mumbling that I couldn't quite decipher. Then I thought I could hear my mother's voice. She was arguing with someone . . . maybe Adam? I was beginning to get nervous again. Between my mental state and the cold, my teeth were chattering beyond control.

A few moments later, Adam reappeared, his demeanor different than before. He was less soft, the determination in his eyes to gain control of the situation was clear. Detective Trudeau was now "on duty."

In a huskier tone than he normally used, he said, "Your father, Peter, and Henry are helping wrangle everyone back inside. A bunch of rubberneckers." He rolled his eyes. "It's sixteen degrees outside. You'd think that would deter them." He said it more to himself than to me, then added, "Your mother tried to come back here, but I convinced her to go back inside, with your father's help. The fewer people contaminating this area the better."

David and Angela took a few steps closer to us. David glanced at me briefly, his eyes bloodshot and filled with tears that threatened to spill forward. He turned away from me, sniffling, and directed his attention at Adam. "I called nine-one-one and they're sending people. They said they're close by and should be here soon."

Adam gave David a curt nod, then said, "What the hell happened back here?"

"I . . . I don't know," David replied, dropping his head. His bottom lip quivered. "My sister . . . we just had a fight . . . I . . ." He inhaled deeply.

"It's okay," I whispered. "Just take it easy for right now." I didn't have the energy to give Adam the stink eye, but I nudged him with my elbow. He needed to lay off a little bit.

David lifted his head. "It shouldn't have happened."

The way he said it gave me pause. It could have been my mind running away from me, but "shouldn't" seemed like an odd word choice. Wouldn't it have made more sense for him to ask "why?" or to be in some kind of denial about it happening at all? I kept my voice level as I replied, "Well, no . . . this shouldn't happen to anybody."

"No, I mean our fight."

"And what exactly were the two of you fighting about?" Adam asked. He folded his arms over his chest. I could sense his tension level rising.

"About whether or not Angela would lead the performance tonight. I told Rhonda to put her ego away and let Angela have this opportunity."

"I'm gathering by the fact that Rhonda took back her position as the lion's head that she was not receptive to that idea." My eyes flittered back and forth between the two.

Angela nodded. "Rhonda was still upset with my clumsiness yesterday and kept saying we couldn't afford to screw this up tonight. David stuck up for me even though he knew it would make her furious. The more he insisted I be given a chance, the more she berated me for my mistakes. I decided to give in and just let her have it. It wasn't worth all the arguing."

"Just imagine if she hadn't been so stubborn," David said. Turning to Angela, he continued, "You might not be here right now."

The weight of his statement hung heavy in the tent. I could feel the repercussions of close calls pushing down on my chest despite the fact that it had nothing to do with me. I kept quiet while the two sorted through their feelings.

"I know." Angela stared down at her hands. "And yet, I don't feel any relief . . . because your sister is dead, my future sister is dead . . . there are no winners here."

David's eyes glazed over and it seemed as though he'd stopped listening. I wasn't sure if he'd acknowledged Angela's response or not. He shook his head, mumbling something incoherently to himself. A few seconds later, he addressed the rest of us in a louder voice: "I said a lot of nasty things to her . . . called her names a brother should never call his own sister." He turned away, perhaps embarrassed by his admission. "It was a senseless fight and now it will be the last words we'll ever speak to each other."

"This is all my fault." Angela covered her face with her hands and began wailing.

Much like her theatrics the previous day, her cries appeared a little more dramatic than called for. And that observation was due to the fact that just a minute ago, she'd been much calmer. It was a zero-to-sixty reaction.

Either she was always this erratic in nature, or she was putting on a show. And if it was a show, was it for the sake of her fiancée or for everyone else?

I checked David's facial expression to see if he'd had any type of feelings about her sudden emotional display.

And I had to admit, it did seem to snap him back into the present moment. The previously glazed look in his eyes dissipated and he wrapped an arm around her waist, pulling her close. He massaged her shoulder as he leaned his head against hers.

Over the awkward silence that followed, the sound of car wheels on a gravel road could be heard outside the tent. A few moments later, I heard a couple of car doors slam almost in unison. Adam poked his head out the curtain to see who'd arrived.

"Back here!" he hollered to someone.

I heard wheels—gurney wheels—bumping along the pavement. I'd become all too familiar with that squeaky sound and was not a fan.

"Step back," Adam instructed. "We need to make some room in here."

The coroner had arrived along with a few techs, and trailing after them were the forensic investigators. Mumbled hellos were exchanged. A few seconds later, a uniformed officer came striding in, nodding hello to Adam. Adam didn't mince words. With authority, he said, "Secure the perimeter and then I want you to take statements. I'm assuming McNeeley and Gonzalez are on their way. I want them to search the entire area for anything we can. Perp, weapon, whatever. Got it?"

The officer replied, "Yes, sir," then left without question.

The forensic investigators held up their kits, and Adam nodded approval. They quickly got to work attempting to secure any kind of useful print.

Higgins, Adam's partner, stepped in next, his dark eyes quickly scanning our provisional backstage area.

I was beginning to feel a bit claustrophobic with all these people showing up.

Higgins was a little bit older than Adam—not old enough to be his father . . . maybe a cool uncle. The only thing giving away his age were the dashes of gray that peppered his otherwise dark brown hair. The two men shook hands, Higgins patting Adam on the shoulder with his free hand. "Figured you'd get roped into this. As soon as I heard the call and where it was, I knew you'd be here."

"Never a dull day," Adam replied.

Higgins acknowledged me with a subtle tip of his head. "Nice to see you again, Lana. Though we have to stop meeting under these circumstances."

"Agreed," was all I said. I didn't have it in me to fake any kind of smile, formality, or pleasantry.

Higgins didn't skip a beat and resumed his conversation with Adam. "Where's our 10–32?"

I didn't know what that meant, but Adam would soon fill in the blanks. The best I'd learned was 10–4 and I think everyone knew that stood for "affirmative."

Adam shook his head. "No potential gunman that I'm aware of at this point in time. I haven't questioned any of the others." He jutted his chin in the direction of the other troupe members.

They'd been huddled in the corner, diverting their eyes from Rhonda's body. They spoke in hushed tones, and I wondered what they were talking about. It couldn't have been one of them who'd done it. Who shoots someone and then sticks around?

In the meantime, the techs had placed Rhonda inside a body bag.

Higgins observed the group of dancers completely unbothered by the coroner's office activity. This was nearly an everyday occurrence for him. Unlike myself, who could feel the hairs on my arms standing at attention as I heard the sound of the zipper dragged across its track.

The dancers must have sensed they were being watched, because they all stopped talking at once.

Higgins slapped Adam on the back. "I'll see what I can find out from these witnesses. Someone had to have seen something. It's not exactly Severance Hall in here."

With his partner on questioning duty, Adam reverted his attention back to me. "You okay? You want a blanket or something?"

"Do I have to stay here?" My legs were beginning to shake. "Can't I go back inside?"

"It'll just be another minute. When Miller gets back in here, I'll have him take your statement first, and then I'll escort you inside."

I clucked my tongue. "Is that really necessary . . . the whole escort thing?"

His eyes held mine. "Yes. We don't know who is responsible for what happened to Rhonda, and where the hell they went. I'm not taking any chances."

The coroner had made some observations and was scribbling something onto some yellow paper attached to his clipboard. He gave the techs a thumbs-up, and they zipped up the bag, placing Rhonda's body on the gurney in preparation to wheel her out.

While the techs began making their exit, the coroner stepped up to Adam. "I'll be in touch once I get back to my office and finalize my summation."

Adam nodded, and the coroner gave him a casual salute before following after the techs.

I was able to breathe a little easier now that Rhonda's body had been removed from the immediate vicinity. When I looked across the stage to where David and Angela had squirreled themselves out of the way, I noticed that he seemed much worse than he had a few minutes ago. Under the circumstances, that wasn't surprising.

David stood, rubbing his hands on his pants. "What now?"

"My partner," Adam said, pointing at Higgins, "is going to take you and Angela down to the station. We'll need a little bit more from the both of you. Most likely your entire team will be heading down there. The ones who were back here anyways."

"What about her?" Angela asked, pointing at me. "She doesn't have to go too?"

I raised an eyebrow. "I wasn't back here at the time. Clearly I didn't see anything." It came out in such a way that you would have thought it was Kimmy doing the talking.

Adam nodded in agreement. "Miss Lee is correct. For the time being she won't be going into the station, but we do reserve the right to call her in at any time."

Miss Lee. I almost rolled my eyes. But I knew him well enough to know that he was being as official as possible so Angela would understand that he was doing his job . . . and doing it the way it should be done.

Higgins came back over, a mini steno pad in one hand, a Bic pen in the other. "How creepy is this," he started. "You're not going to believe what one of them guys said to me."

Adam pinched the bridge of his nose. "Great. If *you* think it's creepy, it's gotta be bad."

Higgins smirked, but it was humorless. Skimming over his notes, he began paraphrasing the information he'd collected. "One guy, Tyson Yeun, said there was an extra God of Smiles back here. He thought he was seeing things because he knew"—he paused, reading over his notes—"that a Mr. Spencer Leung was out on stage. But thought he must have lost track of time and they all got into formation. Now naturally, me being your average white male, I had no idea what a God of Smiles was."

I shivered, imagining a smiling masked gunman . . . or woman . . . staring back at me.

Adam cringed. "I'm guessing you're enlightened now?"

Higgins bobbed his head up and down. "Uhhh . . . yeah."

Adam shot a glance at David and Angela. "And neither one of you saw this?"

Angela shook her head so assertively, I thought it might fly off. "I was already in position; my head was covered with the costume."

David didn't reply.

Adam stared him down. "Mr. Hong, I'll need you to answer the question."

David avoided eye contact, replying in a monotone voice. "I didn't see anything. I had my back to both of them. I heard Angela screaming, and that's what finally got my attention. We didn't hear the gunfire because of the firecrackers."

Adam didn't seem convinced, but it made sense to me. The firecrackers were right on the other side of the curtain. The sound of a gunshot could have easily blended in. But what didn't track for me was David's initial silence. Did he know something he didn't want to share?

Instead of voicing his skepticism, Adam spoke to Higgins, practically turning his back to David. "So then what? How'd our perp get away unseen?"

"Back through there." Higgins pointed to the rear of the tent, which was undistinguishable from the rest. "That's how the troupe entered prior to the show beginning. There's a slit in the material right near the left corner. Guy must have come in with them or shortly thereafter, then zipped out in all the commotion. It's a maze of businesses on that side of the street; our masked man would have had no problem slipping away."

"Can you radio McNeeley and Gonzalez? Tell them I want an extra detail on those side roads that lead into the neighborhood. Turn that business plaza upside down for any type of evidence."

"You got it," Higgins replied. He spun around to acknowledge the troupe. "Okay, folks, we're taking a nice field trip down to the station. Gather your belongings and let's get this show on the road."

I winced at Higgins' word choice.

Sullen goodbyes were exchanged as everyone began filing out of the backstage area. I gave David's arm a reassuring squeeze. Despite my reservations of his behavior, I still wanted to show compassion for his loss. He squeezed my hand before disappearing on the other side of the curtain.

The forensic investigators were still working, and Officer Miller, the one taking statements, circled back to me and gave a polite smile. I put him at about twenty-five or so. He had ruddy cheeks, a clean-shaven face, and ash brown hair that he'd dutifully buzzed. "This should be quick and easy, Miss Lee."

I looked between Adam and Officer Miller. "Would you guys mind if we took this inside? Why don't we go to my family's restaurant? No one's in there and it's warm. I could make us some tea really quick."

Miller regarded Adam for approval.

Adam sighed. "Sure, let's get you warmed up and out of this tent. But when we get in there, don't say a word to anyone, not until you've given your statement."

I held up my right hand. "You have my word." Then I pretended to zip my lips.

We headed back toward the entrance of the plaza, the cold air slapping me in the face. However, it was a welcome relief after feeling caged up in the back of that tent. Cop cruisers were barricading the exits of the parking lot, their red and blue lights bouncing off the plaza walls. Caution tape had been hung to section off half the parking lot.

As we lifted up a strip of tape and neared the doors, we saw that just about every guest that could fit was standing with their hands against the glass, cupping their eyes.

Adam groaned. "This should be fun."

CHAPTER
11

The people standing directly in front of the doorway stepped aside as we neared. Adam placed a protective hand on the small of my back, encouraging me to keep moving.

A cacophony of voices chirped at us as we opened the door. "What's going on?" "Did someone get hurt?" "Who did they take away on a stretcher?"

A quick glimpse into the crowd showed Donna and Ian in a heated discussion near her table at the center of the plaza. Donna was using emphatic hand gestures while she spoke, her lips moving at a rapid pace. Standing on either side were both mayors with their arms crossed and disapproving frowns on their faces.

Ian fidgeted with his tie, his eyes darting back and forth as he nodded compliance to whatever her demands were. I could only imagine what was running through her head.

Adam held up a hand. "Give me five minutes and I will answer a few of your questions."

My mom pushed her way through the cluster of people surrounding us and blocked me from moving any farther.

"Lana, are you okay? What happened?" She squeezed my wrist, unwilling to let go.

"Mrs. Lee—" Adam began.

She wagged her index finger in his face. "Don't 'Mrs. Lee' me. This is my daughter."

My dad quickly appeared from behind her, placing his hands on her shoulders. "Betty . . . it's okay. She's safe when she's with Adam."

My mom didn't budge or let go of my arm. "Where are you going? I am coming with you."

"Mom, relax," I said. "We're just going to the restaurant so I can give Officer Miller my statement."

"Fine, then I am coming too," she said with resolve. Then, acknowledging my father, said, "Bill, are you coming?"

His shoulders slumped. "I better come along so you don't get arrested for something."

She gave him the disapproving side-eye that I was used to receiving. "Let's go."

Adam and Miller exchanged shoulder shrugs, and we continued on to Ho-Lee Noodle House. Megan, Kimmy, and Vanessa were standing outside the restaurant watching our every move.

Kimmy was the first to approach. "What the hell is going on? Where's the dance troupe? Where are David and Rhonda?" She shifted onto her tip toes and scanned the entrance.

"Kimmy"—I reached for her hand—"you should probably know . . ."

Her attention reverted back to me. She studied my face. "What, Lana? You're scaring me."

"Rhonda is . . ." *Dead? Murdered? No longer of this world?* I didn't know how to deliver the news. Especially to such a close friend. "There was . . . well—"

"Lana, dammit! Out with it! My nerves can't take much more."

My mouth opened again, but no words came out.

Megan stepped forward, giving me a sympathetic smile. "It's okay, Lana, go ahead, we're ready." She hooked her arm through Kimmy's and pulled her close so that they were hip to hip. Kimmy twitched at the gesture, but seemed to relax when she realized it was Megan holding onto her.

I inhaled deeply, squeezing Kimmy's hand. "I hate to be the one to tell you this, but Rhonda was shot."

Megan's hand flew up to her mouth and she gasped. Kimmy didn't move or say a word, just stood there staring, most likely in a state of shock. Hearing that someone you know has been shot isn't something you think you're gonna hear on any given day. Make that doubly for such a large celebration as a Lunar New Year party.

"Is she going to be okay?" Kimmy asked. "She's not . . ."

Squeezing her hand, I whispered, "It was fatal."

"Whoa!" Vanessa shouted. "Holy crap, for real?"

My mother clucked her tongue. "Watch your mouth, young lady."

Vanessa tucked in her chin. "Sorry, Mrs. Lee."

Kimmy was unfazed by the dialogue between my mother and Vanessa. Tears began welling in the corners of her eyes as the implications of what I'd told her fully sank in.

Peter had just walked up, his eyebrows crunched together, surveying the dynamic of our conversation. He put an arm around Kimmy's shoulders. "What's going on? What's happened?"

Kimmy thrust her entire body into his, almost knocking him off his feet. He steadied himself and wrapped both arms around her. "Kimmy . . . what's going on?"

Adam cleared his throat. "Megan, maybe you can fill Peter in. I'm sorry to move this along, but we really need to get Lana's statement and Officer Miller needs to get moving on other tasks."

Megan nodded. She rubbed Kimmy's back supportively. "Of course. You guys go on." She gave me a wink and then mouthed, *I've got this.*

"And don't go telling everyone else," Adam added. "This stays between the lot of you until I get Lana situated. I'll come out and make a statement letting everyone know a few necessary things. We've gotta keep some of the specifics under wraps. The gunman is still loose."

Adam nudged me to head inside the restaurant, Officer Miller and my parents following closely behind.

"Mom, would you mind making us some tea?" I asked once we were closed off from the public. Adam had locked the doors behind us so we wouldn't be interrupted.

My mother nodded. "Okay, you sit down." She shuffled toward the kitchen at an accelerated pace.

"Where's A-ma?" I asked. A new wave of anxiety washed over me, and I collapsed into the nearest chair.

My dad answered, "She's with Anna May, Henry, and Mr. Zhang. They're hunkered down at Wild Sage because your sister worried about them getting lost in the shuffle and potentially hurt. I think she was anticipating a stampede or something."

Adam nodded. "I've seen crowds get riled up over less than this, so that was a good call on her part."

My dad nodded. "And how are you holding up?"

Adam forced a smile. "This is part of the job." He looked down at me. "Speaking of which, I'm going to give the guests some bare minimum information. They do need to be careful since we potentially have a gunman still in the area. Are you okay with me leaving you for a few minutes?"

"I'm fine," I said. My voice was shaky so I didn't know how convincing it sounded, but Adam seemed to accept my statement at face value.

He straightened the collar of his shirt. "I'll be back in a few."

I watched him walk out before I regarded Officer Miller. He'd been a quiet and steady presence. Unobtrusive. It went a long way to helping keep me calm.

As he began to talk me through a process I was already familiar with, I zoned out and Adam's parting sentiment reverberated between my ears: *There was a gunman on the loose.*

After taking my statement and filling out the necessary forms, Miller informed me that he would be in contact if anything else was needed. We shook hands, then he thanked my parents for their patience before leaving.

The three of us sat speechless at the table, sipping tea and processing all that had happened.

Adam came back a few minutes later, a scowl on his face, and his suit jacket slung over his shoulder. He hung it on the back of the chair Miller had previously occupied, sat down, and loosened his tie. "Two city mayors being here during a situation like this isn't something I'm used to dealing with."

My parents were seated across from each other in the remaining chairs. Adam was sitting next to my dad, who patted his shoulder in the way that men sometimes do. That sort of "buck up" kind of way. "It's been a hell of a day, son. Take a load off."

Adam leaned back in his chair. "It morphed into a city council forum out there, talking about hot-button issues, gun control and crime rates. I know this is an election year, but this isn't the time or place for that." He shook his head. "The chief is going to have my head when he hears about this circus. I'm surprised the media hasn't shown up yet."

"Actually," I said, unlocking my cell phone and reopening the news clip I'd found, "they *were* out there. This posted about fifteen minutes ago. The few members of the press that were here for the event called in what was going on. I don't know if they're still around, but they know better than to come inside with a film crew tagging along."

"And who knows if any of them were recording with their cell phones from inside." His jaw clenched. "I know you guys have had run-ins with camera people outside."

"Donna put a stop to that real quick," I said with a chuckle.

"She's definitely a no-nonsense sort of woman. I like that she doesn't engage with the media. It helps my job a lot." He took the phone out of my hand and pressed play on the video thumbnail. The sound was muted, and I watched as Adam's eyes followed the subtitles on the screen. "Unbelievable!" he said, handing the phone back to me. His lip curled in disgust. "They've already announced that there's a possible connection with the Hong Dance Troupe. David and his fiancée are in for it now."

The restaurant doors opened and we all twisted in our seats, a little anxiously for my liking, to see who was coming in. It was Peter, Megan, and Kimmy.

Kimmy dragged her feet as she walked. She'd abandoned her heels and purse, which I noticed Peter was carrying. She trudged over to the table next to ours, her eyes and nose red from crying. "Hi, guys."

"Hi." I scooted my chair closer to her. "How're you holding up?"

"How do you think?" she snapped. A moment later, she slapped her forehead and groaned. "I'm sorry, Lana. I'm not trying to take it out on you."

"I know," I said, extending my hand. I tugged at her wrist. "Free pass tonight, Tran. All-you-can-serve snarkiness."

Begrudgingly, she smirked. "Thanks, Lee."

Megan came and stood over me. "How are *you* holding up?"

I shrugged. "I guess I'm fine. I don't know. It's just so weird . . . the whole thing. I don't want to be the one to discover—"

My dad patted the table with force. "Hey Betty, why don't we go out into the plaza and see what we can do to help clean up. Let the kids have some time to themselves."

My mother raised an eyebrow at his suggestion, but after giving me and Kimmy the once-over, she got up without argument and followed my dad out into the plaza.

Megan sat down next to me. "As you were saying . . ." Her eyes flitted toward the door.

Kimmy's lip trembled. "She was going to say she doesn't want to find the bodies . . . isn't that right, Lana?"

I nodded. I realized it sounded a bit insensitive. This was a friend of Kimmy's, after all. It was different this time. "Sorry, I didn't mean to refer to Rhonda as a body. I know you guys were friends."

"It's okay," Kimmy replied. "I know what you mean. I wouldn't want to be in your position either."

"So now what?" Megan asked.

The three words that Megan must have said more than anyone else I knew. I knew where she was going with it.

But Adam was here—and talk about it not being the time or place for something!

"Now nothing," Adam said, his eyes settling on Megan. I knew that he was thinking the same thing I was. "I have my guys out there searching the area. We'll know more, hopefully tomorrow. And if we're really lucky, we'll have someone detained before the sun rises. In the meantime, I'll escort you ladies home. Peter, you can see to it that Kimmy gets home safely?"

Peter nodded. "Yeah, I was planning on staying over there anyways. If it's cool with you, I'd like to get her outta here now."

"Absolutely," Adam replied.

"Come on, babe." Peter held out his hand to Kimmy. "Let's get you home and into some pajamas."

Kimmy glanced over at me. "You cool with that? I don't wanna leave you guys high and dry with all this mess to clean up."

"Don't worry about it," I said, batting a hand in her direction. "We'll handle everything that's left. You've done plenty tonight and you've been through enough. Go home and take care of yourself."

She reached for Peter's extended hand and he hoisted her up. "See you guys later," she said with a limp wave.

Adam, Megan, and I watched them leave. It was time to handle the remnants of tonight's party. I couldn't leave it all for my parents to deal with, but at the same time, I felt like I had nothing else to give.

Before I could get up from my seat at the table, the restaurant doors opened again and Ian came storming in, with Donna trailing behind him.

"Lana," Ian said firmly, "we need to speak—" His eyes landed on Adam. "*Alone*, please."

Adam rose from his seat, fast and alert. He'd always had

a short fuse when it came to Ian. "Hey pal, I don't know who you think you're talking to in that tone. But you better take it down a notch, otherwise we're going to have a problem." His right hand balled into a fist, and his knuckles cracked.

Donna placed a hand on Ian. "Yes, Ian, the detective is correct. That is no way to talk to a lady."

Adam's shoulders visibly relaxed. "Ms. Feng, always nice to see you."

She bowed her head a fraction of an inch. "As it is to see you, Detective Trudeau."

Through clenched teeth, Ian said, "Lana, may I speak with you in private, please?"

Megan cleared her throat and stood from her chair. "Say, Adam, why don't we go find Lana's parents and see what we can do to help with cleanup."

Adam refused to budge. "I'm sure you can handle it without me." His gaze was fixed on Ian, his arms folded across his chest.

"Adam," Megan replied in a singsong voice. "Lana is a big girl; she can handle Ian."

Ian snorted.

Megan—knowing the two men and their general dislike for each other—moved up next to Adam, acting as a buffer. She pulled on his forearm, but addressed Ian. "I wouldn't do that tonight, if I were you. Also, consider my assistance a favor to your cause."

Adam glanced at me over his shoulder. "You want me to stay, doll?"

"No, it's okay," I said. "I won't be long."

With hesitation, Adam allowed Megan to pull him from the restaurant.

I rose from my seat and gestured to the table. "Would either of you care for some tea?"

Ian ignored the question. "Is your boyfriend always such a meathead?"

"Well, my answer is no, Ian." I shimmied around the table to face him head-on. "This isn't an episode of *All in the Family*, Archie."

Donna looked at the two of us. "I don't understand this phrase that you are referencing, but that is no matter right now. We have more pressing things to talk about."

Ian continued, "Do you always run to his defense?"

I took a step closer to him, lifting my chin. "He's being protective and doesn't appreciate your tone of voice with me. And frankly, after what we've all been through tonight, neither do I."

"Oh, don't be so dramatic, you know I am a direct person," Ian said. "You probably wouldn't have taken offense if he hadn't been around." He jerked his head in the direction of the plaza.

"Enough!" Donna's voice rose an octave.

Ian and I went silent, and Donna squared her shoulders. *Let it go, Lana*, I said to myself. To Ian I said, "What is it that you wanted, Ian? I have things to do."

"Well, first of all," Ian replied, straightening his tie, "the plaza is closed for business tomorrow. Donna doesn't feel that we should deal with any more of this after someone has been murdered. Since tomorrow's Sunday anyways, and a lot of the shops have adjusted hours, we'll shut down and resume business on Monday."

Donna interjected, "I know your family usually has dim sum every Sunday, but perhaps you can convince your parents to forego it this one time. It is important that we have everyone here tomorrow to help out."

I nodded. "I'm sure it will be fine. We can always cook something here."

Ian continued. "Now for the other matter. We can't sit

around and wait for the police to figure this whole thing out. This is yet another murder taking place at Asia Village. It will be extremely bad for business."

"What are you getting at, exactly?" I asked.

"If they do not find out who did this before the end of tomorrow, we'll need you to do your thing. Whoever this person is, they need to be brought to justice."

"Me?" I asked. "I'm not for hire, Ian. You can't just demand that I *do my thing*."

Donna held up a hand. "Money is no issue, Lana. If that's what you need, I can take care of your expenses."

I shook my head. "Donna, that's really nice of you to offer, but that's not what I meant. I just meant that . . ." I paused. I knew what I felt, but not the right way to say it. I wasn't Ian's to command. And I resented the fact that he was so cavalier about my extracurricular activities.

She gave me a gentle smile. "Say no more, I think I understand. Woman to woman, allow me to present it this way: I would like to ask for your expertise in these matters. It must be handled efficiently and swiftly, and I'm afraid that law enforcement is never concerned with the latter."

"Donna . . . I . . ." Again, I found myself at a loss for words. Deep down I knew that I wasn't going to let this rest. How could I? Just thinking about the sad expression on Kimmy's face alone sent me into my "superhero phone booth."

"Think it over tonight," Donna said. "It can be discussed further tomorrow once everyone's had some rest."

"Okay, that sounds fair," I replied.

"We'll be going now." Donna reached for Ian's elbow. "Let's go, Ian."

He glared at me before leaving but didn't say a word, storming out ahead of us.

I followed after Donna, intending to inform my family and the others that we could call it a night, but she stopped me before we'd left the restaurant. In a hushed tone, she said, "I know that Ian's delivery of our request was not proper, but he isn't wrong, Lana. I think we both know that this person, whoever they are, must be brought to justice."

CHAPTER
12

The plaza had emptied out except for my parents, A-ma, Adam, and Megan. They weren't cleaning up as I thought they would be, but instead were sitting at the table that had been ours. Mr. Zhang, Anna May, and Henry were nowhere to be seen.

"Where are the others?" I asked as I approached the table.

My mother got up from the table and came over to me, giving me a once-over. "I told them to go home. There is no reason for them to stay." She searched my eyes, perhaps to see if she could decipher my state of mind.

I gave her a weak smile, hoping it would calm her concern. "Donna and Ian said we could go home anyways. The plaza is closed tomorrow, but she wants all of us to come in and handle cleaning up then. She asked if we could skip dim sum."

My mother furrowed her brow. "Family time is important. Where did she go? I will talk to her."

"They left already, Mom. But if you think about it, we'll technically still be together," I said. "What if we cook here?

We could invite anyone who's helping out to eat with us. Might be nice. They're like family . . ."

My mother's eyes went back and forth like the eyes of those kooky cat clocks. She was mulling over my request and I could see she was warming to the idea. Finally, she said, "Okay, this we will do."

Adam pushed out his chair. "Are we good to head out then?"

My parents conceded and everyone got up from their seats. I went over to hug my grandmother, who gave me an extra squeeze and patted my cheek. There was sadness in her eyes, and in that moment, I felt the worst for her out of anyone else. It must have been difficult to not understand everything going on and to have to wait for it to be translated for her. But I knew that she and I had our special bond, and we didn't need words to communicate. I could read her just as well as she read me.

We all made our way to the entrance, saying our good-byes and see-you-tomorrows. My head was starting to throb, and I desperately needed a glass of water. I pulled the master key from my purse, Ian having just given me one as we'd begun party planning.

As I turned around to look the plaza over one last time, my heart sank. Now in the dim light of the moon coming in from the skylights, the decorated plaza appeared abandoned, like a scene out of a post-apocalyptic movie. There'd been such hope at the beginning of the evening for a prosperous new year.

With a sigh, I locked the door. Who would think that a tiny slug of metal could change the course of so much.

Back at my apartment, Kikko danced with excitement at the door. As Megan, Adam, and I entered, her squiggly tail jittered back and forth and her mouth curved up as if in a smile. I patted her on the head and couldn't help but smile back at her. "It's good to see you, little dog," I said to her.

She snorted in response, spinning her body a full three-sixty.

"Let me change my shoes and then we'll have tinkle-time." I straightened, set down my purse, and slipped out of my shoes.

Megan disappeared into her bedroom without saying anything. It dawned on me that I'd been so concerned about everyone else that I hadn't asked how she was doing. Before I went to bed, I'd have to pop into her room and make sure she was holding up okay.

"You want me to take her out, babe?" Adam asked.

"No, it's all right," I replied, opening the entryway closet. "It might be good for me to have a moment to my-self."

He removed his coat, hanging it on the back of one of the kitchen chairs. "All right. Well I'll get into bed then. See you in a few minutes."

"I won't be long." I pulled my zip-up combat boots out of the closet and stuffed my feet into them.

Kikko hopped anxiously.

I grabbed my scarf off the hooks near the door, along with her leash and new sweater. For the holiday, I'd gotten her a red knit pullover that looked like a lion dance cos-tume. It some ways it felt inappropriate, but I didn't want it to go to waste.

I knelt down, and she propped her front paws up on my knee. I stretched out the collar opening, and she stuck her head through. Next, I placed her paws through the arm holes. Kikko barked and did another three-sixty.

Once outside, the crisp evening air stung my cheeks,

and I burrowed my face in my scarf, watching my breath dance on the wind. Kikko skittered over the grass, sniffing with exuberance as she searched for her perfect spot.

I heard a door close somewhere behind me, and I whipped around, with a terrible imagery of a laughing Buddha staring back at me.

But it was Megan, bundled up in sweatpants, Ugg boots, and the puffy Michael Kors coat that I'd gifted her for Christmas.

"What are you doing out here?" I said just above a whisper. It was already past eleven, and I didn't want to be *that* neighbor.

She shuffled over to me, her arms wrapped around her body. "I wanted to see what all that business was with Ian and Donna. I know it wasn't just about closing the plaza tomorrow."

Kikko's head perked up at the sound of Megan's voice, and she wiggled her tail in recognition before going back to her sniffing duties.

"I'm sure you can guess," I replied. "And I'm sure that's why you're out here."

"Well, you know, Big Brother is always watching . . . and listening." Her eyes shifted in the direction of our apartment. "You're gonna do it, right? I mean, *we're* gonna do it?"

I huffed. "Yeah, but I didn't tell them that. Ian practically demanded that I 'do my thing.' It was beyond annoying, and I felt like being difficult."

Megan stared at me. "Huh."

"What?"

"I didn't have to argue with you this time," Megan said, her eyes narrowing. "What gives? You're never this easy to persuade. Usually there is a lot of convincing on my part, and then you're *still* skeptical."

Shrugging, I said, "Meet the new-and-improved Lana Lee."

Megan gave me a wry grin and stuck out a gloved hand. "Detective Riley. Nice to meet you."

After Megan and I had gone back inside, we said good night, and then Kikko and I slipped into my bedroom. Adam was already fast asleep, and I had no intention of waking him. It had been a long day for him, with a stressful ending to boot. No telling what he'd have to deal with in the morning.

And though I was exhausted beyond comprehension, there was a sliver of energy that surged through my body. An anticipation to begin my investigative practices head-on. No remorse, self-doubt, or discouraging remarks attached this time.

Grabbing a set of pajamas and fresh underwear, I tiptoed out of my room and into the bathroom. I turned on the shower and let the water get real hot before stepping under it. I had a chill I couldn't shake, and I allowed the steam to cover me like a thick blanket.

The scene of tonight's events sped through my mind. I imagined a faceless intruder sneaking amongst the other dancers, perhaps in their own costume, and it caused me to wonder if a disgruntled employee had come back for revenge. I made a mental note to ask David if he'd recently dismissed anyone from his troupe.

Then I considered the escape route, which was through the back of the tent—a slit in the curtains that would have gone undetected by an outsider, meaning that the shooter knew exactly how to disappear and in a timely fashion. That side of the tent led to a street that separated the plaza from a smattering of small commercial buildings. They could have easily used the area for cover, then slipped through to the residential area directly behind it.

I'd learned from Adam that residential neighborhoods could provide a lot of hiding places for perpetrators. We're talking in sheds and garages, below porches and decks (if there's access), behind bushes, and so on. He'd even told me a story where he'd found a guy hiding inside the bed of someone's pickup truck.

They could have waited until the coast was clear and then disappeared into the night, thinking they'd gotten away with it. Victory was theirs.

I found myself getting angry at the notion. Imagine the arrogance and audacity of this person to fathom for even a single moment that they could shoot someone in cold blood and then skirt all responsibility. Meanwhile leaving a wake of grief behind.

I shut the water off, finding myself more agitated than I'd been prior to getting in the shower. It was supposed to have been relaxing.

I patted myself dry, then used the towel to wipe the steam from the mirror.

Looking at the reflection that stared back, I thought, *Regardless of how pompous this person might be, there's one thing they hadn't been counting on. Me.*

CHAPTER
13

Adam woke up about thirty minutes before I was even ready to think about opening my eyes. Kikko used my ribcage as a step ladder to observe Adam from a better height while he got dressed. Having a pug knead your midsection is something you can't ignore.

I shifted onto my back and Kikko flopped backward, snorting her discontent at my movement.

"Sorry to wake you, doll," Adam said. "I want to get to the station early before the chief gets sucked into other matters."

"It's okay," I mumbled. "I probably should get up anyhow."

Adam looped a tie around his neck. "I'm not going to bother having *the talk* with you. I think we've gotten to an understanding . . . finally. But just remember two things."

"What's that?"

"Don't interfere with me directly. And, if anyone asks, I did not approve this endeavor of yours. It wouldn't look good for me, especially with the chief."

I laughed. "You know I'd never rat you out," I said.

"And I know we're on the same page—which I want to say I appreciate more than you can understand. But I'd still like your expertise from time to time."

He tightened the knot of his tie, straightening it and smoothing out the fabric. "Off the record, no problem. Hypotheticals are okay. But you know I can't give you specific investigative info."

I held up my hand, which Kikko promptly sniffed. "I solemnly swear—"

"If you say 'that you're up to no good,' I'm not even going to dignify that with a laugh." Adam stifled a smile as he reached for his suit jacket, plucking off a few stray pieces of lint before slipping it on.

Giggling, I replied, "No, I was going to say that I swear I'll keep my line of questioning vague."

"Deal." He extended a hand.

I reached for it, which he used to pull me out of bed and wrap me in a hug. He kissed my cheek. "I love you, doll." He pulled away and looked me in the eye. "No telling what we're up against today, so be good . . . and careful."

"Am I ever anything but?" I said with a grin.

"Babe, on your best day, I don't think you want me to answer that."

The temperature had risen to a whopping thirty-four degrees, and with it came a light dusting of snow. A little bit of ice had accumulated on my windshield, so I broke out my scraper, not wanting to wait for the heater to melt it off. The sound of my scraper against the iced window echoed off the buildings and through the parking lot. I was the only idiot out here at eight thirty on a Sunday morning. How I longed for a garage.

Megan had been fast asleep, snoring to her heart's

content, and I wasn't about to wake her. She'd offered to come along and help at the plaza, but seeing as she had to work later on in the day, I didn't want her to overextend herself.

The drive into Asia Village was pleasant. The roads were clear and covered with salt, and traffic was at a minimum—the one perk of going anywhere early on a Sunday morning in January.

When I turned into the parking lot, my eyes couldn't help being drawn to the stage area, now an oversized monstrosity after the events of last night. The caution tape and curtains billowed in the light breeze, and against the gray sky, it once again looked like a horror movie. Stephen King would have a field day here.

I parked my car and hustled into the plaza, noticing along the way that my parents and Anna May had already arrived. I didn't see Peter's car, but I'm sure he'd had a late night trying to keep Kimmy from falling too far down the rabbit hole of grief. If he was a little on the late side, I didn't think anyone would be surprised or have anything to say about it.

My mother was standing outside the entrance of Ho-Lee Noodle House chatting with Esther and—to my surprise—the Mahjong Matrons. What on earth were they doing here?

I walked up to the group of ladies, the Matrons saying hello to me in harmony.

Esther sized me up. "Lana." She tapped on her shoulders. "Straight, you are slouching again."

With a grimace, I straightened my shoulders. When I was younger, I'd always thought she'd stop doing this by now.

My mother was next to comment. "You look tired today, Lana. Did you not sleep good?"

Out came my eye roll. "I slept fine, thank you very much, *Mother.*"

I addressed the Matrons, ignoring my mother's continuing observations. "What are you ladies doing here today? Did no one tell you the plaza was closed?"

Helen spoke for the group. "Yes, we were made aware. However, we wanted to come help any way we could. We can't stay long because we have a Mahjong tournament today."

I just nodded with a smile. Deep down I knew they'd come to see if there was any information they could take along with them to the tournament. I'm sure it would be a hot topic of conversation.

"So, Mom," I said. "Where's Anna May and Dad? And what do you want me to do first?"

"Anna May is in the kitchen with Dad. They are washing dishes and cleaning up. I will clean up the dining room and then come out here and clean the tables. Esther will help me."

"What about me?" I asked again.

"We owe people prizes," she said. "You go do paperwork and find a way to make this right."

In all the chaos, I had completely forgotten we'd still need to dole out prizes. The guests who bought seats had raffle tickets, and I had the list of names in my office. I guess I'd have to call everyone and have them come back for some type of redo. "Okay, I'll get on that now. Who's going to take care of the stuff outside?"

"Adam said last night we cannot touch this yet. The police want to be sure they get everything they need from there first."

"Ian's going to flip," I said. "The pickup for this stuff was supposed to be first thing tomorrow morning."

"This is Ian's problem," my mother replied. "You do not worry about this."

I massaged my temples, already anticipating getting an earful from Ian about the additional expenses. "Well, I'll call the rental company at least and tell them not to bother coming tomorrow. Hopefully we'll get some kind of answer from the police and get this outta the parking lot soon. I don't even want to look at it anymore."

Helen tsked. "I still can't believe that this happened. On such a day of celebration. What will this mean for the coming year?"

"Surely, nothing good can come from this," Opal replied.

My cell phone rang from within my purse, and the sound caused us to jump. Apparently we were all still a little on edge this morning. When I checked the readout, I saw that it was Adam. "Hey babe," I said with a little surprise in my voice. It wasn't usual for him to call me this soon after just seeing each other. A flutter passed through my belly. "What's up?"

"Hey doll, I just got done with my meeting with the chief. Coroner called first thing this morning. He said he found something odd . . . well, maybe odd . . . he didn't know for sure. In the pocket of Rhonda's costume he found an envelope like the one your grandmother gave you the other night."

"Oh?"

"Yeah, he said there was gold writing etched on the front, then inside he found four one-dollar bills. I told the chief I didn't think it was relevant but I'd ask you about it anyways. We're assuming someone must have given it to her last night, and it's all that was on her at the time other than her clothing. Any clue if that means anything?"

"A red envelope with four one-dollar bills?" I repeated, racking my brain.

The Matrons perked up and gasped in unison. Opal covered her mouth, terror filling her eyes.

Helen asked, "Where was this envelope found, Lana?"

"It was in the pocket of Rhonda's costume," I said. "Why? What does it mean?"

Wendy shook her head, her chin dropping and a frown forming on her lips. "This, Lana . . . this is an omen of death."

CHAPTER
14

"An omen of death?" Adam yelled into my ear. "Did I just hear that right?"

I jerked the phone away an inch. "Yeah."

"Let me talk to whoever just said that," Adam barked. "Please," he added.

I handed the phone over to Wendy. "He wants to talk to you."

With a shaky hand, she reached for my phone. "Yes, hello?" she said, sounding unsure of herself.

She was quiet for a moment, and I could hear him explaining the situation to her. When he finished, she then said, "Well, you see, the number four in our language sounds much like the word 'death.' An old custom we follow is to never give anything that is an amount of four."

More silence. I could feel the palms of my hands beginning to sweat. Even though it hadn't occurred to me when Adam first said it, I knew the information in the back of my mind.

I still remembered my first experience in a hospital elevator in Taiwan while visiting my sick uncle. I'd noticed that the fourth floor was missing. And my mother had promptly explained the reasonings behind this and that no one wanted to be on the floor of death.

Wendy handed the phone back to me. I took it and said, "Are you still there?"

Adam replied, "Yeah, and I'm not happy."

"This would mean that Rhonda was the intended victim after all, wouldn't it?"

"It does appear that way, but maybe it's too soon to say. I need to know more about their switch first. Rhonda and Angela were roughly the same size so it might be easy for someone to mistake one for the other and the shooter obviously had to move quickly . . ."

"But, at the very least this proves that it was without a shadow of a doubt, premeditated . . . with extra care into details and everything." I hadn't really thought that the murder itself had been anything but premeditated to begin with. Considering the intricacies of getting backstage, and having a speedy exit plan, how could you think anything other than that? But, in Adam's line of business, you could never assume anything because sometimes the most obvious clues can be different than what they seem.

"I'm not ruling anything out just yet," he said. "Look, babe, I gotta run. I need to talk to the chief about this. I'll call you later, okay?"

"Okay," I said. "Good luck. Love you and stuff."

"Love you too, doll. Be careful."

We hung up, and everyone stared at me with expectancy. I found myself searching for the right words.

My mother wrung her hands. "This is not our concern." She said it to the group as if she were announcing something as simplistic as the forecast. And though she made it seem as if it was meant for everyone, I knew it was specifically directed at me.

Helen stepped forward, addressing my mother, her eyes sliding in my direction. "Betty, I think we can all see that this is not that easy to dismiss. This is a terrible omen. We must help fix it so it does not bring misfortune on all of us who were at the party."

Folding her arms across her chest, my mother replied, "I think the opposite. If we stick our nose in, we are asking for trouble."

Esther nodded, aligning herself physically next to my mother—the Matrons versus my mother and her most loyal friend. I couldn't fathom who would win this one. None of these women should ever be trifled with.

Helen looked at me for support, and I was a bit apprehensive to take a side, not just because my mother was involved in this standoff, but because my mind was already set on what needed to happen next. I wasn't sitting this one out, but for my mother's own good, it was best she didn't know my intention of involvement.

I winked in Helen's direction. It was such a fast movement, it could have easily been mistaken for a nervous tick. But I think she caught my drift. "You know, I don't say this often, ladies, but my mother is right. Maybe it's best we let the police handle this one. We don't want to align ourselves with evil, after all."

My mother lifted her chin. "Thank you, Lana. I knew you would understand."

Helen sighed. "I suppose you have a point." Her immediate compliance told me that she had caught my subtle signaling.

Wendy, Opal, and Pearl were none the wiser and crinkled their brows at me, confused by my response *and* Helen's sudden change of heart.

My mother, feeling quite proud of herself, clasped her hands together and linked her arm with Esther's "Excuse us, we have many things to do before lunch." Turning to me, she said, "Lana, I will talk to you soon."

"I'll be in my office," I replied as she and Esther walked away.

Helen quickly glanced over her shoulder, and once my mother was out of earshot, she leaned toward me and said, "Lana, I knew you wouldn't let us down."

Once the Matrons had left for their mahjong tournament, I headed into my office, briefly stopping to say hello to Anna May and my dad, who were busy putting the kitchen back together. I didn't bother with too much small talk because I had a lot of thinking to do, and truthfully, any conversation I had with Anna May needed to be private. I didn't think she'd divulge any details about her relationship with my dad listening in.

I shut the door to my office, staring at the pile of paperwork I'd left in a messy stack in front of my keyboard. Even though I'd tried to keep myself organized and up to date on everything that needed to get done, the Lunar New Year's event had taken its toll on me. It had been more time-consuming than I originally imagined, especially with Ian constantly nagging me about this detail or that.

I made a silent pact with myself that I would never allow this to happen again. If he ever wanted me to do something like this in the future, he was going to have to relinquish full control. And after this, if he didn't trust me to complete a project, I'd tell him he shouldn't ask me to help in the first place.

I was still mad at his behavior the last I saw him. He'd gotten really snippy with me, and that was something that didn't happen often. I knew it was because Donna had been there and he wanted to appear assertive and in charge. But the fact was, he wasn't. None of us had a handle on what happened. Adam, if anyone, had taken care of the situation, making sure no one was exposed to the unsightly scene backstage. And he'd made sure that my own anxieties hadn't spilled onto the crowd, which could have potentially caused a panic.

And where had Ian been? I hadn't even seen him outside at any point during the show—the evening fireworks display show that *he* wanted more than anything. The only time I'd caught sight of him was when he was being reamed by Donna. And she was probably scolding him for his lack of presence throughout the night.

I shook my head, trying to rattle the thought free. I was getting caught up in being resentful toward Ian, and there was no time for that. At least not at the present moment.

With a huff, I set down my purse and removed my coat. Shimmying behind my desk, I came to the conclusion that it was best to call my contact, Nelson, at the party rental company and let him know about the delay.

After that, I could tackle some of the paperwork. Once I had a cleared space then maybe I could think a little better and come up with some kind of plan. Not just for the raffle, but for my next steps in solving the Rhonda situation.

I found Nelson's business card among the mess of my desk and dialed the number into my phone.

A receptionist answered and put me on hold when I asked to speak with him.

Seconds later, he picked up the line. "This is Nelson, how can I help you?"

"Hi Nelson, this is Lana from Ho-Lee Noodle House. How are you doing today?" I knew he was a family friend of the Hongs, but I didn't know if anyone had shared the news with him. However, if he'd watched the news last night, I'm sure he knew something.

He was silent for a moment, and I thought maybe the line disconnected. Finally, he replied, "It's been a rough morning. I am still trying to come to terms with it. Rhonda was like a sister to me."

"I'm so sorry for your loss."

"Thank you." He sniffed, then cleared his throat. "So, what did you need?"

"Well, due to the crime scene, the police have sealed off the stage and tent area. They've asked us not to touch anything until they conclude they're done and have everything they need. I'm afraid we need to keep everything a little while longer."

"Oh, I see." I heard him shuffling some papers. "Do you know how long exactly?"

"Not a clue. But my family and I are cleaning up the tables and chairs. I don't know if you want to come pick those up at the usual time?"

"I'll see if I can swing by and haul some of it out myself."

"Okay, that would be great. We're open at nine tomorrow morning, so any time after that would be fine."

More papers shuffling. "So do the police have any idea who could have done this?"

"Not a clue at the moment," I said. "Do you happen to know if Rhonda had any enemies?"

"Me?" He sighed. "Since I left the dance troupe, we'd kind of lost touch with each other. The check-ins between us were getting farther and farther apart. I don't know who could have done a thing like this."

"Was there anybody else that left the troupe recently who might have been holding onto a grudge?" I asked, hoping for even a hint of something I could work with.

"Not that I know of. There's not much new blood that comes through the troupe. Why are you asking about that?"

Since we didn't know each other in the least, I didn't want to explain more than necessary. "Just curious, is all. Something like this is devastating to witness."

"I understand," he said. "Whoever it was, I hope they catch the SOB."

After I'd hung up with Nelson, I got started on my desk cleanup. I'd made it through half a stack of last week's mail when someone knocked on my door.

"Come in!" I yelled.

"Hey, Lee, you got a sec?"

To my surprise, it was Kimmy who was entering my office, not a family member like I'd originally thought. Then I smirked to myself realizing they wouldn't have knocked to begin with.

"Yeah, I got time," I said, gesturing to the visitor chair opposite my desk. "What's up?"

In reality, I didn't have time, but Kimmy didn't look like her usual self. She hadn't bothered with makeup, which was highly out of character. We were similar in that way. *And* she was dressed in a matching sweats outfit she only wore on days she wanted people to think she was going to the gym. I also maybe knew a thing or two about that.

So despite my lack of time, I could sense she probably needed to gab. Not the kind of talk you do with a significant other, but with a trusted girlfriend.

She flopped into the chair as if winded and let out an exaggerated sigh.

"Did you get any sleep?" I asked.

"Why? Because of these?" She pointed below her eyes

which were darkened and puffy. "I did sleep . . . for maybe five minutes at a time. Just a warning, Peter is not in a good mood today."

"That's okay," I said. "It's going around."

"This whole thing with Rhonda's really got me shook," Kimmy said. She was bouncing her leg as she spoke, avoiding eye contact.

"That's normal, Kimmy. It's a pretty gruesome thing to undergo. Don't be so hard on yourself. It's gonna take some time."

I didn't know if I was saying that for her benefit or my own. It wasn't an easy thing to go through, even if the deceased wasn't close to you. You couldn't help but see it every time you closed your eyes. Over time, it melted away, and after a point, I suppose it became just a distant memory that felt more like it had happened to someone else instead of yourself.

Kimmy sniffled. "Well, I can't take it. Just . . ."

"Just what?"

She turned to me. "We'd just talked earlier that evening. You know? And we were like, 'Oh yeah, so and so at the club, what a jerk. And maybe we should get drinks next week after work, blah blah.'" She sniffled again. "And now . . . nothing. Not a damn thing, Lana."

"I know, it's very final."

She closed her eyes, rubbing her temples. "I just want it out of my head."

"Give it time."

"We have to do something," she said, opening her eyes. Her voice was firm and commanding. "We have to find out who the hell is responsible for Rhonda's death, Lana."

"Already one step ahead of you," I replied.

Kimmy raised a brow. "You are?"

I nodded. "Don't sound so surprised. You sound like Megan."

"That'll be a cold day in hell," she snickered.

"Oh stop it."

She held up a hand. "You're right. Blondie was there for me when it counted most, and I won't forget that. But I have to tease—it's become our thing."

"How endearing," I joked. "Anyways, yeah, I'm on this, don't worry. But I need your help if you don't mind. You're the only one of us who knew Rhonda on a personal level. I plan on questioning her brother, but I'd like a little bit of inside scoop."

"Anything you need to know." She leaned forward in the chair, resting her elbows on her knees, fingers steepled. "I'm in this, Lee, one hundred and ten percent. We're going to find this creep. And we're going to make them pay."

CHAPTER
15

- - - - - - - - - - - -

"Okay, calm down, Tim Misny," I joked, in hopes of subduing her anger. I didn't actually think she meant to quote the infamous Cleveland injury attorney's tagline, but the billboard I frequently saw on I-480 advertising his services flashed through my mind.

"Har har," Kimmy shot back, but I could tell that it had softened her a bit. "This is important to me is all I'm saying."

I gave her a reassuring smile. "Believe me when I say I get it. But we have to keep our heads about us if we're going to get anything accomplished and be successful. We can't go into this half-cocked, ya know? That's how mistakes are made."

"I know, I know," Kimmy said. "My hot-headed temper doesn't do me any favors. Peter reminds me almost daily."

My eyes slipped in the direction of the clock on my computer, calculating how much time we had before my mother burst in with a random demand she'd just cooked up. "So while I have you here, let's talk about Rhonda a little bit. What can you tell me about her personal life? Did she have any enemies? Stuff like that."

"Whoa, back up a sec. Why are we focusing on Rhonda's personal life and all that? Shouldn't we be figuring out who hated Angela? She was supposed to be the lion's head."

I took a moment to update Kimmy on the new information about the red envelope found in Rhonda's pocket. It had completely slipped my mind that she wasn't in the know.

Kimmy raised her eyebrows. "What?" She covered her face with her hands and groaned. "This is even worse than I thought."

Silence filled the room. I wanted Kimmy to have the time she needed to process this new information, so I didn't try to console her with some generic platitude, but instead held space for what she needed: compassion.

After a few minutes went by, she uncovered her face, ran a hand through her hair, and then rubbed them on her thighs in a methodical motion. "Okay, let me think a minute. It's hard to say what I know in relation to the dance troupe because other than the drama with her brother and his new fiancée, Rhonda didn't say a whole lot."

"Anything would help," I told her. "How about this: let's start with whether or not she was single."

Kimmy blew a raspberry. "Oh hell if I know, Lana. I mean she had men all over her at the club; lots of regulars would come see her dance almost on a daily basis. She'd joke that all of them were her boyfriends. I don't think any of them were legit in a relationship with her though."

"So as far as you know, she wasn't dating anyone specific then? None of the men seemed closer to her than the others?"

"Well, there was one guy I did notice hanging around

a lot, especially during her shifts. His name is Jax Mercer. I don't know if you overheard her mentioning him the night of the party. He showed up to surprise her."

"And was the attention wanted?" I asked while jotting down his name.

Kimmy shrugged. "I think so? She didn't seem to mind him always being around."

"Did he only start going there recently?"

She shook her head. "No, he used to come in all the time, at least once a week. But then abruptly stopped. That was a while ago though. I could be wrong, but I'd say he's been a solid regular for over six months now."

I tapped my pen against the desk. "Do you think he was more than just a customer and she just wasn't saying anything?"

"If he or anyone else was someone special, she was keeping it pretty close to the chest because I never heard two words about it, from her or any of the others. I can try and ask around at the club. Someone else might know something different. Like this girl that works there who I can't stand." She sneered. "Christine something. She was pretty tight with Rhonda. Whether she's willing to have a conversation with me is another story."

"What's the deal with this Christine girl? Why don't you like her?"

"Oh she's a total snob. Thinks she's god's gift to men. She practically puts down everyone that works there—except Rhonda."

"Do you have any idea why?"

"They knew each other from before," Kimmy said without explanation.

As much as Kimmy enjoyed talking, this whole interview was like pulling teeth. I'd had easier times getting information out of complete strangers. "Before where?"

"I never caught from where. I just didn't care to ask, I guess. It made no difference to me."

"Okay, we can find that out later. I don't know if it would be relevant or not, but it wouldn't hurt to know. If they share some kind of special bond, maybe they went through something difficult together that could lead to a clue. Or there's the alternative: keeping your enemies closer sort of thing. Could she have been jealous about Rhonda's popularity?"

"I wouldn't put it past her."

"What about ex-boyfriends?" I asked, wanting to keep things moving, my eyes periodically making note of the time. "Any crazy exes we need to be on the lookout for?"

Kimmy shook her head. "No recent offenders. She didn't seem too interested in pursuing new relationships or talking about old ones. The only thing she really talked about a lot was starting her own dance studio, something geared toward women. That was her reasoning for working at the club to begin with: fast money."

"What about the dance troupe? Isn't she part owner of the family business?"

Kimmy nodded. "Yeah. David dominated everything though. He never really let her have much say and always argued that he knew best. That she needed to trust him more, blah blah and so on."

"What about their parents? Do they have any involvement with the troupe whatsoever? Or is it David who's solely making all the decisions?"

"She rarely talked about her parents, but I know that they stepped away from it and gave over all control to the two of them. From what I can remember, her father was going to disband the group altogether. But Rhonda begged him not to, and then he agreed—under the condition that her brother take majority control."

I clenched my teeth. "Typical." Hearing things like that made me want to light my bra on fire. But I held back further commentary. It wasn't the right time to get on my soap box. "That's probably why she was worried her brother would try and push her out by having Angela step in, right? Because she didn't feel like her opinion mattered on basically any decision he made. And if Angela is as passive and meek as she's demonstrated, well he wouldn't have any problems with her trying to throw in her two cents on what should be done."

"Yup, Rhonda worried that her brother planned to have Angela eventually take over his spot while he went off and pursued something else. When I asked her what those supposed dreams were, she didn't have a damn clue. But what she did know was she'd sooner quit than take orders from that woman, so she wanted to get a head start on a backup plan."

I snorted. "I can't see that woman running a lemonade stand. Like I said before, from the little bit I saw of her, she doesn't seem like a real go-getter."

"You're not the only one who thought that. Rhonda told me the other troupe members weren't fans of Angela's either. Coulda been simple jealousy though. Didn't want some outsider invading their little group. Rhonda mentioned more than once that they were very cliquish."

I drummed my fingernails on the desktop, focusing on the repetitive clacking sound they made while I thought. There had been six other people backstage at the time the gun was fired. Which meant that though it wasn't likely, they were still suspects. I wondered to myself if Adam had completely ruled any of them out. I wasn't privy to the information of what happened once Higgins escorted all of them to the police station at the end of the night.

The popular theory was that there was a lone gunman

who had escaped through the curtains, but we only knew that information because that's what we were told. What if they were lying all along? What if it was really one of them and they were hiding in plain sight, all protecting one another? Essentially they were one another's alibis. David and Angela would be none the wiser because Angela was already in position beneath the tail end of the lion costume and David had his back to everyone at the time. With the firecrackers as a cover, the killer could operate with some freedom.

But then again, wouldn't Angela have sensed Rhonda falling to the ground? Wouldn't she have screamed immediately, causing David to turn around—like he had—and see for himself the gunman's attempt to escape? How long was Angela screaming before David had noticed what was happening? I would assume a matter of seconds.

And what about the murder weapon? If the shooter had been one of the performers, they would have had to abandon it or dispose of it somehow. Would there have been enough time for that?

"What's going on in your head, Lana?" Kimmy asked, snapping her fingers.

I flinched. "Sorry. I was just thinking about the rest of the dancers and what involvement they might have had. Do you want to take a walk outside with me real quick? I want to see something."

Kimmy shrugged and rose from her chair without asking what I was up to. "Sure, I could use some fresh air."

CHAPTER
16

I gave a vague excuse to my dad, Peter, and Anna May about grabbing something from my car for Kimmy. Peter narrowed his eyes, and I knew that he didn't believe me for a second. He knew me too well. But we kept moving through the restaurant, giving them no time for questions.

Slipping past my mother and Esther, we made our way outside, the frigid mid-morning air slapping us in the face as we made our way to the abandoned stage.

Kimmy flipped up the hood of her coat, her cheeks already pink. "What are we doing out here?"

My eyes scanned the length of the stage. "What if the dance troupe was responsible for this?"

"You think someone in the group did this?"

I shrugged. "Anything is possible. If they're as cliquey as Rhonda said they are, they could somehow be involved." I took a few steps closer to the stage area, eyeing the police caution tape with resentment.

"But why would they kill Rhonda?" Kimmy followed closely behind me. "The only way that theory would pan out is if Angela was the one who was supposed to get a

bullet hole through the chest. And with that whole envelope thing, it's not looking to be the case. Plus, they would
have known about the position switch."

"Not necessarily. If the argument between David,
Rhonda, and Angela had happened right before the show
started, it might have been so last minute that the others
didn't know what was going on. Plus, I was thinking about
something that Adam said about the two women being
pretty much the same size. What if it was just a mix-up?
It would be an easy mistake to make. And then there's the
other option . . ."

"Tell me sometime this year, Lee, before my nose
freezes off my face."

I started to move toward the rear of the metal structure where the backstage tent was located. "What if they
did want Rhonda dead for some reason? And it wasn't a
mistake?"

"Lana, that is the most ridiculous thing ever. They loved
her like family."

"Or so she thought," I replied. "I mean no offense by
saying this, but Rhonda seemed to be extremely emotional
and reactive. I could sense right away that there was an issue between her and David. Maybe one of the others was
sick of her behavior or thought it could ruin the livelihood
of the troupe."

Kimmy shrugged. "I suppose that's fair. She did act out
quite a bit."

We'd reached the area where the back curtain was split,
and I searched the ground beneath it, hoping a shiny me-
tallic object would reveal itself to me. Then I moved along
the edge of the perimeter, stopping on the other side of
where the dancers would have been huddled together inside. I bent down to see farther beneath the stage.

No dice.

Kimmy huffed. "This is stupid. What are you looking for?"

"The gun."

"Oh geez, Lana, you are way off this time."

I straightened. "Hey, we can't rule anything out until we officially rule it out. This is part of it. If you want to be involved in the process, then you have to go through all the paces, not just the ones *you* care about."

"Wow, Lee." Kimmy snorted. "You're really embracing this whole detective thing, aren't you? Gettin' kind of bossy."

"Assertive, Kimmy. There's a difference."

She sucked in her cheeks. "Well, you are the expert, I suppose. You're eight for eight, so who am I to say what needs to happen or doesn't."

"Nine, Tran. I'm nine for nine." I stuffed my hands inside my jacket pocket. I'd forgotten my gloves and my fingertips had started to numb. Nodding my head in the direction of the plaza, I said, "Let's go back in."

Kimmy leaned back, a playful smirk on her face, "Oh snap, look out world, here comes Lana two-point-oh. Extra sassy, and kinda bad-assy."

I glanced at her over my shoulder and gave her a wink. "And don't you forget it."

Back inside the plaza, I went directly to my office, ignoring the suspicious stare from Peter as I passed through the kitchen. Kimmy had gone to say hello to her parents, who'd arrived just as we were heading through the main doors.

My mother and Esther had made a lot of progress since the beginning of the morning, and I'd noted that all the tablecloths had been removed. Kimmy's father and my dad were going to be in charge of folding up the tables and placing them on the wheeled cart that the banquet rental company had left behind.

Ian and Donna had yet to arrive, but I suspected they'd be here shortly. Donna wasn't much for manual labor, and come to think of it, I didn't see Ian helping out in that department unless there was something in it for him. You'd think he'd want Donna to see him doing something productive so she wouldn't harp so much. But I could only imagine why Ian's mind worked the way that it did.

After many distractions and a wandering mind, I'd finally gotten through the rest of the paperwork on my desk when, speak of the devil, Ian appeared in the threshold of my office. I silently cursed myself for not shutting the door.

"Do you have a minute?" he asked. He still had his charcoal fedora and matching wool knee-length overcoat on, which—in my opinion—always made him look like a 1920s gangster. But more than that, it told me he'd just arrived.

Checking the time, I noticed it was shortly before noon, just as I'd anticipated. Without even going out into the plaza, I already knew that the heavy lifting was near done, if not completed by now. "Sure, I have a few minutes. What do you need? Is Donna here with you?" My tone was official sounding. Not the "customer service, how can I help you Lana." But the "office professional, I have a meeting in five minutes so make it fast Lana." I was still bitter over his behavior and didn't want to appear too friendly, lest I give him the wrong idea that he could speak to me the way he had or insult my significant other.

"Donna had something spring up last minute, so she won't be coming today." He took a step forward, removing his hat and brushing at an imaginary piece of lint. "I want to apologize for my demeanor yesterday. It was un-called for."

I let the words hang there for a moment. The awkward silence caused him to fidget with the knot of his tie.

"Donna put an immense amount of pressure on me yes-terday. She expects me to get this handled and wrapped up with immediacy, and I'm afraid I took it out on you."

A plethora of retorts flashed through my mind, danc-ing patiently on the tip of my tongue. I wanted to tell him that it was *his* problem, not mine. And that he shouldn't blame Donna's behavior toward him as a means to speak to me like I was his servant. But I swallowed those state-ments, and opted for a tempered, "I accept your apology."

"I can assure you, it won't happen again," he said, tak-ing another step closer to my desk. "A *true* gentleman does not raise his voice to a woman in such a way."

"Let's just drop it, Ian. You apologized, I accepted."

He cleared his throat. "Very well. So, now that we've cleared the air, I really do need your help with this whole situation. I don't have the faintest idea where to start or what to even do. I tried calling the police station this morn-ing for answers, but they were tight-lipped as ever."

"There's your first mistake. They're not in the business of doling out information to people in our position, espe-cially during an ongoing investigation like this."

"Yes, I know, but one can hope," he replied. "I didn't even consider asking your *boyfriend* for help. I already know his stance on that."

I snickered. "That's a definite no-go for you. He is not at all happy with you and the way you lashed out at me yesterday."

"I can't say that I blame him. I wouldn't be too happy myself if I were in his shoes."

Was that a hopeful glance I caught? I ignored it. "Well,

don't worry your pretty little head. I gave it some thought, and I'll 'do my thing' as you so nonchalantly put it."

He sighed, his shoulders relaxing. "Oh thank God. I'd be lost without you. I could help in whatever way you need me to, and Donna agreed to handle any payment, if that's what you require."

I'd never accepted money for the unofficial help I provided in the past and I didn't feel comfortable doing it now. Not unless I planned on accepting Eddie Price's offer on joining Price Investigations, the agency private detective Lydia Shepard worked for and who I'd teamed up with to help Donna with some personal matters that had sprung up from her past.

"Payment isn't necessary," I told Ian, keeping the rest of my thoughts to myself. "Just don't tell anybody that I'm involved . . . unless it's Donna. It's best this sort of thing isn't publicized."

Ian placed his fedora over his heart. "I wouldn't dream of it."

CHAPTER 17

A few minutes later, my mother waltzed into my office, probably too excited about seeing Ian and me having a private discussion. She held out hope that I'd have a change of heart with Adam. It wasn't that she didn't like him—because truly he had grown on her—but as far as marriage material, she felt Ian was the better choice. Not only was he considered well-to-do, but his line of work was much safer than being a police detective. I wasn't even thinking about marriage, and here she was worrying about my becoming an early widow.

They exchanged pleasantries, and before she left, she said to Ian, "I hope you will join us for lunch."

Of course he said yes—it was more time he could spend torturing me. Plus, there weren't many people on this planet who could turn down my mother's cooking. It was rare these days that she graced the restaurant with her chef skills.

Peter was one of the few who was happy about the lack of my mother's presence in the kitchen. When I'd first taken over as manager, he'd confided in me that my mother "enjoys a good hover." Having known her the entirety of my life, I knew exactly what he meant.

Ian lingered in my office, observing me as I tidied up a few remaining items.

"You can go on ahead," I said without lifting my head. "I'll be there in a few minutes."

"I can wait." He shifted weight from one foot to the other, leaning against the door's threshold. "Perhaps you can tell me your plan of action, seeing as we can't talk about this stuff in front of the others."

"I don't know my plan of action yet." I tapped a stack of receipts on the desktop to straighten them out and paper clipped them together. "All I know is I have to talk to David, and maybe go to the Black Garter."

He crinkled a brow. "Isn't that a strip club?"

"A *gentleman's* club."

Ian pursed his lips. "Semantics."

"Rhonda worked there," I said plainly.

Giving my desk a final once-over, I concluded this was the best it was going to get today. There were too many distractions. I had placed the list of raffle contestants front and center. I would tackle it first thing the next morning, once I concluded what the best way was to handle it. "Okay, let's go, I guess."

"Don't let me rush you," Ian said half-heartedly. "What does the strip club have to do with Rhonda's murder? Isn't Angela who we should be focusing on anyhow?"

I groaned, standing up from my chair. I hated repeating myself, but in this situation it was unavoidable. I quickly relayed the information that was discovered this morning concerning the red envelope.

Ian blanched. "That is atrocious. To think that someone used a beloved tradition to threaten someone in such a way."

"Yeah, it's pretty horrid." I shimmied around my desk.

Ian regarded me with amusement. "You know, you could buy a desk that actually fits in here."

I stared down at the oversized desk, having never considered the idea. It had become part of this tiny room, a fixture of my childhood. I could still see myself crouching under it as a kid, playing make believe and pretending I was hiding in an elaborate fort from some imaginary enemy I had cooked up that day. Which thoroughly annoyed my mother, by the way. Probably because I'd poke her in the leg with my finger, and then sometimes pull her shoe off. "It has sentimental value," I replied.

He shrugged and extended his hand toward the outer room. "Shall we?"

Lunch came and went without anything to write home about. I'm not sure if it was the somber mood that hung in the air, or if everyone was just simply tired from all the cleaning.

My mother cooked an elaborate feast: hot and sour soup; steamed *and* pan-fried dumplings; spinach with garlic and ginger; spicy Mongolian beef with water chestnuts, baby corn, carrots, and straw mushrooms; spring rolls stuffed with pork and vegetables; shrimp lo mein with snap peas, mung beans, and onions—and we couldn't forget the whole fish with its beady eyes.

Aside from that last item on the menu, my eyes and stomach were working overtime, and I happily scooped healthy portions of each item for myself to enjoy. Today was the kinda day where you have to undo the top button of your pants—and truth be told, after everything I'd been through in the last twenty-four hours, I was okay with that.

If Shanghai Donuts had been open, I would have gladly purchased half a dozen doughnuts on the way home.

When lunch was over, Anna May excused herself and headed to the restroom. A few minutes after she'd walked away, I excused myself as well. I wanted to catch her alone and ask her about what was going on with Henry.

When I got to the ladies' room, my sister was in a stall. "Anna May? You in here?"

"You know I am," she replied.

"We haven't gotten to talk recently," I said to the metal door staring back at me.

Anna May flushed the toilet, and after a couple seconds, the lock turned and she swung the door open. "Why do I have the feeling I know what this is about?"

She walked past me, heading for the sinks. I followed.

"Are you avoiding the topic for some reason?" I watched her reflection in the mirror, hoping to catch one of her tells. But her face remained neutral. "I mean, why not say what's going on—unless there's something to hide?"

Holding her hand under the automatic soap dispenser, she said, "It's not anybody's business is all. I'm not hiding anything."

"Anna May Lee, you can't do that. It's rude. Here we are as your family, watching you suffer, fawning over this guy, being depressed, then mad, then . . . numb. You didn't even want to come home from California. And now he's showing up to family dinners and escorting you to parties, and you don't think that deserves an explanation?"

She huffed, rinsing her hands rapidly beneath the faucet. "Lana, it's complicated, you know that. I'm still sorting things out with him."

"But I'm your sister," I reminded her. "We were doing that whole bonding thing, remember? We told each other stuff, and we understood where the other was coming from. Like sisters are supposed to."

Anna May grabbed for the paper towels. "Can you keep things between us? I don't want to talk to Mom *or* Dad about it."

"Yes, of course."

She inhaled deeply. "Henry was helping me study for the bar exam, and we got to talking. We haven't really spoken much outside my time interning at the firm, so I didn't know anything new regarding his . . . *wife*." She said it with venom in her voice. "He told me that she finally agreed to the divorce, and now they're just working out the details."

"Did he show you any proof of this recent development?" I worried because he had strung her along in the past. The only thing that brought his lies to the surface had been an inconvenient photograph of him and his "estranged" wife laughing together in the society portion of the *Plain Dealer*.

Anna May remained silent.

I clucked my tongue. "Oh come on, Anna May, you're smarter than this."

She flung her wad of damp paper towels into the trash. "I knew you wouldn't understand. This is exactly why I didn't say anything to begin with. You're just going to judge me and doubt him, and I don't want to hear it."

"I'm not judging you, Anna May. I just don't believe him is all," I replied, trying to sound compassionate versus exasperated. "Sometimes it's hard to be objective when you're in a situation. Are you sure he's not just telling you what you want to hear so you don't stop talking to him again?"

"You don't know him like I do," Anna May spat. She

spun on her heel and made a beeline for the door. "I can tell he's being honest with me. And that's all that should concern you."

I grabbed her arm before she could pull the door handle. "We're not done, Anna May."

She snorted. "Oh yes we are. I'm not having this conversation with you. Stay out of my business, Lana. You don't know me, and you certainly don't know Henry. I believe what he tells me and I'm not walking away from this again. I love him and that's final." She jerked her arm out of my clutch and swung the door open, retreating at a steady pace.

I stood there, frozen and a little shocked at my sister's outburst. The door closed and my shoulders sank. "Well, that didn't go as planned."

CHAPTER 18

Once lunch was over, Anna May left without so much as a goodbye. I tried to act like it wasn't affecting me, but that was far from the truth. I couldn't shake the idea that my sister was purposely believing what worked best for her based on what she wanted out of the relationship. Did she question Henry to find out if what he told her was indeed factual? Did his estranged wife suddenly give up, just like that? I couldn't even pretend to understand. Mainly because I wasn't the type of person to stick around if the other person was clearly not interested. And that made me question whether it was possible that Henry wasn't being as clear as he made himself seem. Who knew what went on behind closed doors. Maybe his wife had reason to believe that their marriage might be salvageable.

It was speculative on my part, of course. One word of truth Anna May had spoken was that I didn't know jack about Henry. I did like the guy, but I didn't want him bringing his messy life into my sister's. She didn't open her heart to men often, if ever, and I wanted the best for her. She deserved the absolute top-notch sort of man. If

Henry couldn't be that, then I hoped she could see that sooner rather than later. There's nothing like looking back on your past and realizing you'd spent a lot of time consumed by the wrong person. Worse yet is when you knew it while it was going on, but refused to take action.

As I tidied up the restaurant for the following day in hopes of making my morning routine a little easier, I argued with myself that I had more pressing matters to think about—like what exactly happened to Rhonda. I hadn't reached out to David just yet, wanting to give him time to grieve and come to terms with what had befallen his sister. But tomorrow, I'd have to get moving, and questioning him was my first order of business.

Slowly, one by one, our little team of helpers dwindled, heading home for the day. First, Ian left, claiming he had some important matters to handle, but I suspected he was leaving because the food was gone. Esther left next, scolding me one more time about my posture before saying goodbye. Kimmy and Peter after that, and finally my parents.

And there I was, the cheese standing alone. With a few finishing touches in the dining room, I concluded that it was enough for today, and went back to my office to retrieve my coat and purse. I was already daydreaming about the afternoon nap I was planning to take as soon as I finished accompanying Kikko on her afternoon stroll.

I locked up the restaurant and then the main doors of the plaza, my eyes shifting in the direction of the stage as I made my way across the lot to my car. What a relief it would be to have that larger-than-life reminder gone and out of sight. Hopefully, the police would allow us to have the stage disassembled and removed by tomorrow afternoon. And if they just so happened to find the killer before then, well that would solve a majority of my problems.

* * *

I woke up late Monday morning, catapulting myself out of bed at the realization that I had slept through all my alarms. Not only did I have one alarm set on a clock radio, but I also left the snooze option on, *and* had three more alarms activated on my cell phone.

The good news was that I still had thirty minutes before I needed to leave in order to make it in time. Quickly, I mapped out my plan of action: brew coffee, walk dog, dress, throw my hair in a ponytail, and lug my makeup bag to work. No one would know that I'd put my face on in the back of the restaurant. Mr. Zhang and Mama Wu were usually the only ones there before me, and I didn't think Mr. Zhang would comment on my lack of foundation, so I didn't have to worry about my appearance for his benefit.

I wasn't the type of gal to leave home without makeup unless there was some type of emergency or I felt ill. Lana Lee sans makeup usually evoked a lot of questioning. *"What, don't you feel good today?"* or *"Is everything all right with you?"* or my personal favorite, *"You look peaked."* I'm telling you right now, no woman goes about her day wanting to look peaked. And that includes yours truly.

I left the house in a frenzy, almost forgetting my coffee mug, which is not something I handle well. Sure, Shanghai Donuts had coffee, but I prefer to be heavily caffeinated *before* I arrive for the day.

The roads were slick with a thin layer of ice, so I took care making my way to the plaza. A momentary sadness washed over me as I thought about the weather conditions on Saturday and how things might have changed if the forecast hadn't accommodated our show plans. I shook the thought away as I stopped for a red light. No sense in thinking that way; it never led anywhere good.

When I pulled into the parking lot, I noticed two police cruisers parked by the stage. I only saw one officer removing the caution tape, and wondered where the other cop could be.

I parked my car in the employee area and then shuffled my way over to the policeman, who was trying his best to gather the tape up in a neat roll. He was losing the battle.

"Hi there," I said, waving to get his attention. "Are we finally able to take this stage down?"

He glanced up at me with surprise, having been distracted by his task. An attractive young man with a handlebar mustache that didn't fit his baby face. His light blue eyes regarded me with a questioning look. "You the manager?"

"Not of Asia Village, no. But I'm the one who put this event together. I run the restaurant, Ho-Lee Noodle House."

"Oh, you must be Lana," he said with a smirk. His demeanor relaxed and his tone became more personable. "You're Trudeau's lady, am I right? We hear about you at the station all the time."

I could feel my face reddening. With a nervous laugh, I said, "All good I hope."

Ignoring my response, he held out a leather gloved hand, "I'm Darren Shaw, by the way. Nice to finally meet you. You're quite the legend."

"Oh geez, I can only imagine what you guys must think." I reached for his extended hand, giving it a firm shake. Embarrassment was taking over, and my voice squeaked as I spoke. "I'm not really as much of a troublemaker as it probably comes across."

He chuckled. "It's all good. Most of us enjoy seeing

Trudeau get a little hyped up from time to time. He's so even keeled most days, you'd think the man was born in a tie and overcoat."

The mental imagery caused me to laugh. "Well, it's nice to meet you all the same."

"So yeah, uh, Detective Higgins is up in the tent area, taking some final pictures that Trudeau asked for. Don't know for what exactly because forensics already took care of it, but we're just doing what we're told. You can take this down and do whatever with it now. We've got everything we need."

"Oh good," I said, sighing relief. "I can't wait to get it out of here. This whole thing has been a complete disaster."

"You know, forgive me for saying so, ma'am"—he smiled—"but from what I've heard about you, I don't think you should be throwing any more parties."

I detoured quickly around the stage to the tent area to say a quick hello to Higgins. I was hoping that he'd tell me why Adam wanted additional pictures. "Good morning, Detective."

He stood from his crouched position near the opening at the back of the tent. "Mornin', Lana. How are you doing today?"

"I'm hanging in there. Yourself?"

Higgins slipped his phone into his pocket. "Running errands for your sweetheart." He winked.

I'd never really had a one-on-one conversation with him, and I concluded there was no time like the present to try my luck. "Out of curiosity, have the two of you considered that one of the dancers might have faked the whole story? That whole hiding-in-plain-sight thing?"

He rubbed the side of his neck. "We did, as a matter of fact. But you know I can't discuss any of the specifics with you. Police rules and all that."

"Right, right," I said quickly. "I didn't mean—"

"So it's not like I would tell you that we found large boot prints—indicating they potentially belong to a male—leading from the back of the tent and heading in the opposite direction of Asia Village. Or that by the gait of the prints we could surmise that the person was running. Or . . . I definitely wouldn't tell you that those prints disappear suddenly across the street where a set of tire prints magically appears."

His face was deadpan as he relayed the information to me.

"Right," I said again. "So you wouldn't tell me things like that."

"Nope, sure wouldn't." He winked. "Now, if you'll excuse me, ma'am, I have some police business to attend to." He tipped his head. "You have a nice day now."

I wished him a good day and said goodbye to my new friend, Officer Shaw, as I passed him on my way toward the plaza doors.

I was more than grateful that Higgins had given me some info to work with, and I'd have to make sure I didn't accidentally bring any of it up in front of Adam so as not to get Higgins into any trouble.

But I couldn't help feeling a slight disappointment at knowing that my first scenario had been squashed so quickly. At least I knew not to waste any more time considering that one of the dancers had been involved in the murder.

It's honestly the first time in my life that I found the winter weather to be helpful, given that it had left us a valuable clue.

Entering Asia Village through the main doors, I stamped my boots free of the snow and ice that had accumulated from tramping around the parking lot. When I removed the hood that was shielding my eyes, I nearly jumped out of my skin. Standing in front of Ho-Lee Noodle House were a group of shop owners all staring expectantly at me, their faces perking up with interest at my rather loud arrival.

I had a feeling this was going to be a rough day.

CHAPTER
19

I trudged toward the entrance of Ho-Lee Noodle House like I was walking the proverbial plank. I noted that Penny Cho from the Bamboo Lounge was present, which was especially interesting because she was never here this early. The Lounge didn't open until noon. Cindy Kwan from Modern Scroll and my hair stylist, Jasmine, stood closely together, whispering back and forth, their lips moving at what seemed like a hundred miles a minute. Mr. Zhang and Mama Wu stood off to the side, perhaps being the respectable elderly folks that they were, but I knew they were just as eager to gossip.

"Good morning, everyone." I tried a genuine smile, but I could tell I failed by the lack of any response.

Jasmine was the first to step forward. "Lana, my god, you look a mess." Her voice was filled with concern, and her gaze so intense I could almost imagine her calculating the length my hair had grown—even with it in a ponytail. "I have some under eye cream in my bag, if you want some."

Cindy, who was standing slightly behind Jasmine, pinched her arm. "Shhhhh. Why would you say that?"

I groaned, remembering that I hadn't put any makeup on. "I'm fine, just running late today is all. I have my makeup right here." I patted my tote bag. "I wasn't expecting an entourage when I showed up today." My eyes searched the faces of the people I knew so well, waiting for them to explain themselves before I showed my own hand. I already knew they'd come for information.

Mr. Zhang folded his hands behind his back. "Ah, Lana, we have given you quite the surprise. We only come to share our concern. Many things have been said, and we would like to know if they are true."

"What have you heard?" I asked.

Mama Wu cleared her throat. "Is it true about the red envelope?"

They all seemed to lean forward in anticipation of my answer.

I nodded. "Yes, a red envelope was found in Rhonda's pocket after she'd been shot."

Jasmine, Penny, and Cindy gasped. Mama Wu and Mr. Zhang shook their heads.

Mr. Zhang tsked. "This is very unfortunate, indeed. Perhaps we should clean Asia Village to get rid of any evil spirits that might be sticking to us."

Mama Wu nodded in agreement. "Yes, I think this will be very wise."

"I will consult my books to see how we can handle this misfortune." Mr. Zhang bowed his head respectfully to Mama Wu and then excused himself, heading in the direction of his shop.

Mama Wu sighed. "I had hoped that Helen misunderstood."

"I wish she had too," I replied. "It complicates things further . . ."

Mama Wu patted my arm. "Yes, this is true. But we must continue on with our day. Don't lose hope, Lana; the police will make this right. And Mr. Zhang will be sure to keep us protected from any negative energy. He is very knowledgeable about ancient customs."

"Let's hope you're right about that."

"I must go," she said, regarding the group. "Have a nice day, everyone." To me, she added, "Lana, I will make your favorite doughnuts first today. Stop by in a little while."

Penny had stayed silent for most of the conversation, her hands on her hips, disapproval on her face. "This whole thing stinks. Can the plaza even handle this kind of bad publicity? We just made it through the bulk of the holiday season, and we already know it's going to be slow for a few months. Is this going to totally wipe us out?"

Cindy shook her head. "You can't think of it like that."

"Oh yeah?" Penny challenged. "Why not?"

Cindy adjusted her horn-rimmed glasses. "Because someone is dead, that's why. It's not about us. We'll deal with it how we deal with everything else around here, one day at a time."

"I have to agree," I said. "We'll manage."

Penny snorted. "Remember that sentiment when rent is due. Which by the way, I heard Ian is planning on raising."

Jasmine rolled her eyes. "Not this again."

Penny threw up her hands. "Right? Like, hello. He keeps yammering on to me about inflation."

"When did he say this?" Jasmine asked. "The salon always does pretty well, but I need to hire another manicurist, and I can't pinch any more pennies in my budget."

"Just last week," Penny revealed, "he came into the Lounge for lunch and a drink. Give that man a whiskey sour and watch him go. You can't beg him to keep his mouth shut."

Cindy clapped her hands together. "Ladies, can we stay focused? This isn't helping anything."

"Again," I said, holding up an index finger, "I have to agree. Let's just make it through the day." I shuffled a few steps toward the doors of Ho-Lee Noodle House thinking about makeup, paperwork, and murder. You know, just your average Monday morning.

Jasmine stepped closer to me as I inched away and in a loud whisper said, "I suspect Lana has a plan to fix this whole thing. Don't you?"

The other two women moved in closer as well.

"I'd rather not—"

"Hey dudes," a voice said from behind the trio. Without turning around, I knew exactly who it was.

"Peter!" I shouted in relief. "You have great timing."

He arched an eyebrow at my excitement. "Uh, yeah, right on. What's going on?"

"Oh nothing, you're just saving Lana in the nick of time," Jasmine teased. "But that's okay. I already know the answer to my question. I saw your lip twitch," she said to me with a wry grin. "Have a good day, Detective." She winked before heading back to Asian Accents.

Cindy and Penny said their goodbyes, and I dug in my coat pocket for the keys to the restaurant, more than thankful I had an escape route from any further questioning.

Peter watched as the women went their separate ways. "What was that all about?" He jerked his thumb over his shoulder.

"Trust me, you don't want to know." I unlocked the restaurant doors and we stepped into the darkened space. It was cool, quiet, and felt like a sanctuary more than ever before.

Peter shut the door behind him and engaged the lock. "You're probably right about that. I hope it's not what I think it's about."

I moved blindly through the maze of tables to the back wall, flipping on all the lights to the dining room. It was *exactly* what he thought it was about, and I didn't feel like getting a lecture from him this morning. Peter remained unrelenting in his stance against my sleuth-like involvements. "How's Kimmy doing?"

Peter made his way over, his hands holding onto the straps of his backpack as he walked. He shrugged. "I guess she's all right. Better than yesterday morning." He stopped in front of me, his eyebrows crunching together. Tilting his head, he asked, "Did you do something different to your hair or whatever? 'Cuz you look totally different today."

CHAPTER
20

After I'd dutifully pretended like I had no idea what Peter was talking about, I shut myself in my office, more than ready to complete my first order of business: putting on my face.

While I applied my foundation and setting powder, I'd let the messages from the voice mail service play in the background. There was a message from our meat vendor reminding me that he needed our order for the week. One from Nelson at the party rental company telling me he wasn't going to be able to make it that day. And about twelve messages from people who'd attended the dinner celebration, wanting to know what was going on with the raffle.

By the time I was done listening to all the messages and perfecting my eyebrow arch, I only had about ten minutes to finalize a few things before the Matrons' arrival.

My attention kept falling back to the list of names I had to call. I found myself regretting the use of a raffle ticket system and made a mental note that if I ever tried to pull something like that off again, I'd just have people submit an entry form including all their contact information and pick winners by name.

But it also gave me an idea. I smacked my forehead, scolding myself for not thinking of it sooner. I could use this to my benefit and create an elaborate ruse to get everyone back to the plaza. The murderer, if they were one of the guests who had bought a seat, would be invited to return to the scene of the crime. And I could hopefully find a way to specifically talk to David's ex, Whitney Meng, and Rhonda's . . . potential suitor, Jax Mercer. I didn't know what else to call him.

The wheels in my mind finally began to churn at an accelerated rate and I felt relief wash over me. Now at least I knew I had access to two of the people I didn't know how to reach. David was still in my sights, but I didn't know how he would respond to me questioning his ex. I had dreaded the thought of asking for her information, especially in front of Angela.

With my revised plan now in place, I realized there was something else I would need to pull this off quickly: help. I couldn't get through close to a hundred phone calls in a day, especially while managing the restaurant. I pulled my cell phone out of my purse and texted Kimmy, filling her in on my idea, and asked if I could enlist her assistance with making the necessary phone calls.

She readily agreed and that provided me with even more relief. I suggested we split the list straight down the middle, and I told her I'd stop by after the Matrons were situated with their breakfast.

Once I wrapped up my texts with Kimmy, I checked the time, noting I had five minutes left. I quickly shot a message over to Penny asking if she'd like some help getting additional business. After her gripe session this morning, I'd doubt she'd say no to making some fast cash.

With the dinner guests returning to Asia Village, it wouldn't hurt to offer them discounts at the Bamboo Lounge for the day, as a further incentive to get them back without much complaining about the inconvenience. If Penny went along with the plan, it could bring her quite a bit of customers, and maybe some repeat offenders if they enjoyed themselves. And who knew what other money they might spend while they were milling around the plaza.

A few minutes later she responded to my text saying she was on board.

A tingle of excitement ran through my body, and I sprung up from my desk with a renewed sense of pep. Maybe today wouldn't be so bad after all.

When I let the Matrons into the restaurant, trying to appear cheerful and unaffected by the recent happenings, I could sense they weren't buying it. Or they were too preoccupied with their own feelings to notice my attempt.

Helen let out a dramatic sigh as she removed her winter coat and slid into the booth. "I'm afraid we're not very hungry today, Lana."

Wendy nodded. "Perhaps we should just have some rice porridge."

Alarm bells sounded in my head. The Matrons never strayed from their usual breakfast, like ever. In all the months since I'd begun working full time at the restaurant—rain, shine, sleet, or snow—they'd requested the same thing every day. They were more reliable than the postal service. "Are you sure about that?" I asked all four women.

They looked to one another for reassurance and then nodded. The vote was unanimous.

"Okay . . ." I said with reluctance. "Are you sure I can't

interest you in anything else? Pearl, you really love your scallion omelets."

She shook her head. "I could not eat them today. But thank you. I know it is not like us."

The pep that I was feeling prior to their arrival dissipated, and I found myself slinking back to the kitchen with a pit in my stomach. I'd never seen the Matrons this concerned about any of the other happenings in the plaza. I hadn't realized what an impact this would have on them. And that made me wonder who else shared their sentiment. Tradition could be extremely important to people.

When I entered the kitchen, Peter had one earbud in, and was jamming out to his typical morning playlist. He gave me a thumbs-up, which was our acknowledgment that he knew I was coming into the kitchen to place the Matrons' order. No other communication was usually needed.

I held up my hand and shook my head. "Not today. They only want rice porridge. And throw in a dish of pickled cucumbers."

His mouth dropped. He removed his earbud, gawking at me as if I'd just sprouted a third arm. "What did you just say?"

Walking over to the tea kettles and hot water dispenser, I said, "Right? This is unheard of. I could hardly believe it myself."

"Dude, this is like the seventh sign of the apocalypse or something. Not cool." He tsked. "Like who woulda thought this would cause such an uproar?"

"It is pretty yucky though. I mean imagine the God of Smiles shooting you point-blank. It's evil. And then the envelope thing . . ."

"It is primo gnarly, man," he said, moving back over to the stove. He pulled some cooked white rice out of the fridge and spooned it into a pot. "Like, what do you think that chick thought when she got the envelope? I mean, like, if it was me, I wouldn't have thought much about it, except that it's weird. You know I'm not superstitious or whatever."

"You're probably the most practical guy I know . . . well, maybe other than Adam." I began preparing the Matrons' tea, portioning out leaves from the metal container that contained the best oolong directly imported from Taiwan. "I do wish I knew what was running through her head though."

Peter paused, his ladle hovering over the pot. "You're gonna stay out of it though, right? Like, you don't need to involve yourself *every* time. And Kimmy—don't egg *her* on either, man."

"I'm just speculating," I said, turning my back to him. I busied myself with filling the teakettle with water. He could read through my lack of a poker face in under thirty seconds flat, so it was helpful to have a distraction tactic.

"Okay, cool. The two of you tag-teaming for real stresses me the hell out. The amount of gray hair I've accumulated is ridiculous."

"Don't worry so much," I said, closing the lid on the teakettle and placing it on my tray. "Besides, if you need to start dyeing your hair, I got a gal."

After the Matrons had been served their tea and rice porridge, I told them I was stepping out for a minute. I knew they'd be my only customers at this hour of the morning. It's rare that anyone comes in before ten o'clock. Which, to be honest, was preferable most days. The Matrons enjoyed engaging with the other customers that would come in, and there was no telling what they might say, or what secret they might divulge to an unsuspecting party.

Kimmy was pacing the entrance of China Cinema and Song as I walked up. "Geez, there you are, Lee," she said, throwing up her hands. "I've been waiting for you for fifteen minutes."

"Why? I could have just come into the store. It's not like it's a trek."

"My mother is here today," Kimmy hissed. "I don't want her to know that I'm helping you with this. If she finds out, I'll never get her to leave."

Lowering my voice, I asked, "What is she doing here?" I took a peek around Kimmy to see if Mrs. Tran was anywhere in sight. "Are you going to be able to make the calls with her around?"

"She didn't think I could handle being in the shop by myself. I'm too emotional." She rolled her eyes. "I'm in the process of trying to get rid of her. Let me just tell you the show I've had to put on to convince her that I'm fully functional. It's been an exhausting start to my day."

"Well, if you can't get rid of her by lunchtime, let me know and I'll see if I can get Rina to help."

Kimmy snorted. "You know she won't help with any of your scheming. I love her to pieces, but she's the very definition of goody-goody."

"I'm not an amateur," I said. "I wouldn't tell her the secret part of the plan. Besides, I want this to happen on Wednesday, so people have got to be notified by the end of today."

"Don't sweat it, Lee. I won't let you down."

"Thanks for doing this. You're really helping me out." I handed her the second page of the list, having kept the first page for myself. "Oh, and one more thing," I said as she took the paper from my hands and stuffed it into her back pocket. "Don't breathe a word of this to Peter. He's already made it clear this morning that he doesn't want you or me involved in this case. So he can't know the details of what we're doing either."

Kimmy smirked. "Please, Lee, you're not the only one around here who's not an amateur."

CHAPTER
21

— — — — — — — — — — — —

After Kimmy and I parted ways, I quickly stopped in Shanghai Donuts to grab my bag of treats from Mama Wu. When I peeked inside, I found a sugar raised doughnut along with six glazed doughnut holes.

I had promised myself I wouldn't be eating this much sugar in one sitting anymore, but these were special circumstances, and I needed the fuel to keep myself from totally falling apart. It was either that or buy a new purse, and doughnuts were much cheaper than the Jimmy Choo Diamond Crossbody handbag I currently had my eye on.

The pastry bag also provided me a good cover upon returning to the restaurant. No one would question me with a bag of doughnuts.

The Matrons had finished their breakfast and were sipping tea, speaking to one another in hushed tones when I dropped off their check.

Helen fished her wallet out of her purse as quickly as I'd placed the plastic money tray on the table. "Lana, I know that we had our secret moment yesterday while the others were around."

She was referring to my covert wink. "Yes, and I thank you for going along with that. My mother wouldn't like me to disagree with her, especially in front of non-family members."

"I explained this situation to the others," she said, regarding the other three women with a nod. "And we *all* hope that you will handle this quickly." She placed some bills on the tray, including a few extra for a tip. "This must not wait a moment longer. I trust you are already working on something."

The look in each woman's eyes was hopeful. I wanted to reassure them to help put their minds at ease, but I also knew I had to be careful with how much I told them. No doubt our conversation would be circulating around the plaza in no time. I couldn't risk the hindrance, especially after the way everyone came at me seeking answers earlier in the morning.

Deciding to keep it simple, I said, "I have everything under control."

When I extended my hand to reach for the money tray, Helen grabbed my wrist, squeezing it with urgency. "Please, Lana, you must take this seriously. If you do not, great disaster will befall all of Asia Village."

"That's what she said?" Megan gasped into the phone. "All of Asia Village? That's pretty extreme, Lana." I was seated up at the hostess station waiting for Nancy to arrive for the day. As soon as she got in, I'd hunker down in my office and start making phone calls.

"Yes," I replied, my voice low in case Peter decided to sneak up on me. "Like, geez, no pressure."

"Do you really think it's *that* serious?" Megan asked. I could hear the coffee maker in the background.

"*They* think it is. And maybe that's enough, I don't know."

"So what's our next steps?"

I filled her in on the details of my plan to get everyone back to the plaza under one roof. And that I'd gotten Kimmy to help with the phone calls.

"I can be there Wednesday," Megan said. I'm off that day. Robin needed extra hours, so I told her she could fill in for me."

"If you could be here, that would be great. I'd feel better knowing you were at least in the vicinity."

"Did you call David yet?"

"Not yet. I'm waiting for Nancy to come in," I explained. "I'll call him first and see if he can meet with me later today or possibly tomorrow. I'd like to see him before I get everyone back here. It might help me with my line of questioning with his ex-girlfriend."

"Are you going to try and question him alone? I'm still not sure what to think about his current girlfriend . . . fiancée, whatever—what's her name again?"

"Angela. Angela Sha."

"Well, keep me updated. I'll be on computer duty today until it's time to leave for work. I have your compiled list of names jotted down and I'll add Angela to it. I'll see what I can drum up with some internet stalking. Wish me luck."

I did just that before we hung up. We were all going to need a little luck if we wanted to find out who murdered Rhonda.

After Nancy came in, I shut the door to my office and got straight to placing the necessary calls. I started with the party rental company, trying to connect with Nelson, but didn't answer. I left him a message letting him know that the police had cleared for the staging equipment to be disassembled.

Next I called David and asked him if he could meet me for coffee.

"What's this about?" he asked. "Did Ian back out of payment?"

"No, no, nothing like that," I replied. "I just wanted to touch base with you on a few . . . loose ends."

He must not have had it in him to argue the point, so reluctantly, he said, "Okay."

"There's a Starbucks right around the corner from here. Wanna meet there around six?"

"Actually why don't we make it drinks instead. I could use a stiff one," he said. "We could drink in honor of my sister."

"Sure, that's a great idea," I said, the wheels turning in my head. "My best friend is a bartender at the Zodiac. Do you know it?"

"Yeah, it's that kitschy place with all the astrological stuff everywhere, right?"

"That's the one. They have a great happy hour and I'm sure that a few drinks will be on the house."

"Okay, I'm sold," he said. "See you at six."

I felt like a genius setting up the meeting at the Zodiac. Now Megan could be present for my interrogation. She was pretty solid at reading people and perhaps she'd catch a tell that I missed. If there was anything for David to hide, that is. And, as a bonus, Angela wouldn't be there to hinder any of my questions. But, I'd have to find a way to talk with her as well. That was one thing I agreed on with Megan; I hadn't made my mind up about Angela just yet. She was either authentically a damsel in distress or she was a diabolical mastermind.

Not wanting to waste time overthinking the idea, I got back to making my calls. Most people were at work, so a lot of calls went directly to voice mail. It was a little mundane to repeat the same thing over and over again, but at least the process was streamlined and I didn't have to waste a ton of time over-explaining or listening to complaints—or worse yet, questions about the surrounding details.

I was a bit disappointed though when neither Whitney Meng nor Jax Mercer answered the phone. A piece of me was hoping I could have some kind of conversation with each of them that would give me a clue as to where their headspace was. But I'd have to wait for more on that until Wednesday.

After a quick text to Megan to let her know I'd be dropping in with David, I kept it moving, only breaking to check on Kimmy's progress—which was going smoothly since she convinced her mom to leave for the day. And then I took a short break to eat a quick lunch of Hunan beef and vegetables with a side of white rice. Okay, I had a small bowl of lo mein noodles drenched in a tangy teriyaki sauce with a few pieces of grilled shrimp too. But no one needed to know about that except for Peter and me.

I finally finished making all the necessary calls just in time for Nancy's lunch break. In a few more hours it would be time to meet with David.

CHAPTER
22

--- --- --- --- --- ---

The Zodiac is a neighborhood bar located between Asia Village and the apartment complex where Megan and I live. Though the bar is quite popular, it's predominantly regulars, so you see a lot of the same faces, giving you that *Cheers* "Norm!" sort of feel. Which I didn't mind in the least. Now that I was happily taken, I wasn't on the look-out for a potential boyfriend anyhow.

I did from time to time keep an eye out for someone Megan might be interested in, but it was slim pickings since she swore off dating anyone who was a regular customer. I can't say that I blamed her. Imagine how awkward that would be if things went sideways and then they had to see each other on an almost daily basis. No thanks.

I pulled into the parking lot at five forty-five, hoping to get a few minutes to chat with Megan before David showed up. I had no idea what kind of car he drove, so scanning the parking lot told me a whole lot of nothing.

Inside, I ambled over to my usual bar stool, my eyes traveling over the entirety of the room to see if David had beaten me there. From what I could tell, he hadn't.

I liked to sit at the end of the bar nearest the door and against the wall. I preferred to be out of the way of foot traffic and to also have a good perch for people-watching. Leaning with my back against the wall gave me a great vantage point and helped me look inconspicuous as I kept an eye on the entrance. I have great peripheral vision.

Megan was at the other end of the bar chatting up one of the regulars. She did a double take as I sat down and held up a finger to signal she'd be over soon.

I unbuttoned my coat but left it on. Even though the bar was warm, I could still feel the chill of the frigid temperature. Cleveland winters usually had that effect. You felt the weather right down to your bones.

A few minutes later Megan came over with a martini glass filled with a neon green liquid and three maraschino cherries on a tiny, plastic sword. She set it down on a napkin and slid it over to me. "It's an Aquarius Appletini, our current special."

I swiveled on my stool and lifted the glass, giving the drink a good sniff. It even smelled tart.

"Just drink it," Megan said.

Taking a sip, I sampled the liquor concoction, strong notes of sour apple causing my lips to pucker almost instantly. "Wow, that is intense," I replied, setting down the glass.

"I thought you could use a change from your usual whiskey and Coke. Plus, I haven't made you try a different drink in a while."

I'd had my share of appletinis in my college days— which Megan was well aware of—but with my mild advancements in age, I'd come to prefer things on the bitter side in the alcohol department.

"So, what's the plan?" Megan asked, wiping away water

rings from the bar top. "Just straight up interrogation or are we going for the more subtle approach?"

I picked up the plastic sword from my glass and bit off one of the cherries. "I think subtle. He is grieving, after all. I don't want to come at him too strongly and then he clams up. Did you find anything out during your internet search today?"

"Nope. Nada. These people are as boring as can be. I couldn't even find Jax Mercer when I first started. But then I tried out *Jackson* Mercer just to see if that would make a difference, and it pulled up some LinkedIn stuff, which was also boring. And that's about it."

"I was hoping for a different answer."

"You and me both, sister," Megan replied. "When I searched David and Rhonda, nothing came up other than their dance troupe. I didn't have time to completely go through their social media profiles though. Well, David's is private anyways . . . so we're not going to have any luck there. I planned to scour through Rhonda's hot mess during my break."

"Why do you say it's a hot mess?"

Megan blew a raspberry. "This girl posted like every hour on the hour. I'm talking memes, articles, surveys, selfies, what she was eating and where it came from, fashion tips, skincare recommendations. The list goes on and on."

"So she was active on social media is what you're saying."

Megan snorted. "Why do I put up with you?"

I straightened in my seat. "Because I'm charming and cute."

She rolled her eyes. "Well, you charming little thing, don't look now but David is walking through the door."

I held back the urge to spin around in my seat. Anytime anybody told me not to look at something, it was the first thing I wanted to do.

Megan casually waved, signaling him over, and I spun the stool around. "Oh hi, David."

"Hope I didn't keep you waiting long," he said, unbuttoning his coat. He sat down without taking it off, and I wondered if he was as cold as I was. "I see you started without me."

"Hardly," I replied. "I just got here a few minutes ago myself." The clock on the wall told me it was six on the dot. I had thought he'd be at least a few minutes late. Any further gossip with Megan would have to wait until later.

"What can I get you?" Megan asked.

David shrugged. "Whatever Great Lakes you have will be fine."

"We still have a couple of bottles of Christmas Ale," she said. "We also have Burning River Pale Ale, Dortmunder . . . uh, Eliot Ness."

"Let me start with a Christmas Ale while it's still around."

The fact that he said "start" was a good sign. It meant he wasn't going to try and leave in a hurry.

Megan sauntered away, grabbed his beer, and returned with the bottle and an empty glass. "Let me know if you guys need anything else."

David poured his beer, and then held up his glass. "Here's to Rhonda, I hope she's in a better place."

I held up my martini and clinked my glass against his. "Here's to Rhonda."

We sipped our drinks, sitting in an awkward silence after the toast.

Finally, David broke the silence. "So, what is it that you wanted to meet about?"

"Well, first," I said, trying to sound conversational, "how are you holding up?"

He rested an elbow on the edge of the bar, his gaze traveling to the wall of liquors that were neatly displayed behind the counter. "Putting together a funeral for your sister is not something you think you're going to do in your early thirties, that I can tell you. I haven't really slept much the past two nights."

Guilt washed over me for even calling this meeting so soon after Rhonda's death. But I knew I had to do what I had to do. Every day that went by was another day the killer walked free. The sentiment to be gentle, however, was greater than before. "I can't even imagine. How are your parents and Angela holding up?"

"I think Angela is trying to be strong for me, but I know she's bothered by the whole thing." He stopped himself from continuing, but it was obvious he wanted to say more. Instead, he said, "My parents are as you'd expect. A total and complete mess at losing their youngest."

"I'm really sorry." I could feel my heart breaking for him and his family. The bit about Angela being strong kind of caught me off guard, and I wondered if he was being honest about it. She didn't seem the type to put on a brave face, considering the dramatic outbursts I'd witnessed. "If there's anything I can do for you, please let me know. Even if it's just preparing some meals for you and Angela."

"Thank you," he said, his lips curving into a small smile. "I appreciate that."

We sat there for a few more minutes in another bout of awkward silence. I was trying to think of the best strategy to approach the subject, realizing that I probably shouldn't tell David I knew about the red envelope. I didn't think it was common knowledge, though it was all over the plaza. Which made me wonder how long it would take to get back to David now that the Matrons had spread it all throughout our community. I felt a sense of queasiness in my stomach. "It's all just so weird," I said, my words sputtering out like exhaust from an old muffler.

He turned his head in my direction, looking at me for the first time since our toast. "What is weird?"

"The whole thing." I fidgeted with the sword in my glass. "Why would anyone do that?"

His shoulders sank as he turned away again. "I don't know. But if there's anyone who could figure it out, I suppose it would be you, right?"

My body froze. "What?"

He met my gaze. "I happened to stumble on some articles about you on Cleveland.com. You're quite the detective, from what I read."

I silently cursed the *Plain Dealer* and their online forum. It wasn't the first time I'd been outed for my activities by the media. In one article they even referred to me as the Asian equivalent to Angela Lansbury.

"Don't be so surprised," David said, studying my face. "I had a feeling that's why you wanted to meet with me. I can't say that I'm not thankful for the help. Police are slow with protocol, among other things, and I think we could use all the help we can get. Especially after . . ."

I was still processing the information and fixated on the fact that David knew my intentions before having even met with me. So distracted, in fact, that I almost missed his unfinished sentence. Almost. "Especially after what?" I asked.

He leaned closer to me, his voice lowering. "Do you know about the red envelope thing?"

I twirled the sword between my fingers. "Uh, yeah. But just so you know, Adam doesn't make a habit of going around and telling me details about open cases. He only told me because he wanted to ask me if I understood the meaning behind it. And some people happened to overhear—"

He held up his hand and waved away the rest of my explanation. "I don't care about that. I only wanted to know if you knew so I didn't have to explain. And I'm guessing that you understand the implications of what it represents?"

Gulping, I said, "Yes, I get it."

"Okay, I'm glad you understand. Because that night, when Angela and I got home from the police station . . ." He glanced over his shoulder.

"Yeah?" I'd shifted to the edge of my seat, as he turned back around to address me, our faces only a few inches apart.

He inhaled deeply. "When we got home that night, Angela found a similar envelope at the bottom of her purse."

CHAPTER
23

The queasy feeling in my stomach intensified. "Did you tell Adam or Detective Higgins?" I asked.

He shook his head. "I was afraid to admit anything to them. You're the first person I've told."

"Why are you afraid to tell them? They should know. Like right away," I said, surprised at the urgency that slipped into my voice. By outward appearances to anyone else in the bar, you'd think we were just two friends catching up. My body language didn't betray the sick feeling I had or the suspicion that rested just below it. "Angela could be in danger."

David glanced over his shoulder. "I don't think she is . . . and if she is—"

"How could you not think she is?" I spat. "Your sister had an envelope, and we see what happened to her." The whole thing stunk to me, and I was genuinely flabbergasted at his lack of concern for his future wife. "You have to call Adam right away. I can call him for you, actually." I thrust my hand into my purse, digging around for my cell phone.

He reached for my wrist, pulling it away from my purse. "Just hang on one second."

I relaxed my hand, and he released his grasp on me. Opening his coat, he gestured for me to take a look.

My mouth dropped as my eyes landed on the butt of a pistol. From what I could see without him exposing too much in the bar, he was wearing a shoulder holster under his coat, which explained why he hadn't taken it off when he first arrived.

He readjusted his coat, pressing it closer to his body. "So, as I was saying, if she is in danger, I'll take care of it myself."

"First of all," I hissed, "a lot of good it's going to do her if you're here with me. And second of all, you cannot drink and carry a firearm. Do you even have a concealed carry license?"

David pursed his lips. "No, I don't and you don't even need one in the state of Ohio anymore. Besides, I've never owned a weapon in my life. Trust me, though, Angela is safe. Just in case, I have her hiding out in a hotel room under a fake name." He groaned, smacking himself on the forehead. "I shouldn't have told you any of this; you're a cop's freakin' girlfriend."

"I'm not going to say anything," I said quickly. Truthfully, I didn't know if I was currently lying right now or not. This was a slippery slope I found myself on. David had entrusted me with this information. But at the same time, he was playing a dangerous game, and I didn't know if what he said about Ohio law was true. When I had a moment to breathe and I wasn't on the spot, I could make a more conclusive decision and search the internet to see if what he said checked out.

He lifted the empty beer bottle in front of him and began picking away at the label. "I know we don't know each other well, but you have to trust me. I know what I'm doing."

"I don't think you do."

He glared at me. But the longer he stared, the more his face softened. I think he could see that my concern was genuine. "Well, what would *you* do if your sister was murdered, and your fiancée might be next?"

I snorted. "I'd tell the police."

"No you wouldn't," he said, his voice on the edge of becoming shrill. "You'd handle it yourself. Isn't that what this is all about?"

Crap. He sorta had me there. I *would* take matters into my own hands. "Well, I wouldn't buy a firearm and try to handle it *that* way."

He set the beer bottle down, a little harshly, enough to cause Megan to look over. She signaled to the bottle, but David shook his head. She gave us a thumbs-up and then went back about her business.

He turned to me, his eyes wet with potential tears. "You're not going to tell on me, are you? I don't have time to sit in jail . . . if that's what goes on. I don't even know . . ."

"You just told me you didn't need a CCW—"

"I don't," he said, getting defensive. "But if you say I'm a danger to myself or someone else, maybe they will lock me up—and I can't do anything, including protect Angela, if I'm behind bars in jail."

Now *there* was an idea. "Do you even know how to shoot a gun?" I asked.

"Sorta. A buddy of mine used to be in the military and he took me to the range with him a couple times. Nothing serious, just messing around trying to get a bull's-eye. He was quite the marksman. Me, not so much."

I felt immensely uncomfortable. This was a new situation for me. Most of the people I'd been involved with didn't want to have any part in handling things on their own. Half the time they didn't even want *me* involved. "How about this," I said. "How about you don't carry the gun on you and I won't tell Adam that you even entertained it. But I do think I should tell him about the envelope. He has to know that this person had more than one target. It could change the suspect list considerably."

"I'd rather you didn't tell your boyfriend anything. I don't trust cops. Never have, never will." He shoved his stool backward, preparing to stand up. Looking down on me, he added, "I came here thinking you wanted to help, just you and me. If you're involving him, count me out."

I panicked, not wanting him to storm out before I'd felt satisfied with my interview. Other than the existence of another red envelope, I hadn't learned anything useful pertaining to Rhonda, which was the whole reason I'd called this meeting. And if he walked out that door, I knew I'd never get him to tell me another word. "Okay, okay." I pulled on his forearm. "I won't say anything. I promise." I couldn't cross my fingers behind my back, but my legs were crossed, so I hoped that counted.

With reluctance, he slowly sat down again, scooting his stool back in. "You swear?"

"Yes, I won't say anything to Adam."

"Good, because I'd rather not do this alone. I don't know the first thing about doing something like this, and I know you've got enough experience for the both of us."

"But you gotta get rid of the gun first," I said. "That's my deal-breaker. We either do this the right way, or we don't do it at all, and I tell Adam everything. If the gun gets confiscated, then that's your problem." I didn't even know if that was a thing, but I said it with enough confidence that it sure sounded like I knew it was fact.

His jaw clenched. "Fine."

"Where did you get it anyways?" Not having the slightest interest in guns, I didn't make it a point to know the local purchasing spots.

"I didn't buy the gun, it's my cousin's," he said.

"And he just gave it to you?"

"I told him I needed protection, and after what he read in the newspaper, he didn't argue with me." David shrugged. "We're close like brothers; he'd do just about anything for me."

"How thoughtful." I tried hiding the sarcasm from my voice, but I fell flat.

David narrowed his eyes. "Don't be so judgmental."

"I don't mean to be. I get that you see it as a protective gesture, but all I see is that your cousin is helping you with your very own potential murder charge. You really think you'd have self-control when faced with Rhonda's murderer?"

"Yeah, I would have self-control. I'm not a Neanderthal!"

A group of guys sitting at a nearby table had stopped talking to one another and were gawking at us.

I smiled awkwardly at their table, then glared at David. "Shhhh . . . keep your voice down."

He shot an icy glare at the table of guys and they all turned away. In a lower voice, he said, "I wouldn't kill anyone, I just want to protect myself and Angela if we should get attacked."

I almost spat out, *That's what they all say*, but I bit my tongue. "We just have a difference of opinion is all. Let's not get deterred by that fact. We do have a common goal, which is to find Rhonda's killer."

He inhaled deeply, his husky shoulders elevating with the breath. Slowly he released it, his nostrils flaring. "You're right. Let's forget about it. I'll give the gun back to my cousin. It's probably better anyways. My parents would be devastated if their oldest son went to prison right after their daughter was killed."

"I'm glad you can see that. Now that we've gotten that out of the way, why don't you tell me about your sister and if the three of you have any enemies?"

I signaled Megan for another round. This was a much bigger production than I'd originally thought.

For the next hour, David gave me a glimpse into the life of the Hong family. Most of it wasn't especially exciting, which I wouldn't have been inclined to believe, but since Megan had also said basically the same thing, I had a feeling that he was telling me the truth.

I remembered to ask him about letting anyone go who might be harboring some feelings about having been kicked from the tight-knit group. Nelson Ban was the only one who left, but David said that was due to injuries and they were still on speaking terms.

It had been Rhonda, after all, who had suggested the party rental company to me as a way to help Nelson out.

When I moved on to questions about his ex-girlfriend, Whitney Meng, and whether she might be involved in some way, he seemed uninterested and unconvinced that she would go to those lengths to get him back. According to him, the breakup had predominantly been amicable and they were still on a friendly basis.

I wasn't sure how much I believed that, especially if Whitney had any feelings that Rhonda was the sole reason for their breakup. There's no way that would provide an amicable breakup. I was hoping that Kimmy might be able to enlighten me on that topic.

David was equally uninterested when I brought up that someone was gunning—no pun intended—to hurt Angela for something salacious she'd done in the past. His immediate feeling was that if anyone was after her, it would be to get back at *him*. Yet, at the same time he couldn't produce a single reason as to why he thought he'd be a likelier target. It gave me the sense that there was something he wasn't telling me.

Instead, he went on a tangent, informing me that Angela was a "sweet girl" who would "never hurt a fly" and had led a quiet life with a "respectable upbringing."

How he knew that her entire history was squeaky clean with such clarity, I didn't know, but time would expose the truth on that one. No matter what he had to say about her, I still wasn't sold on Angela's perfect princess act.

What felt like a game of Ping-Pong was going nowhere fast. My patience was beginning to thin, and I contemplated another drink. If I had to leave my car at the bar overnight, it wouldn't be the first time. Always better safe than sorry.

It wasn't until I brought up Jax Mercer that David perked up and seemed to take the conversation more seriously.

"Why do you bring *him* up?" he asked, leaning toward me. His fingers were drumming rhythmically on the bar top.

"Kimmy mentioned him to me as someone who was sweet on your sister, maybe a little too much. And he happened to be at Asia Village the night of the party."

He ran his tongue along the top row of his teeth. "Kimmy knows more than I thought."

"Am I missing something?" I cocked my head. "Kimmy

knowing the existence of Jax doesn't really seem all that earth-shattering to me."

David reached for his beer, drained the contents of the glass, then slammed it back down. "If my sister mentioned Jax Mercer to Kimmy, then I'm sure she told her that he's also Angela's ex-boyfriend."

CHAPTER
24

I didn't know the appropriate reaction to this news. An option that cycled through my mind was to immediately jump out of my seat. Another was to rip my phone out of my purse and call Adam right away. Instead of doing either of those, I remained seated with one hand wrapped around my martini glass and a chill traveling up my spine so intense that it rivaled the temperature outside.

This was extremely valuable information, and I knew for a fact that Kimmy hadn't known. Because if she had, it was without question that she would have offered up that juicy tidbit.

I had a string of questions I wanted to throw at David. Why hadn't he brought this fact up on his own? If he'd known that there was a mutual acquaintance—or maybe more—between the women, why wouldn't he bring that up first?

"Did you tell Higgins that when you were down at the station? The fact that Jax Mercer is affiliated with both women is completely and totally relevant." I stared at him, struggling to hide the incredulousness in my voice.

As I studied his face, I tried to gauge whether he was being truthful. Maybe it was the martinis, but I was having a heck of a time trying to figure out if David was sincerely this absent-minded or if he was somehow trying to hinder the investigation by withholding useful information.

But why?

He turned away from me, perhaps realizing I was scrutinizing him. "I didn't think it was necessary because Rhonda made it sound like there was no interaction with him anymore." David's hand balled into a fist. "I thought the guy was old news. But I see now that she must have been hiding it from me if she's talking about him to Kimmy."

"You didn't realize he was at the party on Saturday night?"

He shook his head. "I had no idea. If we crossed paths, then I didn't recognize him."

"So what's his deal?" I asked. Regardless of where he chose to settle his attention, I continued to focus on his profile, unwilling to look away no matter how awkward it was. I'd gotten to that point in the evening where I wanted to make him squirm in his seat, at least a little bit.

He propped his elbows on the bar, steepled his fingers in front of his face, and placed his thumbs under his chin. "The guy is a creep. A stage-five clinger—"

"Okay . . . well what happened with him and Angela? Let's start there."

"Jax likes the ladies . . . especially the Asian ones. They met one day at Koko Bakery. You know it, right?"

I nodded. Everybody in the Cleveland Asian community did. Koko Bakery was on the east side of the city over on Payne Avenue. It was probably the most well-known and well-liked Asian bakery in the entire county. It used to drive the Yi sisters—from Asia Village's now defunct

Yi's Tea and Bakery—crazy, and I hated to admit that I took a tiny bit of pleasure from that.

"Well, he'd pretend like he'd never gone there before and ask pretty Asian girls for help in picking things out. Angela being the kindhearted soul that she is, of course helped him, and fell for all of his pickup lines."

"How do you know that he was using lines?"

"Oh, I know the type," he said, stiffening his shoulders. "Plus, the cashier told me."

"Okay, well then what happened?"

"They dated for about a year and she slowly started to realize he wasn't a one-woman sort of man. She broke things off and he tried several times to win her back, but Angie wouldn't have anything to do with it."

I noted to myself that it was the first time he'd called her Angie. It appeared endearing to me, and I wondered if that was intentional. Was he trying to make me sympathetic toward her by acting more personable? "Okay, but what does this have to do with Rhonda? How did she get involved with him?"

David reached for his beer glass, searching the bottom as if to confirm that it was indeed empty. Fidgeting. I noted that as well.

Finally, he said, "About six months ago, he started frequenting the Black Garter, and claimed that his association with Rhonda was a coincidence, but I don't buy it. I think he sought her out."

"To make Angela jealous?"

He faced me, the muscles in his jaw tensing. "Wouldn't you think so? They just so happened to meet each other and have the connections that they have? This town is small, Lana, but it ain't *that* small."

* * *

After David left, his words hung in the air like a thick San Francisco fog. I was bothered to no end by our conversation. Before heading out, he'd promised me that he would alert Higgins of the connection between Jax Mercer, Rhonda, and Angela. I, of course, would confirm that for myself, because a gross feeling in my gut told me I needed to watch myself around David. With the knowledge he possessed, he could help the police with their investigation, but he'd chosen to keep it to himself. I couldn't see many reasons behind that logic other than some form of guilt. Either he was involved, or he knew who was and was trying to protect them from getting caught.

I stuck around at the Zodiac to chat with Megan about my conversation with David. I knew that she'd overheard a little as she had been checking in with one of her customers near us a little more than she usually would. Which inadvertently gave the guy the wrong idea. After he'd left the bar, Megan came to show me that he'd left his phone number scribbled on a napkin along with a generous tip. The almost illegible handwriting read "Call me sometime! ~Charlie."

While I waited for Megan to circle back around, I texted Adam to let him know I needed to talk with him as soon as possible. He'd been working nonstop on the Hong case, thanks to the mayor's insistence. Not that it was a bad thing because who doesn't want to live in a safe city? But I still wanted Adam to have time to breathe.

Megan rolled her neck from side to side as she approached. "I have the worst kink in my neck," she said, leaning against the bar. "I need to get a massage before the week is over."

"I'm sure *Charlie* can help you with that," I teased.

She slapped the bar top. "Oh you, stop it. I am flattered, but . . . you know . . ."

"Does he come in here much?"

Megan nodded. "He's cute too. I think he does construction, so he's got muscles for days, but . . ."

"But?"

"I don't know." She looked over her shoulder, scanning the bar for a customer in need.

"Don't do that."

She turned back around. "Do what?"

"That avoid-y thing you do when the topic of dating someone comes up. You're so fast to match up everyone else but yourself. It's been a few years now . . ."

Megan pursed her lips.

It was a subject she never talked about and I never brought up. Ever. When the topic *did* somehow come up, we referred to him as "ex-dude." Only that. Megan couldn't bring herself to say his name or to even call him a "past boyfriend."

I understood how she felt because I'd had a similar situation. The illusive ex-jerkface. But the sting for her had been more so than my situation because they'd been engaged for several months. Then, out of nowhere, he announced that he was moving to Florida and that she wasn't invited.

Since that time, she'd refused any opportunity to date, and perhaps she hid behind her rule of "no regulars" to make it harder for herself to find a match.

Megan huffed, brushing stray hairs away from her face. "We have other problems than my love life, Lana. I heard some of your conversation with David, and I am going to cast my vote that he is as shady as a covered porch in Mississippi."

"I haven't heard that analogy," I quipped, trying to lighten the mood. I could tell by the creases between her eyebrows that she was not happy with my previous topic of choice.

She ignored me. "How could he not think it was important information that his fiancée and sister shared a man in common?"

I shrugged. "I'm right there with you. I find it odd. Also, his insistence that Angie is such a saint. I don't buy it for a minute. Especially with her over-the-top theatrical performances. They sure seem like great ways to garner sympathy from him. And then the part where he said that she's been so strong for him in the same breath. It's laughable."

"'Strong' is not a word I would use to describe her."

"And then the second envelope thing. I don't know what to think of *that* mess."

Megan stood up straight. "Wait, what?"

I filled her in on what David had told me about Angela finding a similar envelope in her purse that same night.

Megan let out a low whistle. "Now I'm sure that Higgins and Adam would like to hear about *that.*"

I nodded, leaving out the part about the gun for the time being. I didn't want Megan to know that he'd been armed the entire time he'd been sitting next to me. I was still trying to figure out how to handle that whole thing.

"What did he have to say about his ex-girlfriend, Whitney what's-her-name?" Megan asked, not noticing that I'd gotten quiet.

"Not much, really. But I got the feeling that maybe he wanted to protect her? Maybe. I couldn't get a good read on that one. He said their breakup was amicable and they still talk to each other."

"*Or* it's entirely possible that he's in denial and doesn't want to be any part of his sister's death. If his ex-girlfriend *did* do it, then he'd most likely blame himself. Even though Rhonda is faulted with messing up their relationship—which by the way, so not her fault—I could see how he'd still take responsibility for what happened to her as her sibling."

"True, true. Even if for the simple fact that David felt he needed to protect Rhonda from any harm," I said, thinking about the gun again. There was a sip's worth of alcohol left in my martini glass. I finished it off and said, "Well, we've got our work cut out for us. One interview down, another death envelope added to the mix, and the victim's brother is sketchy."

"And," Megan said, lifting a finger in the air, "exhibit A shows that dating isn't all it's cracked up to be."

CHAPTER
25

As I was leaving the bar, the weather took a turn for the worse. A lake effect snowstorm was coming in, scheduled to bombard our area of the city within a half hour. I hurried home, making Megan promise to close the bar early if needed. What was the sense of staying open if no one could leave their house anyways?

Adam texted me back right as I was getting into my car. He told me he was picking up a pizza and wings and would meet me at my apartment. I felt a sense of relief knowing that he'd be spending the night, but I was also nervous about the new information I had to tell him. I didn't know how he would react. I was still trying to figure out my own feelings on the situation.

The things that David told me had come as such a shock, and I'd spent so much time trying to act casual that I'd spun myself in circles. The fact that another red envelope had been doled out complicated things even further. And that David had kept it to himself instead of going right to the police was suspicious and continued to weigh on me. Though he'd expressed to me that he didn't trust the authorities, I still didn't find it justifiable enough to jeopardize your future wife's safety. At what cost would you put your own grievances aside?

I beat Adam to the apartment and was grateful to have a few minutes to myself. Not only to collect my thoughts and prepare for the evening, but to jot a few things down in my trusty notebook.

After a quick tinkle break with Kikko, we scurried back inside and I gave her an extra treat as a reward for dealing with the iced-over sidewalk. I'd tried booties for her little paws one year, and it did not go over well. To get back at me, I'd found a present waiting for me next to my bed. Without hesitation, I'd donated said booties, and now they were some other little dog's problem.

Now with Kikko situated and happily chomping on some doggy chow, I headed for the bedroom. Kneeling down next to my bed, I stuck my hand under the mattress, blindly searching for the spiral rings of my notebook. The tattered five-subject was home to all my wild theories and contained data I found useful while working on cases such as these.

I'd thought it was on the morbid side to hold onto it, and that if I was ever psychologically profiled for some random reason, I might be invited to a lengthy stay in a room with padded walls. But my PI friend, Lydia, had assured me that there was nothing wrong with me and that reviewing old cases may give ideas on how to solve future ones.

Each time I opened the notebook—this one being the second I'd had to purchase—I couldn't help skimming through the pages. They were stories—albeit grizzly ones—and a part of me relived the happenings over and over again each time I had to use it. I ran my hand over the indentations on each page, feeling the strength I'd used to put pen to paper. It comforted me in a weird way that

I couldn't put into words, but it left me with a realization that I had helped people find closure.

Turning to a fresh page, I considered what needed to be documented. Blank pages hold future stories—some good, some bad, some even sinister. In the case of this particular notebook, it held what felt like ramblings of a mad scientist. But it was for my eyes only, and no one else needed to make sense of it.

I made quick scribbles of the information David had told me, my concerns about his affinity for concealed weapons, and his distrust of working with the police. I also made a few notes about Jax Mercer. I'd have to make a special point to seek him out when he returned for Wednesday's raffle drawing. That's when a fearful thought struck me. What if he didn't show? That thought mutated into, *What if no one came?* No one of relevance to the case anyway.

I'd been so sure of myself, not even thinking that the killer might just not show. I mean, why would they risk returning to the scene of the crime? And could I use their absence as a signifier of guilt?

With my pen hovering in place above the page, I continued to argue the point with myself. Because maybe the killer would come back so they *didn't* appear suspicious. Wouldn't it be more unusual if someone didn't show after having spent money on the raffle?

The buzzer sounded, causing me to jerk my hand, the pen drawing an involuntary line through Jax's name. I stared at it for a few beats and thought how weird it would be if there was some symbolism channeled from the universe through my pen.

Without giving the thought any life, chalking it up to all the superstitious talk I'd been involved in, I capped my pen and shoved my notebook back under the mattress.

The buzzer rang again, and I remembered how cold it was outside. I double-timed it to the door, Kikko barking and spinning circles in front of the entryway. I wouldn't doubt she smelled the pizza through the door.

When I opened up, Adam was holding his cell phone with his finger positioned over the screen. "Out of the way, doll." He slid past me, kissing my cheek as he passed. "Hot pizza, cold cop."

Kikko snorted, following behind Adam and the food he carried, her tail wiggling at hyper speed.

"What took you so long to answer the door? I almost turned into a copsicle." He set the pizza box down on the dining room table along with a brown paper bag and a six-pack of beer.

"Sorry, I was in my room." I inhaled the scents of pepperoni and banana peppers wafting from the box. "How was work today?"

He shrugged off his coat and hung it over the back of a chair. His dress shirt was wrinkled from his holster. Not that he ever wore it when he came over, but nevertheless, the mark of his day was always present. "Typical stuff."

Adam wasn't one to talk much about his work. I had gotten used to it over time. It wasn't exactly a light and airy topic. And the non-criminal activity was office humdrum like the rest of us experienced. Filling out forms, reviewing documents, meetings, and so on. Despite his lack of sharing, I still made it a point to always ask.

"Well, you're not going to believe *my* day." I moved into the kitchen to grab plates and napkins. "I met with David . . ."

"Oh?"

"Yeah . . . you're definitely going to want to hear this." Once I had the necessary items, I returned to our tiny dining area and passed Adam a plate. "You might benefit from having me as an informant."

"In that case, maybe I better have a beer first."

After I'd filled Adam in on everything that David had told me earlier in the evening, he remained silent for several minutes, taking bites of pizza and washing it down with chugs of beer. For the time being, I left out the part about David carrying a gun. A second envelope and the news about Jax Mercer being involved with both Rhonda *and* Angela was enough.

I allowed him time to process while I enjoyed my own plate of food, especially grateful that he'd gotten me teriyaki wings.

We'd moved into the living room, Kikko sitting between us hoping for a handout and a random show on Netflix playing in the background.

"I'm going to call his bluff on the red envelope," Adam said after what felt like eternity. "But I will definitely be reaching out to this Jax person. If David would have told Higgins that information on the night of the murder, we'd have made so much progress by now."

"Wait . . . what? Go back to the bluffing part. What do you mean?"

"Think about it, doll." He set his plate down on the coffee table then wiped his hands on a paper towel. "If Angela received a red envelope too, then it kind of throws out the idea that Rhonda was the target. And at the same time, conveniently sets up this Jax person . . . potentially." He paused, shaking his head. "I'm not one hundred percent sure about that part because he'd be risking a lot if he couldn't get you to bring up Jax without him having to coax you into it. And Jax *is* a plausible suspect."

"But why would he make up the thing about the red envelope? I'm still stuck on that part. You could easily disprove it, couldn't you?" I asked. "He has to know that I would tell you."

"Exactly. It'd be your word against his," he replied. "It could get quite complicated if David wasn't willing to fess up to having it on his own. And I bet you if Higgins went knocking on his door asking to see the envelope, David would act like he had no idea what was going on and try to discredit you. We'd need a search warrant to take it further."

I felt my cheeks warming. "But he asked for my help."

"Convenient, isn't it?" Adam rose from the couch, grabbed his plate, and headed to the pizza box for a second helping. "He wants you to think that you're all buddy-buddy with him, so he can gain your trust, probably to keep you off his scent. I've seen it a million times. The guy knows he's at the top of our list. Both Higgins and I know he's involved somehow, but we can't figure out the angle . . . yet."

I chewed off a piece of crust while I thought about the information Higgins had told me that morning. If they were convinced that the gunman had escaped, then I knew they didn't think David did the shooting himself. Which meant they thought he was teamed up with an outside party. My mind traveled back to David getting the gun from his cousin, and his statement about family members who would do *anything* for you. "I know you're not going to tell me because you never speculate, and I know you don't like hunches. But does that mean you've made some progress in the case that's leading you down that path?"

Adam closed the pizza box and turned to address me. "Let's just say, it's better if you keep your interactions with David Hong very public . . . or nonexistent until this case is over."

CHAPTER
26

Troubled sleep followed that evening. Adam and I had spent most of the night discussing the case, which was unusual for us because he normally would shut down any speculations I had. I felt this was a sign of his acceptance of the new me. Don't misunderstand; he wasn't encouraging me to run headfirst into danger. He was still the protective boyfriend he'd been throughout our relationship, but he was more forthcoming than he'd ever been.

The part that kept me awake was this idea that David had somehow pulled one over on me without my awareness. Though I did have my own suspicions about him to begin with, had I potentially allowed for a soft spot because I knew he was grieving? And that made me question whether I knew he was actually grieving or not.

I stared at the digital clock next to my bed: 2:47 a.m. I tossed and turned for a few more minutes before I decided to wake up Adam. I needed to tell him about the gun. If David was really trying to pull one over on me, then I needed to make sure Adam knew all the details.

Adam had his back to me, and I reached for his shoulder, tugging it gently. "Adam, hey, wake up," I whispered.

"Hmmm," he said, stirring underneath the covers. "What's wrong?"

"I have to tell you something I forgot about earlier," I said. Guilt dripped through the word "forgot" as it came out of my mouth.

He turned toward me, wrapping his arm around my waist. "Uh-huh, what is it, doll?"

"David was carrying a gun when he met me at the bar."

In the darkness I could sense his eyes spring open. "What?"

"He said he had it for protection since Angela got the envelope . . . His cousin gave it to him."

Adam sat up. "Do you know what kind of gun it was?"

"No, he didn't say."

"But he showed it to you?"

"Yes," I said as waves of panic torpedoed up and down my body. I suddenly felt sick. Now that Adam had presented the possibility of David trying to pull the proverbial wool over my eyes, I saw a completely different angle in relation to the gun.

Adam said it before I could blurt it out. "That could potentially be the murder weapon." He flung his legs over the edge of the bed. "Where's my phone? I need to call Higgins."

I couldn't fall back to sleep after that. After Adam got off the phone with Higgins, he told me that his partner was going to request a search warrant for the murder weapon and the red envelope. That seemed to calm him, and he fell asleep shortly after without much trouble.

I, on the other hand, could not get myself to lay still.

Instead of making him stay awake with me while I aim-lessly ruminated, Kikko and I ambled into the kitchen in search of cold pizza.

We were in the process of sharing a piece of pep-peroni when I heard a key slipping into the dead bolt. Kikko, too preoccupied with her greasy treat, didn't even bark once.

Megan, with hunched shoulders, crept into the apart-ment. We always left a light on overnight, so she hadn't noticed me sitting at the dining room table. She closed the door slowly, careful not to make any noise, then re-engaged the lock.

Before she took another step, I said, "You're pretty late tonight, aren't you?"

Megan jumped, whipping around to face me. Her fists were clenched to her chest. "Lana! My god, don't do that! You scared the crap out of me."

I let out a little chuckle. "Sorry, I couldn't help myself. I had no idea you tiptoed around here like a ballerina. I sleep like a rock, you know."

"Oh I know," she said, removing her gloves and hat, "but your dog doesn't."

Kikko snorted.

Megan kicked off her ankle boots and padded over to the table, flipping open the pizza box. She tore off a slice and sat across from me. "Speaking of sleeping soundly, what are you doing up anyways? I thought Adam was here tonight."

"He is," I said, jerking my head in the direction of my room. "Snoring like a bear too. But that's not why I'm awake."

She took a bite of pizza. "So what's up? I still have a good hour in me before I pass out against my will."

I told her about the conversation I had with Adam and

his frantic call to Higgins, along with the details of David and his probable lies.

Megan raised a brow. "Really?"

"Yes, really. Why do you say that?"

Megan shrugged. "I don't know, it doesn't seem right to me. Why would David take a chance and show you the murder weapon? He clearly knows your track record if he'd read about you online."

I sneered. "Because he probably thought I was dumb enough to believe his story. I mean, how stupid am I? He shows me a gun and I just believe some story about his cousin handing it over. I could smack myself."

"I wish you would have told me about the gun sooner. It's creepy to think that he was armed that entire time. Plus you can't exactly do that in a bar." Megan got up from her seat and moved to the fridge. She pulled out a can of Coke and came back to the table. "But don't be so hard on yourself. You have always been one to see the best in people. If he appeared to be genuine, there's no reason to think he's lying. Plus, I don't think his story is total BS. Adam is a lot more cynical than you are . . . He has to be, I guess."

"So what parts do you think are BS then?"

"He might be lying about where he got the gun, but I don't think he killed his own sister." Megan shook her head. "At least I hope not. But I *am* thinking maybe he got the gun by illegal means. You know, something with no serial number or whatever, so it can't be traced. I don't think he'd be bold enough to show you the actual murder weapon. Especially with you being a detective's girlfriend. And I certainly don't think he thinks you're stupid."

"I hope you're right about that," I replied. "But I still feel bothered by this. Since Adam pointed out that something is off, I can't shake the feeling that he's right."

Megan pulled on the pop can's tab, taking a sip. "Well, all we can do is wait and see what comes of this warrant situation. In the meantime, let's focus on these other people and eliminate who we can. I think this Jax person is a more viable suspect anyways.

And who knows what we're going to drum up when we talk to a few more people. Didn't you say something about going with Kimmy to the club to chat with what's-her-name?"

"Yeah, Christine Schneider, I believe. She might know more about Rhonda, or something from her past that might help us figure out what direction to steer ourselves."

"See?" Megan said, popping the last bite of crust in her mouth. "We still have plenty of ground to cover and, for once, fewer dead ends. Let's get some sleep, and this stuff is going to make a ton more sense in the morning."

"You're probably right. My head is a mess, and I'm not thinking as clearly as I could." I stretched my arms over my head. "I better make the most of these next four hours of sleep."

Megan placed her hands on the table and hoisted herself up. "That's the spirit."

We both laughed and I said my good night before heading back to bed with Kikko trailing behind.

That was the thing about Megan. When I was feeling bad or the chips were down, she'd always remind me that there was still a sliver of hope to be found.

CHAPTER
27

Getting up after a measly four hours of sleep wasn't as easy as it used to be. I didn't want to think like that or give life to what they say about the effects of age and slowing down. I hadn't even gotten to thirty yet. As I sat on the edge of my bed trying to will myself into alertness, I considered that my octogenarian grandmother was probably in better shape than I currently was.

Already I could imagine the cautionary lecture from Megan about getting serious with my workout regimen. "That's why you're always so tired, Lana," she'd say.

I'd follow up with a "Yeah, you're right," and then down a half pot of coffee like nobody's business.

Adam had already left about an hour earlier. I remembered him whispering in my ear and me replying with a heavy mumble of "I love you."

Stifling a groan, I finally got out of bed and slid my feet into my new plush slippers—another Christmas present to myself.

Kikko jumped out of bed, giving herself a good shake, and trotted out into the kitchen in search of her water bowl.

I prepped the coffeepot per usual and paused, glancing down at my dog.

Kikko stared up at me, her prominent eyes reminiscent of a Precious Moments figurine. She tilted her head as if to say, *What, Mom?*

I bent down to scratch behind her floppy ears. "Is it just me, or is every day starting to feel like an episode of *Mr. Rogers*? Different day, same cardigan."

Kikko grumbled and scampered off to the front door, where she turned to look at me before spinning herself around a couple of times.

"Yeah, yeah, okay," I said, moving toward the entryway, "maybe I should get myself a couple of cardigans."

Kikko barked.

"I'll take that as a yes." I removed her leash and jacket from the hook, stuffed my feet into my boots, and threw my coat on over my pjs. "I bet Mr. Rogers didn't have to solve murders though."

I didn't know what I expected to happen when I arrived at the plaza. I suppose I thought there would be an entourage waiting for me as there had been the day before. However, the person I least expected to see was the only one standing outside the restaurant.

Part of me was relieved. The other part . . . not so much.

The man had his back to the main entrance as I walked in, but the wool coat and fedora took away any question that it might be someone else.

My stride slowed and I contemplated the possibility of sneaking into the restaurant behind him, never the wiser. But he was too close to the doors and my keys made enough noise to wake the dead, thanks to my Hello Kitty keychain and accompanying tinkle bell.

Hearing the sound, he turned. "Oh good, Lana, you're here. We need to talk."

"Yes, good morning, Ian. I'm doing fine, thanks for asking." I pursed my lips before opening the restaurant door with a little bit of force.

Ian cleared his throat. "Sorry, I'm a little scattered this morning. I was going to call you, but I didn't know if you'd be with Trudeau."

I felt the statement had a dual purpose and that perhaps he wanted me to intimate that he could call me anytime. Instead of responding at all, I gestured for him to follow me into the restaurant, then closed the door behind him, making sure to lock it.

He stood near the entrance while I made my way through my morning maze and switched on all the lights.

Once the room was completely lit, Ian moved to the two-seater table right behind the hostess station wall, the usual table he chose for these morning powwows.

"I see you're doughnut-less," I said with a deadpan expression.

He sat down. "Mamu Wu hasn't finished her first batch yet." Folding his hands on the table, he looked up at me, matching my lack of emotion. Either his poker face was really good or he did not find me amusing.

"Okay, then," I said, pulling out a chair and sitting across from him. "To what do I owe this pleasure?" Maybe it was the minimal coffee I'd had, but I couldn't even hide the sarcasm in my voice.

"What progress have you made on the Hong situation?" He examined his fingernails.

I raised an eyebrow. "Are you serious right now?"

"Do you know me to joke around about these sorts of things?"

"It's been like a day and a half since I talked to you, Ian. It doesn't work like that."

He leaned forward. "It needs to work like that. I have reporters calling me left and right. My voice mail was full yesterday."

"Oh geez," I said, rolling my eyes. "I'm so sorry that your voice mail was inconvenienced. This isn't exactly a walk in the park, you know."

"I'm aware, but I also need to remind you that time is of the essence."

"Time is relative," I replied. As far as comebacks go, it wasn't my best work, but it was my true sentiment on time.

Ian clenched his jaw. "Lana, be serious. This isn't a time to be making quips, jokes, or otherwise. Now tell me what you've got in the works."

"First of all, Ian," I said, matching his forward lean, "as I've had to say more than once, I don't work for you directly, so if I were you, I'd take a different tone . . . again."

Ian pinched the bridge of his nose and sat back with a thump. "You're right. I have to apologize, I haven't been myself lately. It's just Donna and all her demands. It's every day all day."

I folded my arms across my chest. "That sounds like a *you* problem."

"Let me help you," he said, leaning forward again. "At least if I'm doing something, then I can tell Donna that I'm involved and maybe she'll back off a little bit."

I took a moment to consider his request, but my thoughts were muddled with his desperation and Donna's sudden need to hound him every chance she got. I remembered the comments she'd made to me about what she felt was his lack of ability.

Though I wasn't Ian's biggest fan, I didn't hate the guy and I didn't want him to be demoted, if that's where Donna was going with all of this. I dreaded to think of who might take over, what that would change. Or, heaven forbid, what if she asked *me* to take his place?

"Okay, you can help," I said. "I'm just not sure with what." I thought about making him the front man when it came to reaching out to David again, but if David was guilty of something, it felt kind of mean to put Ian in harm's way. Aside from the fact that he'd never done anything like this before, I didn't know if he possessed the tact needed for something like questioning a potential murderer. Best to leave that to the pros.

"What are you planning to do next?" he asked.

"Uhhh . . . well, me and Kimmy are planning on questioning someone later today. Remember I mentioned to you about going to the Black Garter?"

"I recall you saying something about it, yes."

"The woman was a close friend of Rhonda's," I said to help jog his memory. My eyes traveled toward the clock above the door. Peter would be here soon. "But it'll be better if it's just us two ladies. Maybe you can help out tomorrow at the raffle makeup event. We've dubbed it the Raffle Remix."

"How about I do both?" Ian replied. "I can come with you guys today, then do whatever you need me to do tomorrow."

"I think it would be best if just Kimmy and I went today."

"And why is that, exactly?"

I held my breath. I knew I couldn't tell him Kimmy's secret, and as I watched the seconds hand move on the clock, I tried to think of something acceptable to say in place of the truth. "She might be more comfortable talking in front of just women. And we can't take the chance that she refuses to speak with us because you're there."

"Is that the sorry excuse that you're going to run with?" He narrowed his eyes.

"I have no idea what you mean."

"I think you do," he said.

"I'm being honest. You being there could complicate things for us. It's better for everyone if you help me tomorrow."

"I think not." He stood up. "This woman dances in front of a room full of men. I hardly doubt she'd be uncomfortable with me being there. You can't be shy in a position like that. Besides, if anything, you going there at all is even more reason for me to come along. Those places can be seedy, and it would probably be best if the two of you had someone like me to escort you."

I stood as well, trying to make myself appear taller than I actually was. "You know, you're the kind of guy that sets feminism back like thirty years."

He waved his hand as if brushing off my statement and pushed in his chair. "Nonsense. Feminism is alive and well, and don't mistake my concern for anything but what it simply is."

I wanted to argue the point, but I felt it would fall on deaf ears. Why agitate myself further? Besides, I knew the real reason Ian probably wanted to go so badly was to give himself the chance to report back to Donna. I'm sure he'd take great pleasure in telling her that he'd be interrogating someone later that afternoon.

Kimmy was not going to be happy with me. But I'd deal with that burning bridge when it was time to cross it.

I followed after him. "There's just two things you need to know first. Well, three actually."

He paused near the door. "Okay, and they are?"

"One"—I held up my index finger—"you let me lead the questioning. You're there in a backup capacity only."

"Fine. Next?"

I held up another finger. "Do not tell anyone where we're going, especially Peter. He doesn't want Kimmy involved in anything to do with this case. And I know you're going to tell Donna what we're up to. That's okay, but don't tell her where. Just say we're meeting with someone and leave it at that."

"Okay."

"Promise me, Ian."

Adjusting his tie, he nodded. "Yes, yes, I promise I won't say a word to anyone about our location *or* that Kimmy is involved in any way. There. Are you happy?"

"Close to it."

He folded his arms over his chest. "What's your final stipulation?"

I held up the final finger and smiled. "You owe me this many doughnuts."

CHAPTER
28

"No way, Lee!" Kimmy yelled. "No way that fuddy duddy is coming with us."

Kimmy and I were standing outside of China Cinema and Song. It was close to noon, and I'd told Nancy I was heading to the bank a little early today and would eat while I was out. Originally I'd thought we would go to the gentleman's club during the evening, but Christine had an early shift and Kimmy told me that it would be much easier to question her when the Black Garter had minimal business.

"Keep your voice down," I said, glancing over my shoulder. I half expected Ian to be standing within five inches of me, but he was nowhere in sight. An elderly couple passed us by, stealing glances in our direction. I pulled Kimmy's arm and directed her closer to the wall. "I don't want him to go either, but it's the best way to keep him from getting in our way."

"That doesn't even make sense, Lana." Kimmy folded her arms over her chest. "If he finds out my secret, he's going to tell someone; and then before you know it, I'm shipped off to a Tibetan nunnery. Is that what you want?"

I groaned. "Don't be so dramatic. Ian will keep your secret. I'll make sure of it."

She flared her nostrils, then dropped her arms, stuffing her hands into the pockets of her coat. "Fine, but you better make sure you live up to that promise because I couldn't pull off a shaved head."

I bit my lip, stifling a laugh.

"Where is he, anyways? Time is money."

I checked my cell phone to see if I had any missed messages, but there were zero alerts. If he didn't show in five minutes, I was fine leaving without him.

As much as I would have loved that, he showed up at the three-minute mark, rushed and stuffing an arm through the sleeve of his coat. Fedora in place, he gave us a curt nod and motioned toward the entrance. "I'm ready to go. Sorry about that. Donna called and I couldn't get her off the phone."

Kimmy pursed her lips. "It's about damn time, Sung. Didn't you know it isn't polite to make a lady wait?" She tipped up her button nose and strode to the entrance, shoving the door open with both hands.

"What's her problem?" Ian asked.

I reached for his arm, stopping him from taking another step. "Before we leave, there's something I need to tell you, and you have to keep it a secret or I'll never speak to you again."

Adjusting his tie, he said, "Of course. I won't breathe a word to anyone. But Lana, just how many secrets do you need me to keep?"

* * *

Ian had a hard time hiding his shock when I told him about Kimmy's moonlighting gig at the Black Garter. But he understood once I explained to him that she was a server there, not a dancer, and that it was to help her family compensate for the loss in business they'd had since the digital era had taken over. On top of her already meager wages, she'd offered to take a severe pay cut so her family could use the extra money toward rent.

Even though it hadn't been my intent, I hoped that the additional information about struggles within the plaza to make rent would discourage any further ideas that Ian had about raising the costs. He didn't know that Penny had divulged his secrets to anyone else, and it had been sitting on the back burner of my mind since she'd mentioned it.

When we reached the parking lot, Kimmy was standing in the employee area next to Ian's Mercedes. She was frozen, her nose red, but her stubbornness refused to let her show any sign of weakness. She pointed at his car and firmly stated, "Since you're coming along, we might as well take this fancy thing."

The drive to the Black Garter was awkward at best. There were many long periods of silence as we traveled east on I-480, my eye catching the Tim Misny billboard. I almost made a snarky comment to Kimmy about it, but with her current mood, I didn't think she'd appreciate the jest.

We got off at the Brookpark Road exit and continued to the area of the street that was infamous for its gathering of strip clubs and adult shops. It was a far cry from a red-light district, but the area was well known all the same.

The idea of a place like this in the daytime is something altogether different. I knew that businessmen would frequent gentlemen's clubs for meetings or for the supposed great lunch deals that were provided, but to me, it felt a whole lot like drinking a twenty-ounce of Coke for breakfast.

In my mind, it didn't go together. But who was I to judge?

Ian parked near the entrance, only a couple of cars gracing the lot. *Must be a rotten lunch special*, I thought.

Before we got out of the car, I said, "Now remember, guys, let me do most of the talking. Kimmy, try not to rip the woman's throat out; I know you're not a fan."

"Don't worry, Lee," she said, opening the back door, "I think Christine will do just fine with a little good cop, bad cop action in her life." She winked and got out of the car before I could scold her further.

Entering the club during the day was a completely different experience than my first trip there, which honestly felt like a lifetime ago. I remembered how timid I had felt back then, clutching Megan's hand and keeping my eyes solidly fixed on the ground.

Perhaps it was the things I'd been through since then that had made me more comfortable with entering such an establishment, or the fact that I was here with Kimmy and Ian, who were far more assertive and comfortable with themselves.

Kimmy gave a flippant wave to the hostess, who nodded in return and smiled at us as we passed. I would assume that was why she didn't bother asking for my ID, and not because I'd severely advanced in age since my last visit.

With confidence and ease, Kimmy strutted to the bar, leaned over it, and flagged down the bartender. A striking redhead in a revealing top that included the Black Garter logo positioned her hands into finger guns and gave us a bright smile. She sashayed over, blowing an air kiss at Kimmy.

"Lana, this is Autumn," Kimmy said. "We work a lot of shifts together."

Autumn gave me the once-over, a lopsided smile forming. "Lana, you've got a great vibe about you. She'd be perfect, Kimmy."

My cheeks warmed.

Before I could correct her, Kimmy burst out laughing. "No, she's not here for a serving job."

I glared at Kimmy. "It's not *that* funny." I had no idea why I was even offended, but I blamed it on ego.

"Sorry, Lee." Then to Autumn, she said, "We're here to talk to Christine. Is she around?"

Autumn giggled. "Oh, my mistake. I thought you were trying to help fill the empty spot we have now that Raquel is making the switch to dancer."

Kimmy snorted. "Not with Lana, no."

Ian cleared his throat.

"Oh right, this is Ian. Ian, Autumn," Kimmy said with zero enthusiasm, waving her hands between the two.

Autumn stuck out her hand for Ian to shake. In a much sultrier voice than she'd used with us ladies, she said, "It's a pleasure."

Ian extended his hand in a very businesslike manner. His stance appeared stiff and unnatural. "Nice to meet you," he said dryly.

Autumn must have picked up on his lack of interest and released his grasp, giving him a little side-eye as she focused her attention back to Kimmy. I imagined that a girl like Autumn didn't have a lot of men who were uninterested in her. "Did you say you're here for Christine?" she asked. "That's like . . . unheard of."

Kimmy nodded. "It's about Rhonda."

"Oooooh," Autumn replied with a slow nod. "Well, she's still in the back. Her shift starts at one. She came in early to talk with Dominic."

I turned to Kimmy. "Dominic is the owner, right?"

"Yup, good ole Dom," Kimmy said. "Come on, let's go to the back. They like to call it the Green Room around here."

We wove through the tables that surrounded the stage area, a few of them occupied, but no one paid us much attention. A door marked Employees Only was to the left side of the stage. Kimmy pulled a key card out of her pocket and tapped it in front of the activation box on the wall.

A green light blinked and she twisted the knob, holding the door open for Ian and me.

We were greeted with cement walls painted a glossy black, and dim lighting that matched the rest of the club. There were three doors off to the left. The first one had the unisex bathroom symbol on it, the next one read Janitor, and the third was marked Green Room.

Kimmy opened that door and walked in like she owned the place. I followed behind her and Ian trailed behind me. There were three women lounging on the velvet sofas opposite the dressing tables. Relief washed over me at the observation that all the ladies were fully dressed, especially with Ian in tow.

A thin blonde, with legs that seemed longer than the length of my whole body, sat on the arm of the sofa with her back to the door. Her high ponytail was taut, smooth, and damn near perfect. She'd give Barbie a run for her money, that was for sure. She was dressed all in black with leather leggings, stiletto boots, and an oversized sweater that hung off her right shoulder.

She twisted to greet us, but as her eyes fell on Kimmy,

her smoky lids lowered and her burgundy lips pursed. "Well, look what the cat dragged in," she said with obvious disdain. She twisted further to address me. "Mind your company, sweetheart, this one's nothing but trouble."

"Oh stuff it, Schneider, I'm here on business," Kimmy shot back.

I observed Kimmy puff up like a peacock within a matter of seconds. My childhood friend was not one to back down or be intimidated by anybody, so it didn't come as that big of a surprise.

Christine stood, towering over Kimmy's short frame. She was easily five foot eleven without the stilettos. Her shoes added a probable four inches to her height. "What business would that be?"

"Rhonda Hong," Kimmy said, allowing the words to hang there.

Christine visibly softened, her shoulders relaxing. "Why?"

"What do you mean *why*?" Kimmy spat.

Christine leaned against the arm of the sofa. "Why is it your business and what do you want from me?"

The other two women, both brunettes oddly similar in appearance, perhaps twins even, looked at each other, and the one facing us said, "Come on, Mel, let's go."

In short order, they removed themselves from the room, avoiding eye contact as they slunk out the door. My only guess as to their haste was that Rhonda was a sensitive topic and they didn't want to be a part of the storm that was brewing at a steady clip.

Ian took a few steps farther into the room and shut the door behind him.

Christine seemed to just then notice his presence and jutted her chin out in his direction. "Who's the suit?"

Kimmy blew her bangs out of her eyes. "Never mind

him. This here is my friend and associate, Lana Lee. She has some questions for you about Rhonda."

I didn't bother extending my hand. She didn't seem like the type to accept the offer.

A few moments later, I found I was right as she folded her arms over her chest. Her sweater slouched farther down her arm with the motion. "And you are, who exactly? A PI? You definitely don't look like a cop."

Christine, though unpleasant, was quite attractive. And I could see why she thought she was hot stuff. I couldn't find an ounce of fat on the woman, her skin was perfectly tan and flawless, her startling blue eyes—probably contacts—complemented her features to a T. And her face looked perfectly symmetrical, something I'd once read in a beauty magazine was a key determining factor on whether someone was considered "good looking" or not.

She sized me up, and I allowed her to feel as if she had an advantage over me. If she felt secure and unthreatened, she may say more than if she saw me as some sort of competition. I knew how the game of alpha female went. And to think men thought they were the only ones who dealt with that.

"No," I said. "I'm just someone who wants to help find out what happened."

"What would you know about it?" she asked.

"I have a little experience in the department."

"Oh? Like what?"

Her stare was beyond intense, and I had to force myself not to avert my eyes. After all, I wanted to appear unobtrusive, not weak. "I've solved a couple of homicide cases with extenuating circumstances."

She seemed unimpressed, her attention drifting over to the dressing tables.

I followed her gaze, noticing for the first time that there were a stack of boxes on one of the vanity stools. "Did those belong to Rhonda?"

Christine only nodded.

"You guys were close, huh?" I said it with genuine sympathy, forgetting for the time being that she was Kimmy's nemesis. "I know what it's like to lose someone close . . . I'm so sorry."

When she met my eyes for the second time, she appeared more vulnerable than before. Almost like a little girl trapped in a grown woman's body. "Thank you. We were very close, like sisters almost."

I took a step forward, focusing on keeping my voice gentle and level like that of a therapist. "I'd really like to find out what happened to your friend. I only had the pleasure of knowing Rhonda for a very short time, and there are a lot of holes. I need more information on what things were going on in her life."

Christine appeared to be thinking over what I'd said, and I'm sure part of her was wondering if she could trust me. Finally, she said, "All right, I'll play. If you're serious about this, I hope you brought some pen and paper. Because I have a lot to tell."

CHAPTER
29

As luck would have it, I did keep a mini steno notepad in my purse, a habit I'd picked up from Adam. I pulled it out, flipped to a fresh page, and positioned myself on the velvet sofa adjacent to where Christine was sitting.

Kimmy grabbed one of the vanity stools, dragging it closer toward us, as Ian stood by the door like a guard on duty.

I uncapped my pen. "Now tell me, how did you meet Rhonda?"

She sat back in her seat, crossing her legs. "At a dance school for kids. We did ballet and tap together for about four years. Then we lost track of each other. My mother couldn't afford to keep me enrolled, so that was the end of that. Rhonda kept going, of course."

"So you didn't go to school together or stay friends beyond that?"

"No, I grew up in Medina and went to school there. My mother wanted me to go to that specific dance school—I think one of the teachers was a friend of a friend or something."

Medina was just a county over from Cuyahoga, but for most in this area, it was considered far and out of the way.

I made a few notes in my steno pad. "How did you reunite with Rhonda then?"

She laughed. "Total coincidence. I moved out this way to be closer to downtown. I live over on the edge of Brooklyn now. At first, I tried to work at Christie's in the Flats, but I couldn't stand all the traffic on the weekends, so I lasted there about a month before giving up. I decided to give this part of town a try and came to the Black Garter. When I bumped into Rhonda, I knew I had to stay. Sure it's less money, but I deal with a lot less fuss around here—plus, bonus that I got to work with an old friend." She looked down at her hands. "I guess that's out the window now."

Though I'd never been, I was familiar with Christie's Cabaret. It was right next to Shooters on the Water over on the West Bank of the Flats. The place always had a full parking lot, and I couldn't imagine how much money Christine had potentially lost. It made me wonder if she was being honest about her reasons for leaving.

Not finding the specifics of her departure from one job to the next relevant, I decided not to press the issue for the time being and move on. "Okay, so what can you tell me about Rhonda's life since you two reconnected?"

"She was a solid chick," Christine said, staring off. "A real solid chick, and for that reason and that reason alone, I agreed to go into business with her."

That caught my attention. "You guys were going to be business partners?"

"Yeah, we were going to open a dance studio together." She held up a hand. "Not for this kind of dancing, mind you. We were going to teach hip-hop."

My eyebrows raised. "Hip-hop . . . that's totally different

than . . . well, any of the things she was a part of." I scribbled a note in my pad.

Christine leaned forward, trying to take a peek at the
page. "Because it was *my* idea."

Kimmy coughed.

Christine gawked at her, and I used the distraction to
shift positions. I didn't like someone reading over my
shoulder. "So what does that have to do with her murder?"

She turned her attention back to me. "Lots. A lot of
people didn't like it. Dominic, for one. He would lose two
of his best dancers, and whoever else we could drag out
of here. There are a lot of girls here just for the money who
would love an easy out. We were going to offer jobs to
anyone who wanted to be an instructor."

I eyed her carefully. "And Dominic knew about this?"

Christine threw back her head. "Oh did he ever. A lot
of girls couldn't keep their mouths shut about it. Like this
one." She pointed at Kimmy.

Kimmy's mouth dropped open. "I don't gossip. Not
about Rhonda, or you, or anyone. I mind my business and
collect my tips, thank you very much."

Christine snorted. "Yeah, right. You and Autumn have
the biggest mouths in this whole place. Besides, Dominic
already told me it was you guys that spread it around to
management."

Ian took a step forward. "Ladies, can we keep on point
here? It doesn't matter who told whom about what. What
was the man's reaction when he confronted you? And did
he confront Rhonda as well?"

Christine gave him the once-over much like she had
done with me. She jerked a thumb over her shoulder, addressing Kimmy, "Who *is* this guy?"

Kimmy shook her head. "An associate. Don't worry
about it."

Christine sneered. "The way you talk about everyone, you're like in the mob or something."

"Ian has a point," I said. I didn't want to admit that fact, but I was aware of the time, and it was ticking at a faster rate than the contents of this interview. Ian grinned at me and I pretended not to notice. "What was Dominic's reaction?" I asked again.

Christine refocused her attention back to me after giving Ian additional side-eye. "He wasn't happy. He said that there'd be hell to pay if we tried to take any of the girls away."

"He said this to you or to Rhonda?" I asked.

"To both of us," Christine replied.

Kimmy coughed again.

This time Christine, Ian, and I all looked at her.

She wrinkled her nose. "What? I have a tickle."

"You said a lot of people were upset about this?" I said to Christine, getting back to the point. "Like who? Starting your own business doesn't seem like that big of a deal to me."

"It is if other people don't want you to succeed. Let's see . . ." Christine ticked on her fingers. "Her brother wasn't happy about it, and neither was—"

"Hold on," I said, raising a hand. "Her brother was aware?"

"Yeah, he raised holy hell about it. Said she couldn't leave him to do all the work with their family business. He forbade it."

Kimmy and I exchanged a glance. I said nothing but made a note on my paper.

"Okay, who else?"

"A few of her customers. I don't know if you're familiar with someone named Jax."

"I am," I said.

Her eyes widened at my confirmation, but she didn't re-mark on it. She continued on. "He threw a fit. The only reason that dog came in here was to see her. And she led him on, thinking he had a real chance at a relationship with her. Which was dumb if you ask me. But he was not happy in the least. Thought if she went a different direction he'd get the axe." She smirked to herself. "Jax gets the axe. Seems about right to me."

I jotted down that Christine had called him a dog. I detected some jealousy in her voice as she spoke about the adoration this Jax person had for Rhonda. But I also remembered that David wasn't a huge fan of his either. "Okay, who else?"

"Reed Ellington," she said.

Scribbling the name down, I asked, "And who is he ex-actly?"

She dug around in her purse, pulling out a cell phone. "Excuse me a second, I just have to check the time." After giving the screen a longer than necessary glance, she said, "He's one of our regulars, *and* was interested in investing in our future business. But Rhonda did not share the sentiment."

"And why's that?"

"Because he was interested in more than just invest-ing. When I say he was obsessed with her, I am not over-exaggerating. Pair that with the fact that he has an ego the size of Texas and it sure spells trouble to me. I don't think he's the sort of guy who would take too kindly to being shut down. I wouldn't put it past him to take ac-tion over it."

I studied Christine's face, trying to assess if I could find any tells that might give her away. Everything she'd told me felt off in some way, though I couldn't put my finger on it. "I just have one more question."

"Well great, because I need to get going. It's almost time for me to get out there and I still need to change my outfit."

"Do any of these people, outside of her brother, of course, know the symbolism of red envelopes?"

Christine's lip curled. "No. What the hell does that even mean?"

I huffed. "Never mind." I dug into my purse, pulling out a business card from the side pocket. "If you think of anything else—anything at all—give me a call."

She took the card apprehensively, gave both sides a read, and said, "Okay."

But I had a feeling she'd throw it in the garbage the minute we walked out the door.

Back in the car, Ian ran the engine for a few minutes, allowing the interior to warm up. We'd only been gone an hour and I felt the time away was believable for the story I'd given Nancy.

I could hear Kimmy's teeth chattering from behind me. She pulled herself forward on the back of my headrest and said, "I don't like it, Lee. That whole story stinks. I hope you caught my intentional coughing fits."

I twisted to face her. "Yeah, what was that about anyways?"

"She is lying straight through her perfect veneers. Rhonda never mentioned a business partner when she talked to me about opening her own dance studio. And she never mentioned the hip-hop thing either. *Alsoooo*, I never told Dominic anything about Rhonda's plan to leave. I don't think Autumn did either. If Dominic would have approached Rhonda about it, she definitely would have told me. She wasn't the type to hold back on confrontation."

Ian turned in his seat as well. "Are you saying that entire thing was a waste of our time?" He looked at me, incredulous. "Can we not believe a word she said?"

I took a deep breath. "I had a feeling toward the end that could be the case, but I wasn't sure if there were some half-truths mixed in. The thing about Rhonda's brother tipped me off."

Kimmy nodded. "Right? Like she told me that she was worried he didn't want her to be a part of the business anymore. So why would she tell Christine that he refused to let her leave? It doesn't add up."

Ian turned back around, staring at the club for a few beats before putting the car in reverse. "Unless she *is* telling the truth and Rhonda was lying to Christine because she didn't want to go into business with her."

"Wait a minute, Sung," Kimmy said, sitting back in her seat so Ian had full view out the back window. "Are you saying you think that Rhonda was stealing Christine's idea—assuming it was actually Christine's idea to begin with, which I don't think it was, by the way—and was going to cut her out somehow?"

Ian put the car in drive, maneuvered into the apron of the parking lot, and waited for oncoming traffic to pass. "I'm not saying she was going to steal anything from anyone. I'm just saying maybe she didn't want to be in business with her like Christine thought she did. She's a very strong personality, from what I gathered over the past hour. And if Rhonda was already sick of dealing with her overbearing brother, I don't think it's likely she'd want to get in business with someone just like him. It's like jumping from the frying pan into the fire."

I tugged on my seat belt. There was so much to think about, and now I wondered about Christine's motives—if she had any. Was she telling us the truth she thought she knew? Or was she intentionally lying to throw me off a trail? Perhaps *her* trail?

There is that old adage about keeping your enemies closer, and maybe that's the real reason why Christine had buddied up nice and close to her childhood friend.

CHAPTER
30

- - - - - - - - - - - - - - - -

Upon arrival at Asia Village, I realized that I'd completely forgotten about the bank deposit. No one seemed to notice that I'd left without it, so as I made my way back through the restaurant, I decided not to announce my error. I'd have to make my usual stop on the way home to the bank's overnight drop box to avoid bringing attention to this telling misstep.

Ho-Lee Noodle House wasn't very busy, so I took the opportunity to stow away in my office for a short while before I had to cover Nancy's lunch break. I needed time to think over the interview with Christine. Ian and Kimmy had gone on ad nauseam in the car about their own speculations. Normally I would be grateful for potential scenarios I hadn't thought of myself, but today it had felt like a whole lot of senseless chatter. I needed some peace and quiet. Time to think through things without any influence from outside sources.

With the door closed—and locked for good measure—I dug the mini steno pad out of my purse and reviewed the pages I'd scribbled on at the Black Garter. There were definitely holes in the things that Christine divulged to us. But why? And what did they mean?

I pulled out my cell phone and opened an internet browser to search for "Reed Ellington." My heart wasn't in it, and neither was my head. I felt discouraged by the hot mess of an interview with Christine, and deep in my gut I felt like this Reed person was a false lead. I didn't want to do this anymore. I just wanted someone to deliver the answer to me on a silver platter. But that's not life. You have to work for what you want. And despite the fact that I felt like giving up, defeat was not an option. There was too much on the line.

A small glimmer of hope shone through my cloudy demeanor when I found that Reed Ellington was, in fact, a real person who lived in Cleveland, Ohio. It was promising that Christine hadn't fed me a fake name, or a character from a TV show. But it didn't add up to much . . . until . . .

I blinked my eyes several times, bringing the phone screen closer to my face to make sure I was reading it correctly. Reed Ellington was not only a real person, he was the owner of RE: Event Rentals, the rental company we'd used for the banquet.

I snapped my fingers. "Well, how do you like that? Maybe Christine wasn't a total waste after all."

"Think about it, Megan," I said when I'd finally gotten home. "If Reed had a thing for her, and he knew exactly where'd she be, and was familiar with the tent equipment . . ."

After I'd found the information on Reed Ellington and texted Kimmy to share the news, it was time to cover

Nancy's lunch break, so I didn't have much time to myself for the rest of the workday.

I'd texted Megan in between serving tables to make sure she'd be around in the evening. She had the night off and Adam was busy with the case, so it was just the two of us seated at the dining room table with my notebook, her laptop, and massive amounts of coffee. Kikko lounged nearby with her favorite stuffed duck, chewing on its neck.

I extended an invite to Kimmy, but she had plans with Peter and didn't want him to become suspicious if she suddenly cancelled on him. I had a feeling that he was on hyper alert for any changes in behavior concerning his girlfriend. I knew that he'd eyed me up and down a time or two during the day. I was only thankful that he hadn't noticed the bank deposit bag missing from my hands when I'd left at lunchtime.

Megan sipped her coffee. "I don't know, Lana. The whole thing has a funny feeling to me. Reed Ellington just so happens to be infatuated with Rhonda and is the owner of the company you hired for the banquet where she was shot? Don't you think that's a little . . . weak?"

"I think it's genius," I countered. "Diabolic . . . but genius. He's the owner of the company, so far removed from the outward appearance but with all the information he'd need to pull something like that off."

"Do you even remember him being there that night?" she asked.

"Well, no. I didn't know what he looked like until I searched him out online."

"When you saw his picture online, did it ring any bells whatsoever?"

"No, but that's not that weird. I wasn't looking for him

that day. Plus there were over a hundred people in the plaza. He could have easily sidestepped all of us. Technically he didn't even have to come inside. For all we know he was outside the tent the entire time."

Megan tilted her head. "I still think it's planted information, Lana. This Christine chick sounds super unreliable. And I'd be more inclined to think that she did it, and is trying to send you on a wild-goose chase."

I could feel my theory deflating like a balloon with a tiny hole: slow and steady. "It holds water," I said, ignoring my own balloon theory. "I can walk through Ho-Lee Noodle House in total darkness."

"So?"

"Sooo . . . someone who was familiar with the tent structure would have no problem finding the slit in the material to escape through without a struggle. Anyone else would fumble around for a little bit."

Megan let out an exasperated breath. "I see your point, but I still think that it's David or now, Christine. I mean, let's be real, Lana. If this guy supposedly wanted to invest in Rhonda's future business, wouldn't killing her totally remove that possibility? On top of that, if he was obsessed with her, and she led that other guy on . . . what's his name?"

"Jax."

"Right, him. If she led him on, who's to say that she didn't do that with everyone? We don't know that she wasn't 'into it,' like Christine said. She lied about half of what she told you guys. Kimmy confirmed that as soon as you guys got in the car."

She had a point. But I felt it could still be equally as flimsy. The truth was that nothing about this was concrete. With Christine telling half-truths, and David maybe trying to fool me into complacency, I didn't know which end was up. But regardless of that fact, there was this sensation in my gut that I was on to something.

Megan finished off her coffee. "Or, you know what . . . it could even be that Christine and David are in on it together. They're both lying about minor details and maybe they're playing with you."

"But what about the large boot prints leading away from the tent?" I asked, recalling the hints that Higgins had given me. "It would more than likely be a man. Which takes Christine totally out of it."

Megan batted the idea away with a flick of her wrist. "We're also assuming that Higgins was leading to it being a man. He didn't actually specify what kind of boot prints. Also, they could be totally irrelevant anyways. Those footprints could have been there before the tent went up."

There was a sharp, rapid knock at the door.

Megan and I jumped. Kikko sprung to her feet, her duck clutched between her teeth. She let out a low muffled growl.

"Are you expecting anyone?" I asked.

"No," she replied.

"Maybe Kimmy changed her mind," I said, getting up from the table. "I'll get it."

"Okay, I'll refill the coffees," she said. "You do want more, right?"

"Of course I do," I replied over my shoulder. "I'm not done with this conversation."

Kikko followed behind me as I made my way to the door. My heart had gotten a kick start from the unexpected visitor. I was going to have to razz Kimmy about her timing and remind her to consider warning texts in the future.

As I pulled open the door, wondering how she'd ditched Peter for the evening, I was dumbfounded to see that there was no one there.

I didn't make it a habit to say the whole "Hello, is anyone there?" thing because I've seen too many horror movies, and that situation never goes well.

Kikko growled, dropping her duck at my feet. She peered out into the darkness, her ears pricked up.

I was beginning to think we'd misheard the sound and that maybe it was coming from a neighbor's place, but as I began to shut the door, out of the corner my eye, I noticed a flash of red.

When I turned my head, I saw what had been there the whole time. Duck-taped over the peephole, which I'd failed to use, was a glossy red envelope with my name written in black marker.

CHAPTER
31

Megan yelled from the kitchen. "Who is it? Did Tran sneak out after all?"

I was frozen in place, my eyes locked on the envelope. It couldn't be, could it? I was almost afraid to touch it. As if the thing would implode in my very hands.

In the brief moment it would take to light a match, my thoughts burst into a montage of doom. Doubts flooded my mind as I began to feel like I'd taken on too much, had been overly confident in my crime-solving abilities, and was now inviting a shooter into my life. To my doorstep. Someone who clearly wasn't done with their trigger-happy ways.

"Lana!" Her voice was closer now. I saw movement in my peripheral.

Kikko barked, then grumbled, clawing at my leg for acknowledgment.

"Lana?" Megan paused a few inches away from me. "What the hell is that?"

My hand, trembling, reached out to rip the envelope

down. But Megan grabbed my wrist. "No, Lana, don't
touch it. Hang on a sec."

I heard some shuffling around, still unable to tear my
eyes away, and a few seconds later, Megan used her gloved
hand to peel the envelope and duct tape off the door.

"Close it," she said, her tone becoming stern. "Get inside! What if the person who left this is still out there?"
Yanking my arm, she pulled me in, then slammed the door
shut and secured the dead bolt. "What's the matter with
you?"

I closed my eyes and inhaled deeply. "I don't know, it's
like I was paralyzed."

She had the envelope between her thumb and index finger, holding it away from her body as if it were contam-
inated. "Come sit down and drink some coffee. You're
probably shaken up and worn out from all the activity
lately. And clearly you're in shock."

Mechanically I headed back to my seat at the table, feeling slightly nauseous and light-headed. Kikko stayed by
my side, planting herself at my feet and pressing her body
against my calf.

Megan placed the envelope between us and removed
her gloves. "Don't touch it. I'm going to pour you another
coffee, and we're just going to sit and decompress for a
minute."

I focused on the sounds she made in the kitchen. The
coffee filling the cup, the fridge opening, the creamer cap
snapping open then closed, the spoon clinking against ce-
ramic. *Be present, Lana*, I reminded myself.

Megan returned to the table and placed a steaming cup
of coffee in front of me. Notes of vanilla from my favorite
creamer wafted up to my nostrils, bringing me a modicum
of comfort.

"Drink," she ordered.

After we'd spent a few minutes in silence, sipping our caffeinated drinks—and observing the red envelope that took up more space in our minds than it did on the table—Megan once again reached for her gloves.

She looked up at me. "I say we open it first. Make sure we're dealing with what we think. And then we call Adam . . . or maybe even Higgins. If this is what we think it is, which I both think we know it is, it's evidence."

I cleared my throat, rubbing at my neck. It felt like a giant frog sat in the middle of my esophagus. "Okay, let's do it."

Megan picked up the envelope, her eyes flicking in my direction as she flipped it over. It had been sealed with adhesive. Fumbling with the edge of the flap—not easy with knit gloves on—she peeled away at the corner, finally tearing open the tiny envelope.

She pushed on the edges, which inflated the interior, and stuck her gloved thumb and index finger inside, pulling on the contents.

We both saw the familiar green of U.S. currency reveal itself as she pulled the folded money out. Placing the envelope off to the side, she used her other hand to unfold the one-dollar bills.

She counted. "One . . . two . . . three . . ." Holding up the final bill, she said, "Four."

As if there had been any room for doubt on what had been affixed to our door, the wave of disappointment that followed was just the same. There's always that tiny smidge of hope that an idealist holds on to.

Megan let out a heavy sigh. "We need to call Adam and let him know about this right away. He is not going to be happy."

My cell phone, which was within arm's reach, was in my hand in a matter of seconds.

Adam picked up on the third ring. "Hey doll, what's up?"

My eyes fell on the unwelcome intruder lying on our table. "We need you to come over as soon as possible."

"We?" he replied with caution.

"Yeah, Megan's here with me. Someone left us something on our door, and it's not exactly what you'd call a present."

Both Adam and Higgins arrived within a half hour. Megan and I had moved into the living room with our coffees because neither one of us wanted to be near the envelope, which sat abandoned on the dining room table until Adam secured it for analysis in one of his evidence bags.

After they'd determined we weren't in any immediate danger, Higgins went back out into the parking lot to search for any evidence. Adam stayed with us while he filled out a few forms concerning the evidence he would be submitting.

"You guys didn't touch it, right?" he asked, glancing between me and Megan.

We shook our heads. Megan replied, "I used gloves to get it off the door and also to open the envelope."

"Glad you guys were thinking on your toes," he said, scribbling on his form. "It'll help. Especially if we can get something off this. It's doubtful, because we only found a partial on the last one and it didn't match anything we had in the system, but still . . ."

I wished that I could have taken credit for thinking on my toes, but really, if Megan wouldn't have been here, I would have pulled the envelope right off the door. I didn't say as much, and Megan didn't bring it up either.

Megan poured Adam a cup of coffee and brought it

over to him. "Did Lana tell you that she met with Christine today?"

Adam nodded his thanks as he took the mug from her. "Who is Christine?"

"Christine Schneider," I said, being thankful that Kimmy enjoyed calling people by their last name. "She works at the Black Garter and was a very close friend of Rhonda's."

He raised a brow. "And she's relevant how exactly?"

Megan clucked her tongue. "Isn't it obvious? Lana went to see her today, with Kimmy and Ian . . ."

That got his attention. His eyes met mine, but he didn't comment. I had a feeling that would come later.

Megan continued. "They went to ask her some questions about Rhonda's personal life. The woman gives them a complete runaround with all these cockamamie stories, and now we get an evil red envelope on our door the very same night?"

I could tell by the vein popping out of Adam's forehead and the tension in his jaw that he didn't want to bypass the Ian portion of the story, but he seemingly took a few moments to collect himself. "So you're insinuating that this Christine woman is the shooter we've been looking for?"

Megan shrugged, moving back into the living room to sit next to me. "I don't know if she's the shooter herself, but I'm saying that's pretty convenient timing. Maybe she's an accomplice or something?"

Adam massaged his temples. "For the time being, we're running on the assumption that the killer acted alone, but I'll do a background check on her anyway. It most likely is just a coincidence though." He pulled out the mini steno pad he kept in his inside jacket pocket and scribbled down her name. "Lana, can you place her at the plaza the night of the murder?" He said it without looking at me.

"No, I'd never seen her before in my life," I answered with resolve. "She stands out, for sure."

Megan turned to me. "But you even said earlier that the person could have dodged all of us or been outside the entire time. So it doesn't matter if you ever saw Christine a day in your life when you get right to it."

I pursed my lips. "Uh-huh." I never enjoyed it when Megan used my own words against me.

"It would help make it more plausible though." Adam tapped his pen on the table. "Did you get an alibi?"

I shook my head. "No, I didn't really think she was a suspect at the time. I knew she was lying but I didn't know about what specifically."

Megan snorted. "Oh, I'm pretty sure she was lying about everything." She rose from the couch, moving back into the dining area. I could sense the caffeine was having an effect on her. "Did Lana tell you about Reed Ellington? That he's not only the owner of the company she used for the banquet, but he was also obsessed with Rhonda in more ways than one."

Adam leaned to the side so he could see me, as Megan was obstructing his view. "No, she didn't."

"I was getting to it," I said. "All of this just happened today. It's not like I'm harboring information."

Adam held up a hand and redirected his attention back to Megan. "Wait. What did you just say? He was obsessed with her in more ways than one? What does that mean?"

Megan huffed, and I wanted to remind her that Adam wasn't a mind reader. With exasperation, she replied, "He wanted to do business with her in *and* out of bed. Supposedly he wanted to invest in her future business endeavors."

"I see," was all Adam said. He made a few more notes in his pad. Then he added, "We have our eye on someone at the moment, and it's not a female. So this Reed guy could be a viable suspect."

There was a light tap at the door, and then Higgins walked in, stamping his feet on the doormat. Kikko sprung to action, barking as she hopped closer to our new guest. She landed at his feet, sniffed his boots, and snorted.

Higgins bent down, his demeanor lighthearted. "Aw, check you out, little guy. Protecting your mommy?"

"Girl," I said. "Her name is Kikkoman."

Higgins straightened. "Like the soy sauce?"

"Yeah," I said with a sheepish grin. "It felt clever at the time."

He entertained my sentiment with a chuckle, but as quickly as he'd laughed, his facial features became serious once again. I was used to the change in character because Adam also demonstrated this behavior. I called it "putting on his detective hat."

Higgins removed his leather gloves as he approached Adam. "I found a set of boot prints in the snow that appear to have come and gone to this apartment. I followed them out to the parking lot, and the vehicle they left in had tires that are consistent with a larger automobile. Probably a pickup truck if I had to guess. Whoever it was hauled ass outta here, because there are fishtail marks in the snow leading all the way to the main drive."

I rose from the couch and joined the others in the dining area. "So that would eliminate a woman for sure then?"

Higgins furrowed his brows. "Maybe? If the prints belong to anybody of consequence, that is. But with all the foot traffic around here, it's hard to say it means anything. Either way, I took some photographs. Judging by my own shoe size, I'd say it was a men's size thirteen. Which matches the prints we found near the tent."

Adam grimaced. "If those boot prints were from our mystery shooter, that might take Hong officially out of the running. And definitely makes this Christine person a no-go."

CHAPTER
32

\- - - - - - - - - - - -

"Not necessarily," Megan shot back. "Just because Christine didn't deliver the envelope herself, doesn't mean she didn't have something to do with it in some other way."

Higgins looked at the three of us. "Am I missing something? Who is this Christine person?"

Adam gave him a brief rundown.

"Oh, I see," Higgins replied. "We haven't found any evidence that the perp was working with anyone, but you never can tell with these sorts of things."

Megan lifted her chin. "See?"

I rolled my eyes. "Well, regardless, who was at our door? Who would Christine be working with?"

Megan threw her arms in the air. "Literally a plethora of people. Could even be Reed Ellington and she's trying to cover her own tracks by putting the spotlight on him. Or maybe she's in cahoots with someone at the strip club."

Higgins leaned in toward Adam and whispered, "Are they always like this?"

Adam nodded. "Every day."

Megan folded her arms over her chest. "We can hear you. Literally we are right here."

The two men stifled a laugh.

It was different seeing Adam with Higgins for more than a fleeting moment. I'd heard some of their friendly banter in the squad car during times I'd called and caught them in the process of driving to some undisclosed location. But it was another thing entirely to see it.

It was good to know that Adam spent his workday with someone he felt comfortable with, someone who could lighten things up, even if only for a moment.

"Higgs, I need two things from you if you don't mind."

"The world is your oyster, Trudeau."

"Can you put in an order for a plain-clothes to be at Asia Village until we figure out who we're dealing with? Squad car through the apartment property probably wouldn't hurt either. In case they decide to make a second visit, I don't want to get caught with our pants down."

Higgins nodded. "Roger that. Pants down is never a good situation."

Adam smirked, then passed the sealed evidence bag to Higgins. "Second thing, since you're going back to the station anyway, would you mind taking this with you? Technically I'm off the clock, and I have another matter to attend to."

Higgins took the plastic bag from Adam, investigating the contents. "Oh yeah? What's that?"

Adam glanced in my direction. "I have a witness to interrogate."

Once Higgins left our apartment, Megan went to shower, making a big production about washing her hair. I knew it was intentional. Both of us had picked up on Adam's comment that he wanted to speak with me.

We sat together in the living room, coffee cups refilled and Kikko at our feet. She seemed to still be on high alert and kept her attention directed at the front door.

Adam wrapped an arm around my shoulders, bringing me closer to him. I leaned against his chest and sighed. "You're not happy about the Ian-tagging-along thing."

"Not in the least," Adam replied.

I listened to his heart thump in a rhythmic beat. "It's not like I wanted him there. He kinda invited himself and I figured it would be easier to just let him feel like he's being helpful. Donna's really on his case lately." I didn't want to get into the specifics and explain to Adam that I was concerned I would be asked to take over Ian's job. Despite the countless coffees I'd had since the evening began, I was exhausted.

"I don't trust him, Lana."

"But you trust me, right?"

He squeezed my shoulder. "Of course I do. It's not about that. Aside from not liking the guy, I feel like Ian's a liability. I don't want him to get involved, make a dumb mistake, and then put all the blame on you. He doesn't seem to have much accountability for his own actions."

I sat up, reaching for my coffee. "Oh believe me, I know."

"Just be careful around him is all."

"I promise I will be. If I can help it, he won't be going anywhere else with me." I didn't want to admit to Adam that Ian had had some useful insights while we'd been at the Black Garter. But I knew that Adam was right in the end. Everyone I took along with me on my adventures could potentially get hurt or make an error that couldn't be corrected. Kimmy and Megan knew the rules . . . and the risks. And their intentions were always selfless; meanwhile, Ian's were at their core, self-serving.

Adam seemed satisfied with my answer and moved on to the next topic. "Tomorrow is the raffle thing, right?"

"Yeah." I nodded. "We're calling it the Raffle Remix, not that anyone cares. Just something Kimmy and I started referring to it as. Penny's on board too. Everyone will get fifty percent off their appetizers and drinks for two hours after we announce the winners."

He leaned back against the couch, closing his eyes. "Sounds promising. It'll bring a lot of business to Asia Village."

"Do you really think it's necessary to have an undercover cop follow me around?"

He opened his eyes and stared at the ceiling. "It's more concerning to me that you don't think so."

"I feel bad for these people," I replied. "There's more important things they could be doing than following your girlfriend around while she waits tables and doles out prizes."

"Nonsense. You are important. Even if you weren't my girlfriend, I'd want some type of police detail on you. No matter how you spin it, you made someone very unhappy, Lana. And they're not shy about threatening you."

Again, I knew he was right. I didn't want to look at it that way, and since he and Higgins had arrived, I'd pushed down a lot of my feelings about the matter. Detaching myself from the reality that the envelope symbolized something nefarious.

I heard the bathroom door open, and I twisted in that direction. Megan came out in a terry cloth robe and matching towel on her head wrapped into a turban. "You know what I was thinking about in the shower?"

"That you drank way too much coffee?" I quipped.

"No, ya goof," she replied. "Why did we get an envelope at our apartment?"

"What are you getting at, exactly?"

Megan padded into the living room and stood on the opposite side of the coffee table, hands on her hips. "If you were with Kimmy and Ian today, then it's clear that the three of you know the same information. So why did you get an envelope but those two didn't?"

Adam straightened. "Actually, that's a good point."

I shook my head. "We're assuming that they didn't get one. Maybe we don't know about it yet. And on top of all that, you're still operating with the idea that Christine has some kind of involvement."

Megan leaned forward. "Yeah, right. You don't think if they received some mysterious red envelope, they'd call you within seconds? Plus, what are the chances of you questioning Christine today and us suddenly getting an envelope?"

"I did give her my business card," I replied. "Maybe I was first because I'm the leader of the pack?"

Adam turned to me. "Maybe you better call Kimmy and find out if she got anything. Just to be on the safe side. And I never thought I'd say this, but you need to call Ian too."

I scanned the room for my cell phone, spotting it on the dining room table. As I went to retrieve it, I remembered that Kimmy wasn't even home. "Kimmy's at Peter's apartment. So if someone went to her place, she wouldn't know about it until tomorrow."

Adam said, "Call her anyways, and let her know to be on the lookout. If she gets anything, she needs to call us right away. Ian too."

I dialed Kimmy's number and she picked up almost

immediately. "Lee, what's up? I'm in the middle of a Tik-Tok binge and you're messing up my flow."

I filled her in on the events of the evening.

A string of expletives followed when I finished. "So you think I got one too?"

"It's possible," I said. "Especially if Christine is somehow involved."

"Did you tell Sung yet?" she asked.

"No, I wanted to call you first."

"He's going to flip."

I dreaded the thought. Before hanging up with her, I made her swear that if she did receive something that she'd alert Adam or Higgins right away.

"Oh, don't worry, Lee. I wouldn't touch that thing with a ten-foot pole," was her reply.

I called Ian next, but he didn't answer. I left a voice mail with minimal details telling him that it was urgent he call me back as soon as possible, no matter what time it was. I feared that if I told him too much he might try and take matters into his own hands in an attempt to be the hero. It sounded supremely cryptic, but I told him not to answer the door. I could see his arrogance getting in the way, and him coming up with the grand idea to confront the person as a means of resolution to all our problems.

During my calls, Adam had stepped out of the room to make a few of his own. I wondered if he was having a police detail put on Kimmy and Ian as well.

Megan had begun pacing back and forth, which was usually *my* move. But clearly the coffee was keeping her fueled and at the ready. Though if she went for another cup, I'd have to tell her she was cut off for the night. At this rate, we wouldn't be going to bed anytime soon. She began to ramble, "If they didn't get an envelope, then that means it could be that Christine isn't involved like I think she is. But the timing of it all . . ."

"Or she knows that it's me she has to worry about," I offered. "But she'd need to know who Ian was, and Kimmy didn't exactly make it a point to introduce him."

Megan spun on her heel and paced in the opposite direction. "She could find out who he was if she really wanted to . . . I think." She threw up her hands. "Ugh, I don't know. I think she fits. Nothing has happened for days, nothing. And you have one meeting with this girl and now we've got a red envelope too."

"You know that normally I don't believe in coincidences," I said. "But maybe these two instances just aren't related."

"Okay, then who else can we look at?" She paused to stare at me for a few beats, then continued her pacing. "Something triggered it to happen, but what?"

I knew it wasn't a rhetorical question, but I also knew that she realized I didn't have the answer either. She wanted me to come up with a reasonable counter argument, but frankly I was too tired to think about it anymore.

Adam stepped back into the living room, shoving his cell phone into his pants pocket. "I updated Higgins and let him know what's going on. I gave him Kimmy's and Ian's names so he'd be aware of who they were in case they called something in before telling one of us."

Megan stopped in her tracks. "So what are we supposed to do next?"

"Well first, you can stop pacing." Adam stifled a yawn. "For now, the only thing we can do is sleep. And wait for the shooter to make their next move."

CHAPTER
33

- - - - - - - - - - - - - - - -

When Adam spent the night, I wasn't a fan of him being gone by the time I woke up. But on that particular morning, I welcomed it because I had to consult my notes and where my thoughts had gone with the recent turn of events. Now that I'd had a mostly decent night of sleep, my head was a little clearer, and I felt I could sort things out.

Once I'd finished dressing and was content with my makeup session, I sat on the couch with my coffee and notebook, reviewing the little I had written about the case.

Despite my own reservations, I scribbled in the sentiments on Christine as well as everybody's opinion on whether or not she was involved. I placed a giant question mark next to her name.

My gut told me that the person we were dealing with was a man. Aside from the large boot prints and tire marks left behind, it didn't strike me that Christine would kill over her potential grievances. It was possible she had motives, sure. But I felt that she'd use a different skill set to handle her problems. One that used manipulation, not brute force.

And if Ian's theory about Christine not knowing the actual truth was accurate, and Rhonda really was trying to dodge getting into business with her, how would Christine know she had anything to kill someone over to begin with?

That reminded me that Ian had never called back. I checked my phone again to see if I'd missed any recent calls or texts, but I hadn't. It kind of frustrated me. Ian would always take every opportunity to attach himself to my hip, but now when things really mattered, he was nowhere to be found. In my opinion, it spoke largely to his character.

A sliver of a thought crept in that maybe something had happened to Ian and that's why he wasn't calling back. I decided to text him again.

TEXT OR CALL ME BACK! I tapped on the send icon a little forcefully and willed my all-caps message to jar him into responding.

I didn't want to fly off the handle, but I was becoming a little unhinged with each passing day. Part of that was actually thanks to Ian himself. And here I'd thought I was the impatient one. I took a few deep breaths and let the thoughts go, imagining all my worries being carried away in a hot air balloon.

I could do this. I'd done it before and I wasn't going to give up on myself now.

I decided that I'd give it another hour. If I made it to Asia Village and he still hadn't responded, I'd ask Adam if he could have a squad car go to Ian's place.

The half-blank page stared back at me. The top half was filled with question marks next to almost every note I'd made. I knew I didn't quite have the full picture just yet. What was it that I wasn't seeing?

A quick check of the time told me that I had to get ready

to leave. I left a note for Megan on her door that I was heading to the plaza and reminded her to be there around eleven thirty. The event would begin promptly at noon.

As I put on my coat and gloves, dreading to step back out into the cold, I cycled through the encounters I had with everyone who might be involved. I had yet to see sight of Angela since the night of the party. When I'd mentioned it in passing to Adam the previous night, he hadn't seemed too concerned. Everything I'd told him about the second envelope, which David said had been found in her things, had been for the most part dismissed. Now that we'd received our own, Higgins was working on getting a search warrant for the gun, and he included the envelope in his request.

Aside from David possessing the potential murder weapon, Adam thought the rest of what David had said were lies. But how could he be so sure?

More important, did *I* think that David was lying to me? I wasn't entirely convinced now that I'd received my very own envelope. I didn't trust him, but I decided that it would be well worth having another discussion with him. Now it would be my turn to confide in him that I'd become an unwilling member of the four-dollar club. Maybe based off his reaction, I could find some truth—or sniff out his lies.

At least I'd finally have my first opportunities to speak with his ex-girlfriend, Whitney Meng, and to meet Jax Mercer face to face. Maybe once I did that, I'd have a better idea of what the heck was going on.

I grabbed my purse, patted Kikko's head one final time, and left my apartment, mumbling the words to Lizzo's popular song. "It's about damn time."

* * *

When I arrived at Asia Village, I noticed a black town car parked near the entrance. Inside was a man who appeared somewhat familiar, with short, sandy brown hair, aviator sunglasses, and a goatee. He gave me a wink as I passed, and I smiled without making a production. I'd been through this one time before, and I knew not to bring any attention to his presence.

The Matrons arrived at their usual time, and I was happy to see they were looking well. Better than they had in days. As the four women walked into the restaurant, they talked excitedly amongst themselves about the upcoming afternoon gathering. It was refreshing to see them regain their liveliness, so I decided not to tell them about the envelope I'd received. Plus, I didn't want them to broadcast it all over the plaza. If it got back to my mother, I knew I'd have a lot of explaining to do.

Helen smiled up at me as I neared the table with their tea. "We are looking forward to everyone coming back to Asia Village today. We even cancelled our mahjong game."

"I hope you're not disappointed then," I said, setting the teakettle down on the table.

Pearl laughed. "It is never disappointing to see so many people. I'm sure we will learn much today." She eyed her sister, Opal. "Many things about many people."

Opal nodded. "Yes, there is a lot to learn simply by watching."

Even though I hadn't told them I had ulterior motives, I knew they were well aware that they existed. Because they thought in the same manner. I'd picked up a lot of observation tips from hanging out with them every morning.

Wendy tapped her chin. "You know, Lana, I'd like to ask you a question about something I find very odd."

"Sure, go ahead."

"Why did the party company not take the stage away? It is sitting in the parking lot for almost a week now. Do they not need it back?"

I'd been kind of annoyed about that myself but hadn't had the mental wherewithal to get on Nelson's back about it. "Sometimes these companies do that," I improvised. "They might be short-staffed and haven't had someone available to come pick it up. I'll call them again today and see if they know anything more."

Wendy nodded along. "Yes, I think that it's best to call again. I hope they will not charge Ian for this. He seems to get very upset when it comes to money."

"Oh, I know," I replied. "Trust me, he reminds me constantly."

We all shared a brief laugh while in the back of my mind I was aware of the fact that I still had yet to hear from Ian.

"Would you ladies excuse me? I'm going to check on your food."

Helen smiled. "Of course, Lana. No hurry, we will be here for a long time today."

I zipped back toward the kitchen, bypassing Peter, and headed for my office, digging my phone out of my purse. To my immense relief I had a missed text message and a phone call. Both Ian.

I pressed call and waited for him to answer.

He picked up before the first ring even finished. "Lana, where is the fire?"

"Ohmigod, Ian!" I yelled into the receiver. "When I say something is important and to call me back right away, then that's what you do. I've been worried sick over here."

"Really?"

"Yes, really. Where the hell have you been?"

"I'm flattered," he said. "My phone crashed last night. Completely dead. I am just now leaving the Verizon store."

I sank into my chair. "Did you get my message?"

"I listened to it as soon as I got to the car. What happened exactly?"

I relayed the entire story of the previous evening, keeping my eye on the clock above my office door. I didn't have much time before Peter came to see where I'd run off to. "So, I'm guessing you didn't receive an envelope too?"

"No," he replied. "Not a thing."

"I don't think Kimmy did either," I told him. "I haven't checked in with her yet today, but so far it's just me."

"Clearly you ruffled someone's feathers," he said. "We can discuss that more later. I've got to run an errand and then I'll be at the plaza. I'll come by the restaurant if there's time."

I wanted to tell him that it wasn't necessary, but he said goodbye and hung up before I could say anything further.

"What was that about?" Peter asked from my doorway.

I hadn't noticed he was there, or how long he'd been listening.

"Nothing," I said, stuffing my phone back into my purse. I shoved it into the bottom drawer of my desk and rose from my seat. "Ian was just calling to let me know he would be here for the Raffle Remix."

"Dude." Peter folded his arms over his chest. "You're totally lying to my face right now."

"I'm not." My voice sounded shrill as I said it. "He literally just said that. He's coming here." I tried to sidestep Peter, but he blocked me from exiting my office.

"Kimmy already told me everything," he said. "I know what you're up to, and Kimmy too."

"I'm sorry, Peter. I didn't want to lie to you, but you don't get it."

"Sure don't," he said, raising his chin. "Do you get that you're like a sister to me?" After he said it, he focused his eyes on one of the door hinges.

My eyebrows shot up. "That is the nicest thing you've ever said to me."

Peter wasn't big on the whole emotion thing. I knew that he could be very romantic in a private setting because Kimmy had told me as much. But as far as getting mushy in public, he kept it to a minimum.

He'd also grown up most of his life thinking he was an only child. It wasn't until his biological father, the late Thomas Feng, confided his paternity that Peter found out he had two half sisters. And even though they existed, Donna didn't encourage the three to spend time together, so they remained for the most part strangers.

The fact that he would think of me as his sister was a huge deal. It also triggered something in the back of my brain that I'd heard a few other people make references to: chosen family. But I didn't want to lose sight of my own moment with Peter by overthinking everything. There would be time for that later.

I brought myself back to the present and spread out my arms for a hug.

He rolled his eyes. "You're gonna girl this all up, aren't you?"

I laughed. "Yes. Yes, I am."

"Fine," he grumbled. "Just don't go telling everybody we had some kind of moment." He extended his arms and I leaned in to hug his skinny frame.

"I won't tell a soul. You will remain the cool, stoic guy you want everyone to believe you are."

"Uh-huh." He sighed.

After we hugged, he pushed on my shoulders and held me a few inches away. "Lana, I know I'm never going to convince you to not get involved or whatever, but can you promise me one thing?"

I grimaced. "I can try."

"Do what you gotta do, just don't get hurt. And make sure Kimmy doesn't either. I don't know what I'd do if something happened to either of you."

CHAPTER
34

- - - - - - - - - - - - - - - -

The Matrons didn't inquire as to why their food had taken longer than usual to receive, and I didn't bother with an explanation. While they ate, I went and hung around at the hostess station, my thoughts returning to the topic of the interrogations I would attempt at the Raffle Remix. I was banking on a lot, and it made me nervous. Not only did Jax Mercer and Whitney Meng actually have to show up, but I'd need them to hang around long enough to be questioned.

After the Matrons left, promising to see me in a few hours, I slipped into my office again to grab my phone. Peter acted as if he didn't notice me coming and going, and I assumed he was trying to put some distance between our heart-to-heart a mere hour ago.

When I got back to the hostess station, a group of four businessmen came in, clad in similar suits and boring ties. The last one had on a polka-dot tie, so I deemed him the renegade of the quartet.

Once they were seated and happily enjoying an early lunch, I sent David a text, inviting him to join us for the

Raffle Remix. I was hoping to sound friendly and unassuming. I ended with *Bring Angela too!*

More than an hour passed before he responded: *I'll be there, but Angela can't make it.*

It took everything in my power not to ask him why she wasn't available, but I decided not to push it for the time being. Once he arrived and we were face-to-face, I could question him on the topic then.

Nancy showed up at eleven o'clock, all smiles and ready to take over as server while I went into managerial mode.

I was tallying the books when Megan walked into my office, promptly at eleven thirty.

"Reporting for duty," she said, giving me a salute.

"Stand down," I replied.

With a smirk, she sat down across from me in the guest chair. "What's shakin', toots?"

"Not a lot," I admitted. "I finally heard from Ian though."

"Geez, what took him so long?"

"His phone crapped out. He had to get a new one this morning."

"Of course. What better time? So, did he get an envelope?"

"Nope, nada."

Megan's shoulders sagged. "Really?"

"I know you are extremely hung up on this Christine-has-an-angle thing, but I don't think it's her."

"Well who *do* you think did it? Out of everyone, she seems the most likely suspect."

"Does that mean you don't think David is involved anymore?"

Megan shifted in her seat and crossed her legs. "He dropped down a notch on my list, but I don't trust him either."

"I feel like the possibility of his involvement is much greater than Christine's. Plus, the whole boots-in-the-snow thing. If she was involved, then she didn't commit the act herself."

"You own a pair of combat boots, you know."

"But I'm also a size seven," I reminded her.

She pursed her lips. "I know, and I hate you for it."

"My point is the boot prints that Higgins found were much larger. Christine is tall, but I don't think her feet are *that* big."

"Okay, I see your point."

"I think that Reed Ellington as an option is still pretty big for me. We know nothing about him except for the fact that he knew Rhonda, was obsessed with her, and owns the party rental company. After today, I plan to orchestrate a run-in with him. I still have to call Nelson, so I'll ask him about Reed and figure out if it's worth pursuing. We also haven't eliminated Jax Mercer."

Megan tilted her head. "Wait, who is Nelson?"

"Don't you remember? Nelson Ban, the point person for the rental company."

She smacked her forehead. "Oh right. I completely forgot. Which reminds me, I wanted to ask you . . . What's the deal with the stage still being outside? And when I walked in just now, I noticed the banquet tables were on that cart thingie in front of Eastern Enchantments."

I shook my head, letting out a sigh. "I don't know. I called him on Monday after we got the okay to take everything down, and he never called me back. Or showed up like he said he would to at least take the seating equipment. The Matrons mentioned it this morning too. I think everyone's sick of looking at it. And frankly, so am I."

"He better not charge you guys extra for it. That's totally on them."

"Oh believe me, I plan to remind him of that exact fact. If he gives me any hassle, I'll just sic Ian on him."

Megan snickered. "Oh Ian. That poor SOB."

"He brings it on himself," I replied.

"What's going on with that Eastern Enchantments place anyways? I thought they were scheduled to open after the New Year. Did we scare them away with our disaster of a party?"

I shook my head. "No, Ian asked the new owner if she would mind holding off until everything got situated and back to normal around here. He told her he didn't want all the commotion to detract from her opening."

"That's probably a good idea—but when is there a dull moment around here?"

I rested my chin in the palm of my hand, letting out a heavy sigh. "That's an excellent question."

"Speaking of"—Megan twisted in her seat to check the clock above the door—"we've got about ten minutes. You wanna get out there? You have a lectern or something you're going to stand behind?"

"Yeah, it's the same one from the banquet. Since it's still here, I might as well use the microphone. Let me call Nelson really quick and see if he can come by this afternoon."

She rubbed her hands together. "All right. Well hurry up, kid. It's almost showtime."

CHAPTER
35

Asia Village filled up quickly with return guests, and I was glad that my plan had worked out as I'd hoped. My dad and Adam had taken apart the clear acrylic cover that was used to shield the koi pond, so I didn't have a stage to stand on. But Megan and I pushed the lectern to the arched footbridge that went across the pond to give me some height.

The crowd was positioned in front of Ho-Lee Noodle House and Shanghai Donuts, petering out near China Cinema and Song. I noticed Ian standing with Mr. Zhang off to the side of the clustered gathering.

Kimmy hung back by Peter and Nancy in front of the restaurant, guarding the doors. We'd closed the kitchen to give everyone a break and the opportunity to participate.

Megan stood next to me at the lectern to keep an eye out for Jax Mercer and Whitney Meng. We'd come to the conclusion that in the consideration of time, she'd corner Whitney while I went and chatted up Jax. Again assuming both of them would show.

If they were missing from the event, it might be a clue as to who our mystery shooter might be.

I positioned myself near the microphone, donning my customer-service smile. Public speaking was my least favorite part of just about everything, but I somehow always found myself in that situation. "Thank you so much for coming back to Asia Village today. The management and staff apologize for any inconvenience this may have caused, and we hope that due to the"—I paused, struggling to find the appropriate word—"circumstances . . . you understand. We hope that our additional offer of huge discounts during happy hour at the Bamboo Lounge will make up for the second trip you've had to make for our holiday raffle."

A few people clapped, which encouraged me, but then I overheard a guy near the front mumble, "Get on with it," and that caused my hands to sweat. There's always one in every crowd.

I forced my smile to stay in place as I began pulling ticket stubs out of the plastic fishbowl that Megan held. With each string of numbers I called out, someone would wave their ticket in the air, then push through the crowd to receive their voucher.

There were a lot of deflated faces staring back at me when they realized they hadn't won anything.

"Thanks again for participating!" I said with a pageant wave. "And congratulations to all of our winners!"

The hush that had sustained itself erupted into a discord of chatter. I was pleased to see that most people went in the direction of the Bamboo Lounge, no doubt making Penny a very happy woman. I saw a few people meander over to the Modern Scroll and a group wander toward Chin's Gifts.

Megan whispered in my ear. "I saw Whitney. She was talking to David. Did you know he was coming to this?"

I nodded. "I invited him last minute. I want to talk with him one more time."

"Jax Mercer is also here, but I lost track of him. Hopefully he went to the Lounge."

"Great, let's get moving. Help me push this thing back over by the tables." I nudged my chin to the front of Eastern Enchantments.

As we situated the rolling lectern next to the dolly of stacked tables, a familiar voice behind me asked, "Do you need help with that?"

I hadn't heard anyone walking up to us, so it caused me to jump, knocking into Megan's arm.

Nelson chuckled. "Sorry to startle you. I got your call about coming to pick up the equipment. Sorry it took me so long; things have been crazy lately."

"No problem," I said. "Ian's been on my back, which is the only reason I really wanted to make sure it got done." It wasn't totally true, but Ian being the scapegoat for my persistence wasn't the worst thing I'd ever fibbed out. "I hope I'm not messing up your day."

"Not at all," he said. "I'm not able to take the stage today, but I can get these tables and chairs out of here."

"That would be great," I replied. Truth be told, I was disappointed he wasn't removing the stage too. "Maybe tomorrow you can get the rest?"

"Yeah, I'll have the other guys come. They have the large moving truck; I just have my pickup."

"Lana"—Megan grabbed my arm—"we need to be going . . . to take care of that thing."

"Oh right, that thing," I said with a nod. "Nelson, do you mind if we have a chat after you're done loading up the tables? I have to be somewhere right now, but I'd really like to sit and talk if you have a few minutes to spare."

He raised a brow but didn't question my request. "Sure, it won't take me long."

Megan pulled again on my arm.

"No rush," I said, allowing Megan to lead me away.

"Geez, Lana," she said once we were out of earshot, "yap it up, why don't you?"

"Sorry, I didn't want to be rude. He got here pretty fast after my call."

We hurried to the Bamboo Lounge, which was now packed with people taking advantage of happy hour. Inside, Megan spotted Whitney sitting at the bar. "Damn, look. She's sitting with David. She seems awfully cozy sidled up next to him, doesn't she?"

"Want me to distract him?"

She nodded. "Naturally."

"Do you have a plan on how you're going to get her talking?"

"Nah, I'm just going to wing it," Megan said, elbowing me in the side. "Of course I have a plan."

I clucked my tongue. "Which is what?"

"I'm going to poke the bear and bring up Rhonda's tragic end. I figure with us seeing her and David chatting, it'll give me a different segue into the topic. I was originally going to ask her what she thought about that night, but now I can really amp it up by asking more personal questions, like what her connection to David is. Naturally, she'll tell me, and I can ask if she was close with Rhonda. That should really get her going."

"We have one shot at this, Megan."

She grabbed my hand. "I know. Now come on, let's go."

Making our way through the dense crowd that had filled the Lounge, Megan let go of my hand as we got near the two former lovers.

"Hey David, you made it!" I placed a hand on his shoulder.

He flinched. "Lana, hey. I was just uh . . . catching up with an old friend. You haven't met Whitney, have you?"

I'd noticed that Whitney's eye twitched as he used the term "old friend." "No, I haven't had the pleasure." I stuck out my hand. "It's nice to meet you."

With some reservation, she extended her hand as well. "Hi. Whitney."

I gave it a firm shake and then in my most apologetic tone said, "I hate to interrupt, but would you mind if I stole David for a few minutes? I just need to go over some final monetary details."

I could tell by the sag that infiltrated the smile she'd had before Megan and I inserted ourselves that she was beyond disappointed.

"I'll keep her company," Megan offered with a wide grin. "I'm Megan." She shimmied into the empty space next to Whitney. "I could definitely go for a drink."

Whitney visibly forced herself to smile, but it came out flat. "Sure."

David furrowed a brow. "What's this about, Lana?"

"Let's go over here," I said, pointing to the secondary exit that led directly to the parking lot. "It'll be quieter."

He said to Whitney, "I'll just be a minute."

Whitney, who had begun fiddling with her earlobe, gave him a curt nod. I suspected after what she'd dealt with when Rhonda was around, she wasn't exactly a fan of women ushering him away. It caused me to wonder if perhaps there was more going on between them than met the eye.

We stood near the doorway, away from the lump of people that occupied the rest of the room. The secondary exit was only unlocked after hours since the Bamboo Lounge stayed open later than the rest of Asia Village, so we had a little wiggle room.

"What do you want?" David asked, his attention split between me and watching over Whitney.

In the minute that we'd separated from them, I noticed that Kimmy had arrived and was hovering over Megan's shoulder.

In a hiss, I replied, "What are you doing to that poor woman? Are you leading her on?"

"What? No! We're just talking. It doesn't mean anything. She was giving me her condolences."

"Where is Angela?" I asked.

"She's at home with the flu. Are you my mother? What do you want?"

I huffed. "I'll just get right to it. Did you lie to me about the red envelope thing?"

He jerked his head back. "No. What would give you that idea?"

"I think it's awfully strange that you didn't think it was necessary to tell the police."

"I told you I don't trust them," he said through gritted teeth. "It's that easy. What business is it of yours what I do with my life anyways?"

Placing both hands on my hips, I jutted my chin out. "It becomes my business when I get a red envelope on *my* door. So you'll have to excuse me if I refuse to tolerate your lame excuses or flippant responses. Getting threatened doesn't exactly make me warm and fuzzy."

His face went pale and his eyebrows shot up. "You got an envelope too? When?"

"Last night. This person was at my private residence. Do you understand how that makes me feel?"

He exhaled and ran a hand through his hair. "Yeah, actually, I do know. Well, sorta. I mean the person didn't come to our house, but they were right there in the back of the tent with us." He shook his head. "The bastard was within inches, mingling with the entire group. And no one noticed. It's unnerving."

His eyes held mine. "I'm sorry I got you into this, Lana."

I took a step back. "Wait, you really did get a red envelope, didn't you?"

"Yes, I told you that."

My arms rested at my sides. "And Angela is genuinely at home sick?"

He nodded. "Yeah. Personally, I think she's sick from all the stress. Normally she's healthy as an ox."

"So you were telling the truth about your distrust of cops?" My eyes fell to the ground, my mind going a hundred miles a minute. Had I read the entire situation wrong? Had Adam's opinion of my previous conversation with David sent me this far off course?

David threw his hands in the air. "Yes, Lana. I have been more than honest with you this entire time. I have no reason not to be."

"So then tell me why."

"Why what?"

I flared my nostrils. "Why don't you trust the cops? You never did give me a specific reason."

"Have you watched the news?" he said, stretching his arms out. "Or how about any murder documentary ever made in the history of ever?"

I pursed my lips. "That's not the best reason."

"Maybe not for you," he said, lifting his chin. "But it is for me. I've seen how this kind of thing goes. You try to help the cops by telling them all this stuff, giving them the details they need. And before long, they're looking at you like you're the one that did it because they can't find anybody else. They want to wrap everything up in a neat little bow." He folded his arms over his chest. "But they're not going to do it with me. I'll handle it myself. They can't protect Angela anyways. It doesn't work in the movies, and it doesn't work in real life."

I couldn't tell if he was really this jaded or was putting on the best acting of his life. I wasn't naïve and knew well enough that the police took a lot of flak, but I didn't think it was deserved as a whole.

I also didn't know if it was the best time to mention that Adam and Higgins were working on getting a warrant to search his house and business at the present moment. With his level of paranoia at police conduct, he might be liable to do something that would further incriminate him.

It was probably best that I talked with Adam first and let him know what David had just told me. Maybe he'd know a better way to work through the situation.

So instead of making things worse by filling him in on all that, I just said, "If you go through life looking at everyone as a bad person, then that's all you're going to find, David. Adam and Higgins are both good guys. You have my word."

He turned away, his eyes flitting back to Whitney. Sadness passed over his face and he studied her from afar. "Rhonda treated her like—" His eyes narrowed.

"David?"

He took a step forward, craning his neck. With a sneer, he asked, "Is that Jax Mercer?"

I followed his gaze and spotted the man he was referencing. It was indeed Jax Mercer. "I was hoping he'd show," I whispered.

David clenched his fists. "Yeah, so was I."

CHAPTER
36

David lurched forward, heading in the direction of Jax Mercer. I grabbed his arm, trying to pull him back, but he shook me off with ease. "Stay out of this, Lana; this isn't your mess to deal with."

A few people who had been standing in the way quickly moved, and I followed closely behind David despite his protest. "What are you doing?" I asked. "You're making a scene."

Jax was making his way toward Whitney, Kimmy, and Megan. From this angle, it appeared as though he was getting ready to hit on them.

David must have thought the same thing because he quickly blocked Jax from taking a step farther. He held his arms out. "Where do you think you're going?"

Whitney peeked over the top of David's shoulder.

Jax straightened his posture, puffing out his chest. "What business is it of yours?"

"I'm making it my business," David replied, matching the stance of his opponent.

The two men inched closer to each other.

My attention was momentarily diverted to Kimmy, who stood opposite me. The glimmer in her eyes was familiar, and she resembled a lioness getting ready to pounce. I didn't believe in telepathy, but I willed her with my mind to not get involved.

David took another step closer to Jax. "You're gonna want to get out of my face, Jax."

Jax snickered. "Oh yeah?"

David clenched his jaw. "Yeah. You should leave. Now."

"It's not your place to tell me to leave," Jax spat. "You can feel free to try and make me though. Go ahead, make an ass out of yourself. See what happens. Wouldn't be the first time."

That particular statement seemed to intensify the anger that David was already experiencing. He pulled his arm back, his hand balled up in a tight fist.

I took a step forward, slowly. "David, this isn't the place." My eyes darted around the room wondering if my undercover cop was lurking nearby watching this spectacle.

"Shut up, Lana!" David growled. "I told you to mind your own damn business."

And that is when Kimmy lost her cool. Barreling forward, she squeezed herself between the two men, pushing David away. The unexpected force caused him to stumble back a few feet.

Kimmy, who without her stiletto heels was much shorter than David, stormed after him, her index finger inches away from his face, and yelled, "Don't you dare tell my friend to shut up. Who do you think you are anyways? Talking to women like that. Shame on you, you big jerk!"

I, being in a state of shock, had frozen. But thankfully Megan sprang to action, grabbing onto Kimmy's elbow and pulling her back. Kimmy tried to shake Megan off, but Megan held on tight. "Oh no, you don't," Megan said, tugging harder on Kimmy's arm as she squirmed. "Take a beat and cool off."

Kimmy huffed, her eyes shooting daggers at David. "Yeah . . . whatever." She finally shook Megan off and spun around to storm in the opposite direction. But Jax held up a hand to stop her.

He stared at her, his hand frozen in midair. His neck jutted forward. "Hey, I know you, don't I?"

Kimmy, still fuming, bawled up her own fists. "Get away from me!"

His eyes widened as recognition set in. "I do know you! You're one of the cocktail waitresses at the Black Garter! That's why I recognize you!"

Kimmy's face reddened. "You got it wrong. I don't know you, now get out of my way!"

She slammed her shoulder into his as she stormed off and out of the Bamboo Lounge.

Penny had been standing a few feet away on the opposite side of the bar. I knew she'd overheard the whole exchange.

Meanwhile, David was in the corner near the hallway that led to the restrooms with Whitney seemingly consoling him. He was breathing heavily, staring at nothing, but didn't seem as if he was going to assault Jax for the time being.

Megan stood across from me. Our eyes met and she shook her head. She mouthed, *What the hell?*

I shrugged my shoulders.

Jax was still standing there, blotting at a large spot of alcohol that had spilled onto his plaid button-down with a cocktail napkin. He mumbled to himself, but over the noise I couldn't make out what he was saying.

I decided if I was going to confront him, it was either now or never.

I signaled Megan with my eyes about what I planned to do, and she gave me a thumbs-up before going over to check on David and Whitney. It was probably best that David be kept busy while I had my talk with Jax. I didn't want him to interrupt with another display of testosterone.

I took a step in Jax's direction, and he held up his hands in defense. "Whoa, there. Are you coming after me too?"

"No, I just want to talk to you. Mind if he we step out into the plaza?" I pointed past him in the direction of the entrance.

He smirked. "Not at all. You can't get me out of here fast enough. A guy can't enjoy a midday drink, it seems." After he glared a final time at David, he made his way out into the plaza. He stood off to the side near the property management office. Ian poked his head up from whatever he was reading on his phone, his eyes flitting between me and Jax. I was a hundred percent sure he wanted to know what was going on.

He gave me a thumbs-up, but there was question in his eyes. I nodded that I was okay and turned my attention back to Jax.

"So what can I do you for?" he asked. His voice lightened and he appeared playful. I wondered if that was part of his charm act.

"I wanted to talk to you about Rhonda Hong."

"Oh?" His demeanor changed instantly. With his chin tucked in, he focused his gaze at his feet. "My poor little Rho."

Poor little Rho. It actually sounded sincere. From outward appearances, he didn't seem to have the swagger and finesse that David and Christine had warned me about. What he looked like was a regular guy who was attractive and probably had confidence in himself. That alone could sometimes give people the wrong idea. Confidence was often mistaken for arrogance and vice versa. Keeping that in mind, I decided to drop any accusatory path I might have considered taking and allow his emotions to lead me. "I'm sorry for your loss."

"Thank you," he sniffed, and then met my eyes briefly before settling his attention on something off in the distance. His eyes had reddened and were rimmed with tears. The kind that were involuntary and could not be faked. "I still can't believe she's gone. I wake up sweating in the middle of the night, thinking it's a nightmare. But it's not. . . ."

It was as if his suffering was palpable, and I felt a twinge of pain stab me in the chest.

He shook his head and cleared his throat. "Sorry, I don't mean to dump on you. It's all been very hard. What did you want to know?"

I did my best to shake away any residual feelings and press forward with my task. But my mind was clouded with random thoughts and waves of compassion. And a question that had been niggling at me since it flew out of his mouth. "What did you mean when you said that David had made an ass out of himself before?"

Jax's mouth opened, and then he closed it again.

"I'm not close to David . . . I hired the Hong Dance Troupe for the Lunar New Year party. So if you're concerned about me saying anything to him, you have nothing to worry about."

Of course, this was me guessing that maybe because he had seen me approach him with David, it meant that I was on the side of his nemesis.

He seemed to consider this for a moment and then said, "David didn't like the fact that his sister and I were close.

A lot of people didn't. They tried to discredit our relationship and our true feelings for each other."

I shook my head, my eyes blinking rapidly. "Wait a minute, you guys were in a relationship?"

Jax inhaled deeply. "Yes, and we were engaged."

"What?"

He sighed, passing over my surprise. "It's such a relief to just say it out in the open. We hid it from a lot of people because it doesn't look good."

"What do you mean?"

"With her line of work at the club, it wasn't attractive that she was in a committed relationship or about to get married. A lot of these men go to those places with the fantasy that all the women are available and there for the taking. It would hurt the money she made if people knew the truth." Then he added, "Kinda like bartenders. A lot of them give the appearance that they're single so they can flirt with their customers and get better tips."

This I knew well enough from things that Megan had told me. "So, you weren't concerned that she was stringing you along?"

He laughed. "Not at all. Rhonda wasn't that kind of woman. We loved each other through and through. She was planning to leave the club after she made enough money to pay for her own dance studio. I offered to pay for it, but she said she needed to do it on her own. I wasn't going to argue with her on it. I knew it was important for her confidence. David was always putting her down and trying to convince her that she couldn't live without him."

I stayed silent for a moment to process what he was saying. His admission did line up with her wanting to leave the club and start her own business. She wanted to do it on her own, so maybe that was the reason why she'd been dodging Christine? "So what happened with David then?"

"Oh, well we had a confrontation a few months back when Rhonda and I were out at a club downtown. We ran into him and Angela and it got pretty ugly. He shoved me and knocked me into a group of guys. A bunch of drinks got spilled and he embarrassed the hell out of his sister. And he made a lot of accusations that night. It definitely shifted their relationship."

"Like what kind of accusations?" I asked.

"The main one was that I'd intentionally matched up with his sister to make Angela jealous. Ang and I weren't even that serious. We met at some bakery and she seemed like such a sweet girl. We went out a couple times, but we weren't monogamous or anything. She didn't seem all that into me, so when she broke things off, I walked away peacefully."

I compared the story Jax was now telling me with what David had said to me in the past. A lot of it lined up, but it was always amazing to me how much perspectives on the same situation could vary.

By Jax's relaxed stance, it seemed as though he was being honest with me. He wasn't distracted by our surroundings, nor was he squirming for an easy out. So far, those small facts were working in his favor.

"How did you happen to meet Rhonda then?" I asked.

"I've always gone to the Black Garter from time to time. They have a great lunch special. You can't get a quality steak that cheap anywhere else in town. So I'd go every Saturday afternoon. But when I met Rhonda, it was love at first sight."

"And did she feel the same?"

He shrugged. "I don't think so. But I started going more often. I'd always ask Autumn when her shifts would be so I could plan out when to go." He chuckled at the memory. "After a time, I suppose that I grew on her. We'd start chatting about this or that, and I finally mustered up the courage to ask her out. I was surprised when she said yes. And I guess, as they say, the rest was history. I didn't have any delusions going into it. I know they're there to make money, and I respect that. Hell, I couldn't get up there and dance for everyone."

The ease he'd used to tell me the story of him and Rhonda flowed so naturally, I felt it couldn't be mistaken for anything other than the truth. It saddened me at the thought that their feelings had been genuine for each other, yet invalidated by the people around them, and perhaps by circumstances themselves. Regardless of the sympathy I felt for their interrupted love story, I had to use the practical part of my senses to distinguish whether or not Jax had any involvement in her murder.

Both my mind and gut were in agreement. He wasn't the shooter I was searching for.

"Why do you want to know about Rhonda anyways?" he asked, shaking me away from my thoughts.

I didn't know if I should be honest with him about why I was snooping around, so I just said, "There are some things that don't add up for me."

"You're not the only one," he said. "I still can't figure out why anyone would want to kill Rhonda. She didn't do anything to anyone."

"What about Whitney Meng?" I asked. "Do you know anything about her?"

"Whit?" he said, jerking a thumb over his shoulder. "David's ex?"

"Yeah, her. I heard that she was upset over Rhonda breaking up their relationship."

Jax snorted. "You're joking, right? Rhonda didn't break them up . . . well, not in the way David made it sound anyhow."

"I don't follow."

"Whitney isn't exactly a saint. She was cheating on David with someone in their troupe and Rhonda caught them. Rhonda was the one who exposed the infidelity and so David blamed her, as if she were the one that made Whitney do what she did."

I could feel my heart quickening. That was definitely information I hadn't been privy to prior to this conversation. "Do you know who the other person was?"

Jax shook his head. "Rhonda wouldn't tell me, for some reason. I don't know if she didn't want to admit it to herself or what."

"So the only people who know are David and Whitney?"

Jax shrugged. "Maybe? All Rhonda said to me was it hurt her beyond repair because the guy was like a second brother to her. She vowed she'd never bring it up to anyone to protect his character."

In that moment, I felt immense clarity crash into me like a tidal wave. Unbeknownst to Jax, he had provided the final piece to the puzzle.

CHAPTER
37

"Would you excuse me a moment?" I said it as more of a courtesy because I hadn't planned on waiting for him to answer.

I heard him mumble "Okay?" as I hurried back into the Bamboo Lounge in search of David. I had to ask him if my theory was correct. Deep down I knew that it was because I'd heard those words before. Those *exact* words, and there was no mistaking them. Rhonda had said them to me the night of the party as she thanked me for hiring the rental company, and that was the thought that had struck me as I'd had my heartfelt conversation with Peter earlier that morning.

It had caused me to wonder about David's relationship with the person Rhonda had mentioned, and if there would be any jealousy that sprung from it. I could have never guessed there'd be another component to the story.

And even though I felt the clarity down to my very toes, as Adam always said, it never hurts to have solid confirmation. And there was still a chance that I was wrong.

But between the pickup truck, the large work boots, the knowledge of both how the troupe operated and the banquet rental equipment, plus the fact that the person was well-versed in Asian superstitions, I felt the answer had been staring me in the face the whole time.

I could have smacked myself for not having realized it sooner, but I put those feelings on the back burner. There was always time in the future to berate myself.

Megan must have sensed me somehow because she turned in my direction as I neared. She slowly rose from her stool, noticing the sense of urgency with which I moved. Suddenly she paused, her gaze traveling past me, and her eyebrows furrowed low over her eyes as she locked onto something going on behind me.

At the same moment, I felt a firm hand wrap itself around my bicep. I jerked, nearly jumping out of my skin. But that only caused the person to hold on more forcefully.

They spun me around, and my heart skipped a beat as our eyes met.

As I'd feared, it was Nelson Ban.

The grin on his face dripped with sarcasm. "Hey Lana, don't forget you were looking for me. Didn't you want to chat?"

Swarms of people stood around us, but no one seemed to notice what was going on, probably dismissing it as commonplace. Just two people trying to find each other in a crowded bar.

"Let go of my arm," I said, struggling to make my voice heard. That giant frog had resumed its solid positioning squarely in the middle of my throat. "There are too many witnesses."

He gripped tighter. "Oh, we'll be leaving. Together. Nice and quiet. You wouldn't want me to endanger these other nice people, would you?" With his free hand, he pulled open his jacket, exposing a shiny silver revolver strapped to his chest. My mind flashed back to the similar encounter I'd had with David, and I wondered if everyone was carrying guns these days.

Nelson shook me. "Their fate rests in your hands. I know you have friends here."

"More than you think," I said with any remaining defiance I could muster. "There's an undercover cop watching us right now." I actually had no idea where he was, but I was hoping he'd noticed me running into the Bamboo Lounge like my hair was on fire.

Nelson brought me closer, wrapping his arm around my neck. His warm breath tickled my ear, and he whispered in an amused voice, "I have no problem upgrading you to a hostage."

He held me so close I felt the gun pressing on my rib cage. I didn't know what to do. If I screamed for help, there was no telling what he might do to me, or who else he might hurt.

"Okay, fine," I spat. "I'll come with you, just don't hurt anybody in the process."

"There, see? Was that so hard?" He loosened his grip so he could look me in the face. "We'll get out of here, nice and quiet. Let's go for a drive and have that chat you so desperately wanted."

Panic sent spasms of tingles flowing through my arms and legs. I couldn't leave with this guy. If I did, would anyone notice? Would the undercover cop suddenly come to save the day? I couldn't take the chance. I needed to slow Nelson down a bit so I could think about what to do. Maybe I could signal to someone else in the plaza to call for help. Did Megan even know I was in danger? She'd been with us earlier as we'd talked, so would anything seem out of the ordinary?

Maybe Kimmy was around somewhere. I tried desperately to remember the signal for being held captive, but I couldn't think straight. The wheels in my head were spinning at a furious rate and all that resulted was chaos.

Nelson whipped me around to face the exit but held me in place. Whispering into my ear again, he said, "Nice and slow, don't forget. We're going to walk out together and then through the plaza. Don't look or talk to anyone. Just keep it moving. You'll see my truck in the parking lot to the left. That's where you walk, nowhere else. If you try to run, I will not hesitate to shoot you."

I nodded in compliance. "I'll come with you but I'd like to ask a question." I tried my best to keep my voice level, but each word shook as it left my mouth.

"I'd rather we didn't have any back-and-forth until you're safe and sound in my truck."

I continued on anyways. If he was going to hurt me later, what difference did it make? It was clear to me that he wanted to escape, so I had to take the risk that he wouldn't do something to me here. "Did you love her like she loved you? Like a sibling?"

I felt his body tense against mine. He squeezed my arm. "You're talking about things you don't understand."

"Well then, mansplain it to me." The bite in my tone shocked both of us. I could feel a little bit of Kimmy's influence surging through my body like a sleeping bear waking up from winter hibernation. I didn't know what triggered it, but I did everything I could to hold onto that feeling.

His hand slithered from my shoulder to the side of my neck, where he applied enough pressure to make me want to gag. "You think you're tough, don't you?"

"Clearly you have me at a disadvantage," I replied, remaining stoic. "So just tell me. What is it that I don't get?"

Through clenched teeth, he hissed in my ear. "What happened to Rhonda was unfortunate. It wasn't my intention to hurt her, but there's nothing I can do about it now, is there?"

His anger was amping up after admitting the mistake he'd made, but I pressed on with my questioning anyways. "Then it *was* Angela you were after all along?"

"If you want to look at it that way, sure. But it's really about your boy David over there. He hit me where it hurt, so I wanted to pay back the favor."

"But why give both women an envelope? If you never intended to hurt Rhonda, why threaten her too?"

He pushed me a couple steps forward. "It was supposed to buy me some time to disappear. Make the authorities look somewhere else. I'd say it worked, wouldn't you?"

"Then why didn't you leave? Were you planning on finishing the job and killing Angela after all?"

There was a young couple standing near the entrance who noticed us and began to stare. I felt Nelson tense up again, pulling me closer to him. "Act natural, Lana."

I widened my eyes at the couple. Hoping they'd get the message. But both of them looked down at the same time, pretending as if they hadn't noticed anything.

My heart rate continued to accelerate. "Angela." I repeated her name. "Were you planning on killing her too?"

"Would you shut up?" He nudged me forward.

"Hey!" a voice shouted from behind us.

A hush fell over the bar. I was confused as to why, but then I heard the cocking of a gun. "Everyone get down on the ground!"

That's when I realized it was David who'd yelled across the bar. I heard a few yelps, including from Megan, and a lot of shuffling as people did as they were told. The couple in front of us held their hands up in surrender and slowly crouched to the ground.

David yelled again. "Let her go! She doesn't have anything to do with this."

Nelson abruptly released me to confront his aggressor, and I turned in time to see him remove his own gun from inside his jacket. "David, old friend, I thought we've been over this. I don't take orders from you anymore."

CHAPTER
38

- - - - - - - - - - - - - -

The scene in the bar was like something out of a bank heist movie. It almost felt as if I was having an out-of-body experience. But searching for Megan's face snapped me back to reality. She was hunkered down near David, next to Whitney, who also appeared as if she could go into shock.

Nelson seemed to remember that I existed, and while he kept his gun trained on David, he twisted his head to get sight of me, and then reached his free hand out to grab my arm again. "You're not going anywhere, Lana. After all, I have you to thank for orchestrating this whole thing."

David held his gun with both hands. You could tell he wasn't familiar or comfortable with holding it. My only hope was that Nelson didn't notice the same. "Leave her alone, she didn't do anything to deserve this. This is and has always been between you and me."

Nelson sneered. "Of course it has. I'm glad you realized it. Well, you and me . . . and her." He waved his gun in the direction of Whitney.

David's jaw clenched. "Wait, it was you?" His eyes darted over to Whitney. "Did you know about this?"

Whitney shivered. "I don't know what you mean. I don't know anything, I swear."

David refocused the gun and his attention on Nelson. "You killed Rhonda, you pile of—"

Nelson waved his gun in a scolding manner. "Uh-uh, old friend. Watch your language when ladies are present. You always were a bit of a brute."

"Answer me!" David yelled.

Whitney jerked at the venom that emanated from his voice and made herself smaller by leaning farther back toward the bar, lowering her head as if she would meld into the polished wood if she tried hard enough.

Nelson pulled me closer to him, wrapping his arm around my neck. "Yeah, I did it. You deserve to be knocked down a peg. And if anyone is going to take away your happiness, I'd rather it be me. It's just a damn shame it was Rhonda who paid for the problems *you* caused." He said it so nonchalantly that it sounded even more treacherous.

David's eyes filled with tears. "You got what you wanted anyways. Whitney and I were through. What more did you want from me? Wasn't stealing Whitney from me enough?"

Nelson took a few steps closer to David, dragging me along with him. "Your disgust at our feelings for one another, your casting me out of the troupe, well, it brought so much shame to our girl, Whitney, didn't it babe?" He nodded his head in Whitney's direction, made eye contact with her, and puckered his lips. "Couldn't handle the heat of all those eyes looking at you sideways because you fell in love with your boyfriend's best friend."

Whitney's gaze immediately dropped to the floor, mascara-streaked tears dripping down her cheeks.

Nelson sneered at her before focusing his attention back on David. "Finally, when we could be together, she wants nothing to do with me. So not only did I lose the love of my life, but I lost my chosen family, and a great career path—thanks to this injury that you probably did on purpose!" He yelled the final word so loud that it made my ears ring. I cringed trying to move my head away from his mouth.

David groaned with such a fury it would have rivaled the Incredible Hulk. "You're an idiot. All of that is your own damn fault! And your injury was an accident! How many times do I have to tell you that!" He was beginning to hyperventilate. His body rattled with each jagged breath and his eyes moved back and forth like a Ping-Pong ball. I could see him catastrophizing and realizing the impact of events, his sister's senseless death perhaps throwing him over the edge.

Suddenly he became very still and the room filled with a thick, uncomfortable silence. His eyes were rimmed with tears that threatened to spill any moment should he blink, but his arm rose with a rigid, calm focus as he set his sights on Nelson. The unfamiliarity of holding the weapon no longer seemed to be there, and I watched in slow motion as David's index finger pulled back on the trigger.

I squeezed my eyes shut as I heard the bullet burst from the barrel of the gun.

CHAPTER
39

Silence followed and I realized I was holding my breath.

In an instant, I felt Nelson jerk his body as he stumbled to the side, and I pried an eye open, turning my head to see that the bullet was lodged in the wall behind us. I released the breath I'd been holding onto for dear life.

No sooner had I felt a sense of relief at David's poor aim, Nelson was again dragging me along with him. But as he raised his arm to take a shot at David, a petite woman in a baseball cap and Cavs hoodie rose from her crouched position at the edge of the bar and whipped a pistol out from I could only guess where. She aimed it at Nelson and yelled. "FPPD! Drop it now!"

Nelson flung me in front of him as protection from the undercover cop's gun.

With a blank expression and a smooth tone, she said, "I wouldn't do that if I were you. There's no way out of here. You're totally surrounded."

I felt Nelson trembling behind me. "I highly doubt that."

Out of the corner of my eye I saw two figures stand from a table next to the windows that overlooked the parking lot. I tried to move my head, but Nelson held on to my neck so tightly I could hardly see much of anything off to the side. The only thing I could make out was that they had baseball caps on.

Then I heard Higgins' voice, "You really are, Mr. Ban. This is my partner, Detective Trudeau, who I'm sure you already know. The lovely lady you're staring at right now is Detective Dorbin, and our buddy, Detective Cain, is just outside those doors with a few officers who have shiny handcuffs just for you."

Nelson shimmied so he could see Higgins better, but he didn't respond. I imagined he was thinking about his next move and the likelihood of escaping in one piece.

He'd begun to sweat, and I could feel the moisture from his body seeping onto my clothes.

Higgins kept talking. "Right now, you have one murder under your belt. Don't make it worse by taking another life. Nobody in this room did anything to you."

In a low voice, Nelson replied, "He did," his eyes landing on David.

David's stance had changed from the riled-up version he'd been just moments ago to a crumbling mess. My guess was that he'd shaken himself up by actually firing the gun. I don't think he realized how lucky he was that he'd missed.

Higgins edged closer while Adam stayed farther back, closer to the line of tables that sat against the wall behind us. I was losing sight of him, but knowing he was there gave me a sliver of hope.

I'd already decided that if Nelson faltered whatsoever and loosened his grip on me, I'd elbow him in the stomach and make a run for it. The thought of having a plan did little to calm me down though. I needed to be at the ready.

Higgins paused, now only a few feet away from Nelson and me. He said, "Okay, well, screw that guy, right? Do you think he's worth it? The time you'll do? Then you've got no one to blame but yourself. But if you go with us now, and don't hurt anyone else, we can try and help you."

Nelson snorted. "I'm going to jail any way you spin it. My life is over thanks to him, so what do I care?"

His arm lifted once again and in that same moment, Adam yelled, "Lana, duck!"

I yanked down on Nelson's arm, clawing into his forearm. His grip loosened and I thrust my body to the ground. Adam flung himself over me and grappled with Nelson. I heard a loud crash as the two bodies went flying into a table, knocking it over in the process.

I watched the gun clank haphazardly to the ground, fearful that it would go off. But it landed with a thud on its butt and then fell onto its side.

I felt a collective sigh resonate throughout the room as Higgins lurched forward to seize the abandoned weapon.

In the meantime, Adam had positioned Nelson flat on his face, reciting his rights to him as he placed the handcuffs aggressively around his wrists.

Higgins came to stand over the two men. Satisfaction edged through his features, a sarcastic grin forming on his lips. As Adam helped Nelson to his feet, Higgins said, "See? I told you not to do that. Me and my partner don't mess around."

After Nelson had been taken away, two uniformed officers approached David, who was getting his very own pair of handcuffs for his use of a firearm inside an establishment. I avoided any eye contact he tried to make as they escorted him out.

Megan and I sat next to each other in a booth while everyone cleared out of the Bamboo Lounge. Penny had provided us with fresh cocktails before tending to the mess that had been left in the aftermath of the standoff.

If she was upset about my bringing this mess to her place of business, she didn't say so, and I would save any apologizing on my end for a time when I wasn't shaking from the inside out.

Megan took a gulp of the drink in front of her. "Ugh, what is this?"

"Probably straight whiskey," I said, sniffing the glass. The ice cubes rattled back and forth as my hand shook.

Megan held out her hand and placed it over mine. "You're okay. We're all okay."

I snuffled, that awkward double breath you take after a bout of crying, and nodded my head. "I know. It's just . . ."

"I was scared too," she said, releasing my hand. "I kept trying to think of a way to get you free. Then I noticed that Adam was sitting by the window. I tried to signal you with my eyes, but you were kinda distracted."

"I had no idea he was here."

"Talking about me again, I see?"

I looked up to see Adam standing over me clad in a Cleveland Cavs hoodie much like the undercover cop who was at the bar.

I sprang up from the booth and wrapped my arms around his broad shoulders. He lost his footing, but quickly regained it, enveloping me in a fierce hug. "Whoa there, doll. You've already knocked me off my feet once."

I pulled away, smacking his arm playfully. "You're a jerk." I was somewhere between laughing and crying. I felt emotionally raw and knew that he was making light to help ease some of the tension weighing down on me.

He pulled me close, kissing the top of my head. "I got you, doll. Even when you don't know it, I got you."

Higgins returned and made some gagging sounds. "You guys are making me sick with all your lovey-dovey stuff. It's bad enough I have to listen to it in the car, but now I gotta witness it firsthand?"

Adam chuckled. "Don't be jealous. You know, Megan here is single, but make no mistake, she isn't a damsel in distress. Neither of these ladies are." He wrapped his arm around my waist and gave me a squeeze.

Megan blanched. "Geez, Trudeau, put me on the spot, why don't you?"

Higgins laughed, his face becoming red. "Seriously, man. Your timing is no bueno."

"What will happen to David?" I asked to keep both Megan and Higgins from further embarrassment.

Higgins rubbed the back of his head. "Well, he's going to get slapped with reckless endangerment, aggravated assault, if not attempted murder, and illegal discharge of a weapon."

Adam held up a finger. "*And* don't forget possession of an illegal firearm."

Higgins drew a checkmark in the air. "Ah, right, can't forget that."

Megan slumped against the table. "I can't say that I feel bad for him. The guy was unhinged to the max. Who knew that he'd go that far? I didn't think he'd actually try and shoot Nelson."

"Me either," I said. "Thank God you guys were already here." I turned to Higgins and Adam. "I wish I would have known sooner though. My life flashed before my eyes. I thought I was a goner."

Adam held me tighter. "You wish? *I* wish I would have

known sooner that Nelson had you captive. It wasn't until Megan did the eyeball dance that I understood the severity of what was going on."

Megan lifted her head. "The eyeball dance? Next time, I'll send out a smoke signal. How about that?"

A burst of laughter escaped me at the absurdity of the conversation. As I scanned their faces, I realized there were no other people in this world I'd rather go through hell and back with. "Think larger," I said to the group. "The bat signal would be more apropos."

EPILOGUE

In the days that followed, the Matrons strolled through the plaza with extra pep in their step and attributed the success of Nelson's arrest to the prayers they had painstakingly recited on repeat along with Mr. Zhang.

The feeling was contagious and a sense of peace flowed through the plaza once again. Not only was Nelson Ban safely behind bars awaiting trial, but David was behaving himself while out on bail.

Though Ian and Donna had both agreed to ban David from ever returning to Asia Village, they did allow him an apology tour where Higgins and Adam oversaw his conversation with Penny Cho. On the advice of his attorney, he promised that he would pay for any and all damages that had taken place at the Bamboo Lounge.

It was a welcome gesture, and Penny readily accepted the offer.

When all the details were finalized, Higgins and Adam escorted David Hong out of the plaza and hopefully out of our lives forever.

In the time since David's arrest, the Hong Dance Troupe

was disbanded and the dancers went their separate ways. But there was word through the grapevine—aka the Matrons—that they planned to start a dance studio in honor of Rhonda.

As far as Nelson's statement went, Higgins oversaw the whole thing, which included an explanation of Nelson's intentions by leaving both Angela and Rhonda a red envelope. Which—as he'd admitted to me—was his way of keeping the police off his scent for as long as possible. He figured it wouldn't take much for someone to make the mutual connection the women had with Jax Mercer.

For that, Adam apologized for not believing that David had told me any truths whatsoever.

Nelson also admitted to following me around, including back to my apartment where he'd so kindly dropped off the red envelope that Megan and I had found taped to our door. He claimed he had no intention of actually hurting me and said it was an empty threat meant to scare me out of digging any further.

Supposedly it wasn't until the moment he saw me talking to Jax that he suspected I knew more than he'd realized. He'd come to the conclusion that Jax would be the only person who might know about the sordid triangle he was involved in.

For the sake of Megan and me, Higgins ordered that Nelson clarify if he had worked alone or if Christine Schneider or anyone else had been involved.

Nelson took full ownership of his actions and claimed to have no idea who Christine Schneider even was.

Megan's ego was a little bruised from the discovery that she had been off the mark, but she bounced back pretty fast and vowed that next time she wouldn't allow herself to get so caught up in her own self-assuredness.

After I *kindly* reminded her that we weren't hoping for

a "next time," I also jogged her memory that she'd displayed the behavior I was usually reprimanded for and offered that next time she found a lecture coming on, she might want to reconsider and remember this instance.

In response, I got a playful pinch on the arm.

Ian had taken some of the credit for Nelson's detainment and had secured his good graces with Donna once again. I let it go because if it would keep Ian firmly in his position, I could stop worrying about what we as a community would have to endure with a change in management.

I hadn't seen Reed Ellington in person, but Ian told me that he had visited the plaza offering apologies for everything that occurred with his delinquent employee who had obviously been terminated from his job. He'd also offered a discount from the original price we'd been quoted, and an even more generous discount toward a future party.

While I appreciated the sentiment, I told Ian that I needed a break from any type of party planning in the foreseeable future.

He didn't argue the issue.

As for Kimmy, her disappearance before the showdown had been opportune and I'd been relieved she hadn't had to go through it with us. Of course, being Kimmy, she was thoroughly disappointed that she'd missed out on the action.

"The only reason I left," she explained, "is because I didn't want Jax to keep screaming about how he knew me from the Black Garter."

Which was exactly why the two of us were currently sitting next to each other at the bar at the Bamboo Lounge. Kimmy had asked me to accompany her while she swore Penny to secrecy. From what we had deciphered, she was the only one who had overheard Jax's announcement.

If anyone else had heard what Jax had said that day, it hadn't been circulated through Asia Village. And there was more of a chance of aliens being real than that happening.

Penny poured us two of her infamous drinks—the Shanghai Shimmer—and slid them across the bar top. "Don't worry, Kimmy, I won't tell anyone a thing about it."

Kimmy leaned against the bar. "How can I be so sure?"

Penny laughed. "I don't want to see the outcome." She tapped the bar good-naturedly and sashayed away to wait on another customer.

"I guess I better be super nice to Penny in the future so she doesn't get any wild ideas." Kimmy took a sip of her drink. "So anyways, how are you holding up? You're always at the center of it. What the hell was that even like? I can't imagine."

"Trust me, you'd rather not know."

I lifted my glass, the memory running through me like a bolt of lightning.

In the instant it had taken the bullet to sail across the room, my life had flashed before my eyes. Every mistake I'd ever made, every moment of serendipity that had brought me to that moment, and every hope I had for the future existed in that frozen slice of time. I understood exactly how short life was and could be.

One thing I noticed was that I hadn't had any regrets weighing me down. I understood that everything had always happened as it should. Each mistake a lesson to learn from, every chance encounter deeper than at first glance, and the importance of hope propelling you forward to an unknown destiny.

Later, when there was some distance between me and what had happened, I would probably question myself on all of that. But as I'd stood there that day, hanging on the balance of life and death, the words of a poet I'd read in college rang through my mind. Charles Bukowski reverberated crisp and clear, as if I'd traveled back in time to that classroom from my freshman year, still seeing the lines printed carefully on the page: "It has been a beautiful fight. Still is."